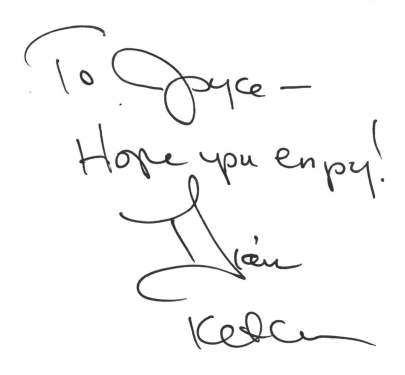

To Joyce —
Hope you enjoy!

[signature]

Naples: Paradise
Can Be Deadly

D0735056

ALSO BY DIANE KETCHAM

The Vanishing A-list
Long Island: Shores of Plenty

Naples: Paradise Can Be Deadly

a novel by

Diane Ketcham

This is a work of fiction. Names, characters, places and incidents are either a product of the author's imagination or are used fictitiously, and all events and conversations are the pure invention of the author.

THIS BOOK OR PARTS THEREOF, MAY NOT BE REPRODUCED IN ANY FORM WITHOUT PERMISSION

Tidelow Press

For information, contact:

Tidelow Press
Author #228
300 Fifth Avenue South, suite 101
Naples, Florida 34102

Or visit **www.tidelowpress.com**

FIRST EDITION

Copyright 2013 by Diane Ketcham
All rights reserved.
ISBN: 0979755581
ISBN-13: 9780979755583
Library of Congress control number: 2012955589
CreateSpace Independent Publishing Platform
North Charleston, South Carolina

To Roger,
Whose love of great literature humbles me.
Here's the lighter side....

PROLOGUE

If only he had left a few seconds sooner. If he had just sneaked away when he first saw them. But he couldn't believe what he was seeing. He knew the man. He knew the girl. And what was happening – he couldn't move. Five seconds, ten. Finally reality returned. Get out of here. Now! Get help for her. And for himself. For just as he started to leave, the man looked up. Oh God, that look.

Now he was on his horse, kicking, kicking, willing it to go faster. "Come on Charlie, come on boy." For a moment there was no sound behind him. Maybe he had gotten away. But then he heard the door slam, and the truck engine start. And he knew. The man was coming after him.

If only he hadn't stopped. His whole life was if onlys, bad decisions that kept piling up. If only he hadn't taken his horse tonight. A date on a cow horse in Naples, Florida was stupid. Ritzy Naples where people rode in Mercedes and BMWs. His horsepower was an aging quarter horse. But his girlfriend pleaded "Oh Cody, there's a full moon. Take me for a ride." And he knew what that meant. So he had, and they had – the greatest sex ever. But now he was riding for his life, on a horse that had never been used for anything but herding a few steers.

If he hadn't taken the shortcut. After he dropped her off, he could have gone down the long dirt road from her house to the main road, and then taken the side streets to his trailer. But he decided to cut through the open fields where all you ever saw were cattle grazing. But not tonight. No, not tonight. He had seen –

He couldn't forget those eyes, killer eyes that were coming after him. And now this stupid full moon. He and his old white horse were lit up like that "Rhinestone Cowboy" movie. And there was nothing ahead but open fields.

His horse gasped and wheezed as it tried to gallop faster. What was one horsepower against 300? He could hear the truck's engine roaring, but no headlights lit the field. Why weren't the lights on? Because he's going to kill you, stupid, and he doesn't want anybody to see it. No reason for headlights anyway. The damn moon lit up everything.

The engine sound grew louder, gaining. Why had he even stopped there? Because he heard the music, Tom Petty belting out "Free Fallin." So he headed toward Tom's voice and the cluster of scrub trees it came from. He jumped off Charlie and sneaked nearer. A black truck with its music system blaring was parked about hundred feet from a clump of bushes. From behind the bushes he heard grunts and gasps. He thought he'd find one of his friends moonlight screwing just like he had been. But when he looked through the bushes and saw who was there and what was happening, he froze.

"Come on, come on Charlie."

Up ahead a twinkle of brightness. A light was on in his friend Billy's trailer. Billy's home. Billy's got a gun! Only a quarter mile, if only he could make it there. But then the truck lights came on. "Oh God. He's going to kill me. He's got to after what I seen."

He kicked the horse harder. He could see two lights now. "Come on Charlie, come on, we can make it." And suddenly Charlie was flying. For a brief second, horse and rider were airborne. Then they tumbled to the ground. He never heard the shot. A bullet pierced Charlie's chest. Horse landed with a thud. So did rider. The truck screeched to a halt. "Oh Charlie," he whispered, gently touching the dying horse's neck. Then he looked up. And he saw those killer eyes.

PART I

Trouble in Paradise

Chapter I

Okay, how do you spell diarrhea? Stop reading, look away and try to spell it. No, really, try. You can even use your imaginary blackboard and finger pen. Can't do it, can you? Ask somebody else how to spell it. They can't either.

That's how I started a newspaper column I wrote about common words nobody could spell. Diarrhea topped the list. Now I was down on my knees cleaning up mountains of it. Well, maybe not *mountains*. My mother always says "You are so dramatic." But a 90-pound Labrador Retriever defecating on white carpet on the 18th floor of a hi-rise is beyond normal cleaning skills. And mine have always been limited.

"Why now?" I said to the big black blob lying so dutifully near me. Why just two hours before one of the most important events in my life, my debut as the congressman's new "lady friend," or whatever the Naples elite would call me? Tonight all eyes would be on me, and I needed to get my mind and body ready for that. Instead I was trying to clean up whatever went into my dog Willie and came out on the expensive carpet labeled Stainmaster. Only these stains were not being mastered at all. And of course it wasn't one spot. No, when Willie goes, he goes like a duck. So the trail stretched from the living room to the front door which is where I should have taken him when I heard the first whimper. But how was I to know he was going to erupt like Mount Vesuvius?

All right, I might have missed a whine or two. I'm busy writing a book, and sometimes I don't stop when nature calls Willie. So Willie waits, usually.

Scrub, blot. Scrub, blot. This was not what I had in mind when I agreed to give up reporting and move from New York to Florida. But I was coming off the worst year of my life at the same time I met the best thing in my life, that being the congressman.

James "Wit" Whitman looks like a young Harrison Ford and makes love like – well who to compare him to? I mean this is a man you can not get enough of. At least I can't. When he asked me to move in with him, I said "When?" Since his congressional district covers Southwest Florida, that meant moving to the beach in sunny Naples. Not bad, huh? He could have represented Fargo. But I didn't think about the consequences of bringing with me a very large dog, now with a very large bowel problem.

"Today!" I shouted at Willie, grabbing another stack of paper towels. "Today you had to have diarrhea!" Willie understands words like "water," "outside," and "din-din." But diarrhea? How *do* you spell it? "D-i- a –"

The ringing phone stopped the spelling. I looked at caller ID. Wit. Should I ask a congressman how to spell diarrhea? I simply said "hi."

"Hi Jazz."

My real name is Agatha Jasmine. That was my mother's idea. It's a long story. No time now for that version. But in the *USA Today* bullet form, I hate my given name, so I'm Jazz to my friends and A.J at work. The bus billboards identify me as "A.J. Billings, New York's most famous Pulitzer Prize winning reporter." My mother identifies me as "Agatha Jasmine, the daughter who never calls."

Wit told me he was running late. He still had another meeting at his downtown district office. Would I mind picking him up there when it was time for the party? Not at all. It would give me more time to clean up the mess. That too, I didn't tell him.

"Take my car," he said. "It's more comfortable."

I've got a rental, a Ford Focus with a crunch in the right front fender, thanks to a bad parking job at a local shopping center. I like that car. But Wit wouldn't want to arrive in Port Royal, the wealthiest area of Naples, in a dented compact. Since congressmen usually drive U.S. made cars, and Wit and his family have enough money to buy Detroit, driving American for James Whitman means driving a big Cadillac Escalade for work, and a Corvette on the weekends.

One last scrub, blot. Okay, enough with the cleaning. Time to think about what to wear. I headed for the bedroom, Willie loping behind me. A dozen dresses lay piled on the giant bed. Why do people have such huge beds in Naples? Maybe to go with the huge rooms. It's been quite an adjustment from New York living, with its cramped apartments and don't make eye contact with anyone, to this seaside land of mega homes and smiley hellos. I could only imagine what the mansion and people would be like later.

We were scheduled to attend a fundraiser for all the Republican candidates in Collier County. Unfortunately, I moved to Florida in the midst of Wit's first real campaign contest. So on this night Wit would be the star. And I would be what? The star's let?

I picked up the short black dress with the open back. Showing bare skin seemed to work down here. How much time did I have before getting ready? Maybe I could write for a little while. Flopping on the bed, I opened the laptop and pulled up my manuscript.

After leaving my job at the *New York Tribune*, I started writing a book about what happened to me last year. I call it "The Vanishing A-list." It's a chronicle about the kidnappings and murders I covered and how I, too, became a victim of the crazed maniac who orchestrated them. I still find it hard to talk about. "Read it in my book," I tell people.

A few keystrokes and I lost the current world. An hour later I was still typing. For some reason I glanced at the clock. Five o'clock! I was supposed to pick up Wit at 5:30. A quick shower, put on the Victoria Secret's matching little black bra and thong – Wit loves the thong—pile my 'getting-too-long-I-need-a-trim' brown hair on the top of my head, apply makeup faster than a Lancôme counter at Christmas time, shimmy into the little black dress, put on my designer shoes, no stockings – nobody wears stockings in Florida – walk Willie one more time, and by 5:31, I was in the underground parking.

The black Escalade sat in a space between two concrete columns. Getting it out had become a phobia. I backed out slightly then tried to turn the wheel a little, then backed out some more. It was taking too long. Darn, just do it. I backed up and heard a crunch. Oh Lord, what did I hit?

Chapter 2

I jumped out of the car. The right rear had grazed the last column. The white column was now streaked with black, and the black Escalade was now streaked with white.

No time to wipe off of the damage, if it could be wiped off.

Driving down Gulf Shore Boulevard, I called Wit's office.

"Congressman Whitman's office," answered Jennifer, the cheery receptionist.

"It's Jazz Billings. Would you tell the congressman I'm on my way but a little late?"

"Yes Miss Billings. No need to rush. I don't think he'll mind." Twenty-something Jennifer made 34-year-old me feel like an old lady.

Traffic wasn't bad and I found a parking space on Fifth Avenue only a block past his office. The congressional office is on the second floor above a bank, although you'd never know it was a bank. Everything in Naples looks like a Beverly Hills movie set with the beautiful facades and interiors. Instead of taking the elevator, I raced up the stairs. "I'm here," I shouted. No one greeted me, so I sat down on the waiting couch. At least that's what I called the beige leather sofa when I first got to Naples. Now it's the sex couch. Wit and I had fantastic sex on it a few nights ago. We went to his office to pick up some documents. Being the only two there, one thing led to another, and there was no waiting on this couch.

I gave the couch a fond pat and searched through the pile of newspapers and magazines on the mahogany and granite coffee table. Flipping through the pages of the *Naples Daily News*, I landed on one of my favorite parts, the Police Report. It's the local crime gossip page made up of little paragraphs about every arrest in the town. In Naples, DUIs are the big news, with domestic violence a close second. But the domestic violence usually consists of pushing your partner. In New York it would mean dismembering them.

A headline caught my attention.

Deputies searching for missing North Naples Man

Was this one of those "silver alerts?" In Florida, if a little old person goes missing, the police call it a "silver alert." But no. This was different.

"Collier County sheriff's deputies are asking the public's help in finding a 22-year-old North Naples man who is missing. Cody Mullins was last seen around 11:00 p.m. Tuesday night, leaving the house of his girlfriend Cassidy Moran on Willow Street in North Naples. Deputies said he left her house on his horse. Mullins is 6 feet tall, of average build, with brown hair. He was wearing jeans and a blue denim shirt. Anyone with information on Mullin's whereabouts, or his horse, is asked to call the county sheriff's office at 555-9300."

A man, and a horse, disappeared? I love this police report. Wait a minute. Cassidy Moran? Could that be the Cassie I met at the Y tennis lesson?

Wit and his friends play tennis, so I thought I should learn too. I took a lesson. Cassie and I were made partners. We were terrible but had such a great time together, we went to lunch afterwards. I really liked Cassie. I meant to call her. What was her last name?

Cassidy Moran. Was Moran her last name? Cassie was Irish. We kidded about that. Moran? Yes that sounded right. It had to be her and now her boyfriend was missing. I definitely should call her.

Cassie, however, disappeared from my mind when I heard the singing. A male voice. Who was singing? Was that Wit? Was he *singing*?

"Born to beeee w-i-i-i ld." A woman laughed. Then an office door opened and Wit and the still laughing woman walked toward me. I had never met this woman. I certainly would have remembered her. Dressed in a teal suit, probably size two, she was elegant and blonde. A perfectly colored blonde. The medium length hair was gorgeous, swept back from her face like a sculpture. How much did that cost? And the outfit. Prada? The suit had to be Prada, or is it Pravda? I self-consciously adjusted the neckline of my on-sale-at-Macy's black dress.

"Oh James, I can not believe you remember that song," Miss Elegance said. Wit was beaming at her, beaming like an idiot. Suddenly he noticed me. "Oh hi," he said.

He turned back to the woman. I couldn't believe it. "Oh hi?" Like "My driver's here." How about "Let me introduce you to the woman I sleep naked with every night."

"Mara, I'm sorry," he told the woman. "I have to get to Carson's fundraiser. I'm supposed to introduce him, so I've got to be there soon. Sorry you can't make it. Jed will call you tomorrow with that information." He turned back to me. "I don't think you two have met. Mara Parkin this is Jazz Billings, my – ah – house guest."

He didn't say that, did he? What was wrong with him?

Mara extended her hand. All I could see was the diamond. Hard to miss. About a four-carat glob perched on her right ring finger. No ring was on her left. Figured. Up close she looked about 40. It was hard to tell with all the Botox pumped into her face. Not a line anywhere. But there was definitely some mileage in those eyes.

"Well you are a lucky woman," she said, giving me the once over. "Staying with James, I bet you have secrets to tell."

I offered a demure smile. I felt my lips purse. I didn't even know I could purse my lips. "I think it's getting late, *DEAR,*" I said to Wit. I never call him dear. That jolted him into a curious glance in my direction. At least he now knew I was there. A quick exchange of goodbyes and we were in the car.

"Houseguest?" I said. "*Houseguest?* Is that what you call the person you have incredible sex with every night. Or maybe you don't think the sex is incredible anymore."

"The sex is incredible," he said, staring straight ahead at the road.

"Well then what? *What?*"

For a few seconds, he didn't speak. Then he turned toward me. "The election is six weeks away. I've got an opponent who's attacking me on every front. This is a conservative district. Jazz, I just don't know what to call you. We're living together. But you said 'Think of it as temporary.' So what do I say? Once the election's over, we can say, or do, anything we want, but for now… "

Wow, that hurt. Our relationship was so fragile. I was still so insecure in it.

It had to be that woman, "Who is she?" I asked.

"Who? Mara? She's a Washington lobbyist. We're working together on the oil drilling legislation."

"But you were singing to her. You don't even sing to me. Born to be Wild? What was that about?"

"Mara and I go way back. We were just remembering an evening. It was nothing. Nothing."

I turned toward the window. What a day. Willie's bowels, the Cadillac crunch, then this Mara who gets sung to. And now there was this party where I would be gawked at by hacks and hangers-on.

Boy, this day is murder, I thought. I had no idea how prophetic that thought would be.

Chapter 3

The further south you drive on Gordon Drive, the bigger the homes. The mansion estate of developer Ross Davids looked like a Tuscany villa. Lights illuminated the massive shrubbery and trees surrounding it. A long brick-paved driveway led to a circular area in front of the house. The driveway was big enough for 20 cars to park, but a valet was whisking them away as fast as people exited them.

This was one of the few mega mansions I had seen where the owner actually lived there full-time. In Naples the slogan should be "the more they pay, the less they stay." Most of the multi-million dollar condos and homes near the gulf are used for only a few months, or even weeks, a year.

Wit and I hadn't talked much on the way there. He seemed preoccupied and I just didn't know what else to say. Yes, Wit finally had an opponent. Republicans in Collier County usually run unopposed. One party rule takes on new meaning down here. But for this election, a new independent party called the Bring Back Prosperity Party, or BBP, had an entire slate of candidates running, including someone against Wit. The new party seemed to have incredible funding. It was plastering the news media with negative ads urging voters to get rid of all the incumbents.

To counter those attacks, the local Republican Party needed to raise more money, especially for the incumbent chairman of the county commission,

Carson Wicklow. BBP money was coming in from all over the country. The BBP commission candidate had already raised $650,000, versus Carson's $250,000. For Southwest Florida, these political war chests were mind-boggling. Nobody ever thought to put a cap on campaign financing for local offices. There was never a need. Until now.

Carson is a good friend of Wit's and the fundraiser was primarily for him. Wit not only has his own money, but as an incumbent in Washington he has access to lots more. It's Carson who needs the help. Carson had been in the banking business. With the turn in the economy, he was not as wealthy as he once was. He couldn't afford to finance his own campaign.

He and Wit went to Harvard together. I had met him a few times. A nice man. His wife died years ago, leaving him with twin daughters to raise. According to Wit, the girls, named Cara and Chasen, were seventeen, beautiful, and turning Carson prematurely gray.

Two valets simultaneously opened the driver and passenger doors allowing Wit and I to get out at the same time. In front of the mansion's huge wooden doors, a twenties-something female in a thigh-high tight red dress waited, clipboard in hand. No need to check our names. "Good evening Congressman Whitman," she said. "And this must be your" – big pause – "guest." As she opened one of the doors, she smiled broadly at me. I forced a smile back and walked into a mammoth foyer. In the middle stood a cascading fountain. A fountain inside a house? A few people stood near it, barely missing the spray. From another room I could hear conversations and piano music.

"Congressman, good to see you." Mack Solan, the new head of Collier's Republican Party, rushed over the minute he saw Wit. Solan had come down from Washington to help his friends in Naples with the election. He was put in charge of the local party even though he was from Virginia. "Carson's in the study," he said. "It's over here on the right. He's with some of our big contributors. I know he would love you to join him." He looked at me. "Is this your new lady friend?"

"Yes, this is Jazz – ah A.J. Billings."

"I'm sure she would like a drink or some food. I can escort her while you join the commissioner."

Wit looked at me questioningly.

"You go Wit, I'll be fine." After all this was my new life. He headed to the right and I headed to the left, trailing behind the man who had not spoken directly to me. Welcome to the South.

The hallway opened into a large living room that overlooked a blue-glowing pool. Lush landscaping surrounded it. If there were any neighbors, no one would know it. Solan led me to the part of the living room where a long table of food had been set up. With a sweeping gesture like "here you are," he quickly disappeared.

As I surveyed the food, I also surveyed the wealth on display. Talk about bling. Gold and diamond jewelry draped the suntanned necks, arms and ears of Naples elite. And what thin bodies. Both the men and the women looked like staying fit were their careers.

Everybody seemed to know everybody else. Nothing is worse than entering a cocktail party and knowing no one. My eyes scanned the room looking for any friendly face.

Over in an alcove I noticed a good-looking blonde girl, maybe 16 or 17. She didn't look happy. In fact she looked almost as if she was in pain. Welcome to the club, I thought. What was she doing at a fundraiser like this anyway? Then I remembered. Carson had twin daughters. She must be one of them.

I walked over. "You don't look so glad to be here," I said. The girl appeared startled to have someone talk to her. She really was a knockout, like a junior miss with that ironed-looking long blonde hair and stunning blue eyes.

She glanced at me, offering a half smile. "You must be A.J. billings, the reporter."

"Yes, although I'm not doing any reporting right now. But how did you know who I was?"

13

"You're one of the few people I don't know. And you're younger than most here. You're living with Wit, aren't you? Everybody's talking about it."

I ignored the remark. "You're one of Commissioner Wicklow's daughters, aren't you?"

"Yes. I'm Chasen Wicklow."

"I've heard about you and your sister. Is she here too?"

"No." She looked around the room as if to confirm it. "Cara's always late. But she should be here soon. Everybody says she loves to party."

"And you don't?"

"We're not very much alike. But Wit probably told you all about us."

"All I heard was that you are identical twins, gorgeous and your father can't wait until you are old and dumpy-looking."

She smiled, that half smile again. I wanted to loosen her up.

"Twins. You and your sister must be something at school. Have you tried fooling the teachers? You know, sitting in on each other's classes, taking each other's tests?"

"We don't go to the same school."

I was confused. "Really?"

"Oh you don't know about Triesen's, do you?" Chasen smiled, fully now. "That's something you could write about. I go to the Community School here in Naples. It's a local private school. But Cara, she's the family's 'wild child,' as my father puts it. So she was sent to the Triesen Academy. It's a small private high school for girls who need – what do they say – a little extra attention. It's out by Ave Maria. Many people don't even know it exists."

"I didn't even know Ave Maria existed. What is that?"

She laughed. "It's a small town east of here. It's got a big cathedral and a university. Triesen is nearby."

"And Cara goes there? Does she live at the school?"

"Part-time. She also commutes home. Well actually she's driven home, by limo. Triesen supplies them. It's not your ordinary school."

"It must be strange not being with your sister in high school."

"We haven't spent much time together lately, even out of school. We haven't agreed on things for a while."

"Oh that will change. I bet in the future you'll be good friends. I know someone with two daughters. They hated each other growing up but now both are married and the best of friends. I'm sure that will happen to you two."

That half-smile again. "Things don't always turn out like people plan."

I didn't know what else to say. So I just smiled at her. Suddenly Chasen tensed up. She was staring behind me. I turned to see what she was looking at. Two men were headed in our direction.

"I have to go," she said. She quickly turned and headed in the opposite direction toward the pool area. So did the men. They seemed intent on getting to Chasen. And nobody was smiling.

Chapter 4

Alone again. In the past whenever I had been at parties like this, I was reporting. So I could walk up to anyone and start interviewing them. But what to do when you are a guest and so on display? I walked back to the food table and watched as people watched me and pretended they weren't talking about me, which of course they were.

My mind drifted to all that happened today. What would Wit say about another Willie problem? His building allows small pets. Willie, however, is not small. The condo board said it would make an exception for the few weeks that I and "the dog" would be staying there. This was after all a trial living together. Nobody expected it to last. A liberal New York newspaper reporter with the conservative congressman James Fennimore Whitman? Please. People would put up with me and Willie for the short time until Congressman Whitman came to his senses and moved on to a more suitable relationship. So they left us alone, until last week when Willie attempted to mount a Maltese in the elevator. The condo commandos – that's what I call the board of directors – sent a letter ordering me to meet with them about the dog problem. A sex-starved and now loose-bowelled Labrador Retriever would not be tolerated in the building. The commandos would probably say Willie had to go, which meant I would too. What would Wit say?

Where was he? I was getting tired of looking at the vegetable platter. I decided to walk out to the pool area and the temporary bar there. I asked for a glass of chardonnay. I don't really like it but it's socially acceptable and I needed to be socially acceptable. As I sipped my wine, I moved off to one side of the bar. The two men who followed Chasen approached from the other side. I finally had a chance to look at them. One was very big, in height and girth. He looked like a former football linebacker. Dressed in a baggy black suit, his buzz cut hairstyle reminded me of the good old boys from the Florida panhandle where I did a story once. The other man was as dapper as could be. With an Armani suit and stylish gray hair, he looked like an older model for Ralph Lauren. Two more opposite people there couldn't be in Naples. But here they were, deep in conversation, and not even noticing me as they ordered drinks. I tried to listen and caught a snippet of the conversation. The big man was talking. "Don't worry. We just need to talk to her. I'll take care of it."

Suddenly I felt lips on my neck. What? Wit. Wit was actually nuzzling my neck – in public. The open back dress does it every time. Well probably with a Scotch or two, also. He smiled at the two men. "Hello Sheriff. Hello Ross." They shook hands.

"Have you met Jazz? Jazz, this is our County Sheriff Bub Walker, and our host for tonight, Ross Davids. Ross is one of the most successful developers in Naples. He did Crescent Cove Towers."

"Oh I love that building." I held out my hand. Davids took it, but his eyes avoided mine. I don't like people who don't look you in the eye. That, however, was not a problem with the sheriff.

"Well, well, the congressman's girlfriend. You're that New York reporter, aren't you?" He grabbed my hand, practically leering at me. His drawl was old-time Florida. "I hope you're not going to be writing anything negative about our beautiful Collier County." County sounded like cow-tee.

How could such a good old boy be elected in a place like Naples, which was so cosmopolitan?

"I'm not reporting any more," I said. "I'm working on a book."

"Oh right, about how you were a sex slave."

"Not really." I did not like this man.

"Now that's nothing to be ashamed of. Sex is what many of us live for, right Ross?"

Ross Davids looked embarrassed. "I think I better go talk to Mack," the developer said. "Nice meeting you," he added in my direction. Still no eye contact, and he was gone.

"Miss Beellings, if you do decide to be a reporter again, you should come tour my department. I have the best police department in the state. And I'd be very glad to personally give you a tour." He squeezed my hand as he said "personally." Then he continued to hold it. I noticed the big shiny watch on his wrist. It had so many dials it probably told him when to pee. Was it a Rolex? Could a sheriff have a Rolex? I was about to shake his hand loose when he finally let go. That was only so he could grab his glass on the bar.

"Got to get a refill somewhere else," he whispered to me. "This bartender doesn't know shit about making a good drink. Congressman, see you and Miss New York later." He winked at me and headed into the house.

I didn't even wait until he was out of earshot. "I don't like him," I told Wit. "Is he up for reelection? I'd like to donate to his opponent!"

"He's not the most diplomatic," Wit said. "But he's been effective here. Everybody's scared of him because he's so unpredictable which I guess gives us good enforcement. Before Bub, we had a sheriff who everybody liked. But he moved out of state to be with a sick relative and that left the sheriff job open. Bub won in a three way race last year. The two better candidates cancelled each other out. He's not up for reelection this year. If he were, he'd probably win in a landslide."

"A landslide?" Someone else joined the conversation. "A landslide victory, now that would be nice." Carson Wicklow put his arm around me.

"Hi Jazz," he said, kissing me on the cheek. "Your man has been very helpful to me tonight."

"I'm glad. Oh I just met your daughter."

"Which one?"

"Chasen."

"Ah Chase, my quiet one."

I didn't think she had been so quiet.

"Have you seen Cara?" The commissioner asked. "She was staying over at school last night but promised she'd be here."

"No, I haven't seen her."

"Well, she'll be along." He turned to Wit. "It's probably time for the 'money please' sermon."

As if on cue, Mack Solan banged for attention on a portable mahogany podium that had been wheeled into the center of the living room. Wit and the commissioner walked over to him. Everybody else followed.

After the speeches, which seemed to be given by half the room, I looked forward to going back to the condo with Wit and sipping a little cream sherry. Then I'd tell him about the rug and the car. Tell him? He'd soon see both.

From across the room Wit gave me the "let's go" nod. I headed toward him.

He and Carson were shaking hands with the people who were leaving. Only a dozen or so remained.

"A real good evening," Carson said. "I think we raised about $100,000 for my race alone."

"Two more minutes and we're out of here," Wit said. It hadn't been so bad after all. Then everything changed.

The sheriff rushed in from outside. He hurried over to Carson and whispered in his ear. Carson turned pale. "I have to go," he said, heading for the door.

Wit grabbed his arm. "What's wrong?"

"Something's happened to my daughter."

"Which one?"

"I don't know."

Chapter 5

Carson ran out with the sheriff. Wit continued shaking hands until only Ross Davids was left. After another thank you to the host, we headed for the car. The ride home had even less conversation then the ride there. Wit was deep in thought. "I don't know if I should call him yet," he finally said. "But I've got to find out how serious it is. He lives for those girls."

He never noticed the car scrape and he barely reacted to Willie's accident on the rug. He was too preoccupied. He decided to call Carson's administrative assistant. Key advisors usually know everything. But the assistant said he hadn't heard a thing. Maybe it wasn't as bad as we were imagining.

Actually it was worse. The phone rang at 2:00 a.m. Wit grabbed for it and accidentally hit the speaker button so I heard everything. It was Carson. His voice quavered. "She's gone, Wit. She's gone. She killed herself, right here in the garage."

"Carson, who's gone?"

"Cara, my Cara, she's dead. My housekeeper Marita found her. Marita was out all day. It was her day off. When she finally got back home, she found her, there." He broke into sobs.

Wit looked at me as he said into the phone, "I'm so sorry. What happened?"

"She left the car running in the garage and she died from carbon mon-oxide poisoning. She was dressed like she was going out. Maybe she was coming to the party, instead… Marita called 911. She couldn't reach my cellphone. I guess someone called the sheriff."

"Did she leave a note?" The lawyer in Wit kicked in.

"No, not that we've found yet. But what else could it be? Chasen is catatonic. She won't talk. Her whole body is shaking. I called our doctor. He's going to give her something to calm her down. I don't know what else to do. Oh Wit I'm a real mess." He started sobbing again.

I never heard a man cry like that.

"I'll come over right now," Wit said. "I'll be there in 15 minutes."

"You don't have to."

"I want to. I'll get dressed and be right over. Have they – is the body still there?"

"Yes, but I think they are going to take her away soon. I guess they have to make sure everything is as it seems. But the sheriff said it's pretty obvious it was suicide. He keeps talking about wild kids and how emotional they get. I wish he'd shut up. Oh God, Wit, I don't know what to do. I've got to be strong for Chase."

"I'll be there soon Carson. Just hold on."

Wit hung up the phone and grabbed me. He held me so tight, I could barely breathe.

"Cara committed suicide. I've got to go to Carson."

"What can I do? Do you want me to go too? I could maybe stay with Chasen?"

"No. Oh I don't know. Carson has a sister, I'm sure she'll be here by tomorrow. The doctor will give Chasen something tonight. You go back to sleep. I'll call you in the morning. There will be a lot to do. He's got his private life and then his public life to deal with on this."

"Why would she commit suicide – and right before the election?"

"I don't know. She was emotional about things. But she always seemed such a survivor to me."

"Do we really know it was a suicide?"

"Jazz, please, I don't need you being a reporter right now." He gave me a quick kiss then grabbed a pair of jeans and a polo shirt. His loafers went on without socks. I often laughed about that. But not now. "I'll call," he said.

"I love you," I said – to no one. He was already in the living room searching for his keys.

This was not how it was supposed to be. I needed to support him with whatever happened. "I'm coming with you!" I shouted. "But I've got to get dressed." I grabbed the first thing I could find, the dress I wore to the fundraiser. It seemed appropriate. It was black.

Chapter 6

Normally the Wicklows' street is dark and quiet. But on this night nearly every house had lights on. Police cars lined the road near Carson's house, which was bathed in light. Off to one side of the driveway, a crowd of neighbors gathered. Two deputy sheriffs kept them behind a yellow crime scene tape that stretched across the front yard and the driveway. The doors of the three-car garage were up and two small BMW convertibles could be seen parked side by side. Cara and Chasen's cars? Must be. A group of police technicians huddled over the silver car on the left.

Wit grabbed my hand as we headed for the front door. One of the sheriff's deputies stopped us.

"Sorry sir, you can't go in there."

"I'm Congressman Whitman and Commissioner Wicklow just called and asked me to come."

"Sorry sir. I have orders. No one can go in there."

"Who's in charge here?"

"Sheriff Walker is here."

"Well go tell him Congressman Whitman is here and Carson Wicklow wants me inside."

The deputy looked confused. Should he leave his post to find the sheriff? The answer was made for him.

"It's all right Al. I'll escort the Congressman in." I didn't have to turn. I recognized the old Florida drawl and felt the possessive arm drape around my shoulder.

"And look who else is here. Why Miss New York." The sheriff pulled me closer and whispered "You like excitement, don't you?"

I glared at him.

But Walker kept whispering. "Don't get your imagination going wild here. It's just another suicide. These kids can't take the pressure."

Before I could respond, he let go of me and motioned for us to follow him into the house. Carson sat in the living room. He seemed oblivious to the police officers milling around. Then he saw Wit and rose from his chair. Wit rushed to him and the two embraced.

"I'm so sorry Carson." Wit's eyes welled up. "I'm so sorry."

"Me too," I said. Carson turned and gave me a hug as well. We all sat down on the sofa.

"I don't know what to do," the father said.

"Can I help with Chasen?" I asked. "Where is she?"

"The doctor gave her something. It knocked her out. Marita's watching over her. I've never seen her like that. I don't know what to do."

"Well I'd start planning a funeral if I were you," the sheriff said.

I couldn't believe it. How could a man be so insensitive? I wanted to slap him. I even made a move to get up, but Wit jumped up first. "Sheriff, can I have a word with you?"

"Sure Congressman." The two walked into the hallway. I couldn't hear the conversation, but I could sense Wit's anger. The sheriff, however, wasn't fazed by it. Wit was gesturing and the sheriff was nodding with a silly smirk. What were they saying? I couldn't stand it anymore so I got up and walked over to them.

"Of course there will be an autopsy, Congressman," the sheriff said. "It's a formality. It will be done. But it's not going to show anything else,

I'm sure. The kid killed herself. It's too bad for the commissioner with the election coming up and all. But hey, what do they say? That's politics." He smiled at me and walked away.

"Why is he like that?" I asked Wit.

"Well for one thing he hates Carson," Wit said. "As chairman of the commission, Carson won't take anything from him. They got into it a few weeks ago about the sheriff's budget. Carson got the other commissioners to agree to cut about $5 million from it. But let's not talk about this now. I've got to get back to him." He nodded toward Carson who sat on the sofa staring into space.

Not knowing what to do, I walked around the room looking at the numerous family pictures. Over the fireplace was a painting of a seated Carson with Chasen and Cara standing on either side. The girls were about 10 and dressed like little princesses in pink dresses. On a side table nearby were more photos and a pile of untouched mail. I picked up a glass frame that held two pictures. One showed Carson, Chasen and Cara opening presents in front of a Christmas tree. The other was at the beach with Carson watching little Cara and Chasen run toward the waters edge. On the wall were the standard school photo head shots. Two looked like they were taken recently. It was amazing how much the girls looked like. I assumed the twin with more make up and her hair pulled back was Cara. I stared at the photo. Seventeen, beautiful, and so much to live for. How could she kill herself? Why would she kill herself? What could happen in your life that would make it so unbearable you couldn't go on? And looking like that?

All my life I wanted to look like that. I have always felt insecure about my appearance, what with the unruly brown hair and the freckles. Nobody ever thought a girl with freckles was pretty. You were cute. Cara had no freckles. She was one of the most beautiful girls I had ever seen.

As I put the glass frame down, I noticed a piece of paper on top of the mail. I picked it up. There were only five words, "We need to talk, important!" It was written in that teenage flowery writing with a heart over the i instead of a dot.

Did one of the twins write it, or was it given to a twin? Could it be one of the last things Cara saw? I would have to mention this to Wit.

"What are you looking at? Still playing reporter?" the sheriff had come up behind me.

"There's a note here. It might be important."

"That's none of your business." He grabbed the note from my hand. "This should go to my crime scene people." I felt like telling him where to go. Instead I went back to Wit and Carson. The sheriff stared at me, then turned and walked away. I watched him. Instead of handing the note to the crime scenes officer nearby, he walked down the hall. Then he stuck the note in his pocket.

Chapter 7

The next two days passed in a blur. Carson wanted everything to go quickly. He said he couldn't bear the pain of the mourning going on and on. Wit did what he could to help, but there really wasn't much to do. The funeral home was handling it all. One night was set aside for a wake, where people could pay their respects to the family, and the next day would be the funeral and burial.

As soon as I could, I told Wit about the sheriff and the note. He said forget about it. Our focus should be on Carson and helping him get through this.

So there we were at the wake for a teenager – with an open casket. As I looked at Cara, I couldn't get over the incredible likeness of the two sisters. That was even more eerie when Chasen arrived wearing the same royal blue dress that her sister wore in the coffin. I started to walk over to greet her, but Chasen showed no sign of recognition. She appeared as if in a trance. Medication? Maybe. She headed toward the casket, but her way was blocked by a pack of girls who raced over. They hugged her and offered words of sympathy. She barely reacted to them.

As I watched, I noticed another woman watching them too. The face was so familiar. Who? Who is that? Then it hit me. It was Beth Johnson, a reporter I used to work with in New York. I couldn't believe she was in Naples. I rushed over to her.

"Beth what are you doing here?"

"Jazz?" We hugged. "I could ask you the same question. How are you? It's so good to see you." We hugged again. "I'm working here," she said. "After The Trib, I was in Boston for a while, but my husband wanted to move to Florida. So here I am. I thought I'd report for a few more years. And when this job opened, I took the crime beat for the *Naples Daily News*."

I guess I looked amazed because she hurriedly went on. "I know, it's a small paper. But there's much less pressure here. I mean look, this isn't even a crime, but any death is unusual in Naples. So I'm covering this. But what about you? What are you doing here? I thought you'd get another Pulitzer for those stories last year about the young celebrities disappearing."

"I needed some time off. I'm writing a book about what happened. And I got involved with the local congressman here."

"James Whitman?"

"Yes, I'm staying with him for a few months to see how it all works out."

"You and Whitman? Wow, I never thought you would settle down."

"I'm not sure I have."

"Well good luck with that. This is really something isn't? Look at the crowd, and the funeral tomorrow will be even bigger. Are you going?"

"Yes, Wit is a good friend of Carson's."

"Right. Wicklow's really destroyed by this, isn't he? And Chasen, how odd to wear the same dress that your dead sister is going to be buried in. You'd expect her to wear black."

"Yes, it is odd. I heard the sisters didn't even dress alike when both were alive. But they were twins. Maybe it's her way of saying good-bye."

Beth said she had to run. She needed to interview someone. Wit was busy talking with a man I didn't know. So I wandered around the funeral home. Groups were collecting according to their social set. The young beautiful people of Naples all clustered near the front door, the better to see and be seen. The older crowd of political friends, business associates, and government aides gathered in the viewing room. I wound up there too. About two dozen floral displays surrounded the casket. I started reading the cards of who sent them.

The groups of people chatted, until as if on cue, all heads turned when Chasen finally broke free from the girls and walked to the casket. The room fell silent as she kneeled down in front of her sister. What was it like to see a mirror image of yourself lying there? Was it as if you were witnessing your own death? She leaned over to kiss her sister's cheek. Because I was nearer, I saw what many others could not. As Chasen kissed her sister she put something under Cara's pillow. A note? A little piece of jewelry? I couldn't tell.

As Chasen stood up, she noticed me. This time the eyes focused. She stared and there was a look. I couldn't read it. One thing was sure. It wasn't friendly. Was she upset that the token to her sister had been seen? Why did I get that look of—of what?

Chapter 8

"*A funeral for a teenager is painful to watch. When life is just starting, to have it end ....*" I stopped writing. I had picked up my notepad to jot down some thoughts while I waited for things to start. But now the church was full. How many people were there? With the supporters of Carson, the young Naples crowd, and the curious, it was standing room only. I could see through the open front doors more people lined up down the steps.

Although Cara had gone to an all girls school, she had no shortage of male friends. The boys wore blue blazers with khaki pants and casual shoes, but no socks. The girls were in light flowery dresses. I felt like I was at a school dance, not a funeral.

In front of me sat a group of girls who couldn't stop talking about the tragedy.

"She would *never* kill herself," a blonde with short curly hair said to the statuesque brunette sitting next to her. "Never!" The blonde repeated. Then she noticed me staring at them. "Sorry, are we too loud?"

"No, I'm interested in what you're saying. Did you go to school with Cara?"

"Who are you?" the brunette asked.

"I'm A.J. Billings. I'm sorry. I'm just curious."

"A.J. Billings? Are you that reporter from New York?" the blonde with the Orphan Annie hairdo asked. "Are you doing a story on this? Are we going to be in your story? I'm Sarah and this is Krista. We went to Triesen with Cara. We can tell you some good stuff. Cara was our friend and there is no way she would kill herself without telling us."

I almost started to laugh. I don't think she realized how funny that sounded. Fortunately the processional started down the aisle. "I'll remember that," I said to them. The sheriff kept assuring Carson it was suicide even though the final results of the autopsy weren't in yet. But the way these girls were talking? Interesting. Very interesting.

I tapped the blonde girl on the shoulder. "Do you have an e-mail address or a cellphone number I can have. I'd like to get in touch with you both."

"Sure, here's my card. Krista, give her one of your cards."

They both handed over little white cards with their names and contact information, including cellphone numbers, email addresses and lots more. Facebook, Twitter, blogs – the social media list goes on and on. Teenagers with business cards? I realized I didn't have any cards for my new life. But then what would I call myself? Official lady friend?

The organ music started. I watched as Chasen and her father, holding hands, walked behind the casket to their seats in the first pew. Wit sat there waiting for them. He said I could sit there too, but I felt more comfortable in the back.

By the end of the funeral mass, and after Carson's touching eulogy, there were few dry eyes in the church. As we left the dark vestibule, the bright sunshine was jarring. It was as if a curtain lifted. People started talking and laughing as they headed to their cars and back to their lives. I thought of how Carson's and Chasen's lives were now changed forever.

Walking down the church steps, I noticed a group of police officers in dress uniform standing at attention. In the middle stood Bub Walker. He saw me and winked.

For a second, I thought he was going to pucker his lips into a silent kiss. At a funeral to be like that? Such a wicked man. Was there anything this sheriff wasn't capable of doing?

Chapter 9

The day after the funeral Wit and I were back to our morning ritual of sitting on the back balcony, or lanai as the Floridians call it, reading the morning papers. Below us, boats headed out for a day on the gulf. Wit's newspaper pile consisted of the national papers. He subscribed to the *New York Times* and the *Wall Street Journal.* I, of course, got my Trib so I could see what my former colleagues were doing. But I also enjoyed reading the two local papers – the *Naples Daily News* and the *Fort Myers News-Press.*

Because of Cara's death, the papers were stacked up.

I reached for the latest edition of the Naples paper. With Beth now writing for it, I was anxious to read her piece on the funeral. It was the front page story with a large photo of the "grieving Commissioner" with his arm around Chasen as they followed the casket out of the church. Beth Johnson reported that 600 attended the funeral and almost as many went to the burial in the cemetery by Vanderbilt Beach.

I couldn't get over the cemetery, so close to the Gulf of Mexico. The land had to be incredibly valuable. Yet somehow a cemetery started there. And once a cemetery, land stays a cemetery. So the mourners almost had a water view as Cara's coffin was lowered into the ground. Of course Beth didn't report any of that. She listed the dignitaries who attended and what the minister said.

A thorough piece. I probably would have done more of a feature story. It was hard to read any article without comparing it to what you would have written. I scanned the following pages until I got to the Police Report. And then I remembered. I hadn't done anything about Cassie and her missing boyfriend.

I had never even held a tennis racquet before I signed up for the Y class. But I borrowed one of Wit's and headed for the courts off Pine Ridge Road. About 15 women attended the introductory lesson. Cassie and I were the only ones not in expensive new tennis outfits. I had on my old black yoga outfit covered by a pair of shorts. She wore a T-shirt and cut-off jeans. We instantly bonded, even though our lives off the court were so different. Cassie was in her twenties and had never been out of the state of Florida. She barely graduated from high school, she told me. I was in my thirties, a graduate of Northwestern University and Columbia Journalism School and had traveled the world. But Cassie probably had been happier with her life then at times I had been with mine. She loved nature and worked in a nursery out east. She talked of her boyfriend – must be that Cody Mullins—and how he worked on a cattle ranch in a rural area of Collier. Cassie adored him.

"Wit, I forgot. I know somebody in the Police Report." I rifled through the stack of old papers and found the issue that mentioned Cody Mullins. "Wit, are you in the middle of something?"

"What? Just reading more about the off-shore oil debate. It never ends."

"I said I know somebody in the Police Report. Remember me telling you about Cassie who I took that tennis lesson with? I think her boyfriend is missing." I read the short article to him. "I'm going to call her. Just let her know I'm thinking of her."

I got out my phone and pulled up Whitepages.com on the internet to find Cassidy Moran's phone number. Cassie told me she lived with a female roommate. Would she even have a phone listed in her name? But there was a Cassidy Moran on Willow Street. I dialed the number and got voice mail.

"Cassie, It's Jazz Billings – from the Y tennis lesson. I read in the paper about Cody. If there's anything I can do, please call me. You can reach me on my cell at 212-555-5968."

A few hours later Cassie called back. "Jazz, oh it was good to hear from you. I am really falling apart here. Didn't you tell me you were a reporter or something?"

"Well yes, but I'm not now. I'm working on a book."

"But maybe you can help me. The police don't seem to care about Cody. They act like I'm bothering them whenever I call. But I know something is wrong. Maybe you could talk to them? Or investigate somehow?"

"Cassie, I don't know what I can do."

"Could we at least just meet and talk? I can tell you about Cody and maybe you could give me ideas where to look? I'm really afraid something bad has happened to him."

"Sure, when do you want to meet?"

"Today? If you could come out here, I could show you where I live and where he lives. Nobody's heard from him since the last night I saw him when he left my house."

Why not? Time to take a break from writing. Doctors have warned me not to stay on the computer too long with the carpal tunnel syndrome in my wrists.

"Okay, when?"

"I could get off work about 3:30. I can give you directions."

Wit said he would be late coming home. He was going to the campaign office after a meeting in his district office. So it would work. And I missed the investigating. Maybe I could help.

"Okay, where do I go?"

Chapter 10

About 20 miles from downtown Naples, new Florida gives way to old. The small house Cassie rented faced a street of dirt. Her mailbox, stuck on a wooden pole, was out on the main road a half-mile away.

Redheaded Cassie answered the door in green shorts, a black Lynyrd Skynyrd T-shirt and a yellow Corona in her hand. "Want one?" she asked. "It's 5 o'clock somewhere."

"Sure," I said. I had never been to Cassie's house. I had never been in any Southwest Florida homes except for mansions and luxury condos. This seemed more real life.

"So ask me questions," Cassie said, grabbing another beer out of an old avocado-colored refrigerator. "Like you would if you were doing one of your stories." She stuck a lime in the bottle and handed it to me.

The first question I had to ask was about the picture of Chrissie Evert hanging on the wall. Chrissie Evert? What was that about?

"It's a funny story," she said. "When I was in fifth grade I had a teacher who always called me Chrissie instead of Cassie. So kids thought my name was Chrissie. 'Just like Chrissie Evert,' the teacher said. I didn't know who that was, but I wasn't going to tell her. So I went and asked the librarian. She found a magazine with a story about Chrissie Evert. I liked the way she looked and that she played tennis. Tennis was such a rich person's sport. So I thought someday I'm going to be like Chrissie Evert. I got her picture and put it on my wall. I've had it for years and I finally took that tennis lesson. That's when I met you. But I guess I'll never be like Chrissie Evert."

"You can do a lot of other things."

"Right. I can't even find Cody."

"Well tell me about that night."

"I asked Cody to take me for a ride on his horse. Did I tell you his horse is missing too? I mean how do the police explain that? Well they don't. Nobody's seen Charlie, that's his horse, since that day. He's white, like the Lone Ranger's horse. So people would notice him if they saw him. Cody and Charlie, they were so cute together." Her eyes filled with tears.

"Go on," I urged her.

"It was such a beautiful night. A full moon lit up the sky. I thought it would be fun to ride out in the fields. We lay on a blanket and looked at the stars, and made love. It was so romantic. Cody has this sensitive side. Nobody sees it, but he can be really sweet. Anyway, we came back here and my roommate was here so he left pretty quick. I thought he'd call me that night, but he didn't. So the next morning I called him. There was no answer. I called about an hour later, and then another hour. I always got his voice mail. So I called the foreman of the ranch, Luther Minner. He said Cody never showed up for work. Then I knew something was wrong. I called the police. They said you have to wait 24 hours for a missing person. So I called his friend Billy. He hadn't seen him, but he's not working right now so he came over when he heard how upset I was. We went to Cody's trailer. There was nobody there. We – well Billy – said it would be okay if we went in. But the door was locked. Billy did something to the door and we got in. There was no food out like he had breakfast or anything. I don't think he ever made it home, and Charlie was gone. There's a little shed next to the trailer where he keeps Charlie. But no Charlie and no hay out for Charlie like he would do every morning. And his little horse trailer was there. So I called the police again and they said I still had to wait. Then I called his auto mechanic. But he said Cody hadn't called him. Now it's been five days. What else can I do? Jazz do you think he's dead? Oh God, is he dead?"

"Cassie stop, you don't know that. Did he owe anybody money? Could he have just gone away for awhile? And what's this about a mechanic? Is his car gone too?"

"He has a truck and it broke down about 10 days ago. It's with the mechanic. I've been giving him rides. And he's not like that – running away from somebody. He doesn't do drugs. He works out. He even goes to church with me. I know something bad has happened to him. But nobody but me and Billy seem to care. He doesn't have family here. I don't know much about his family. He came from Texas. Maybe you could talk to the detective who they put in charge of his missing person's report. Maybe if he thought somebody important was interested he'd do more."

"I don't know what I could say."

"Would you just talk to him, please? You could tell him you were doing a story about it."

"What's his name?"

"Detective Richard Folgers."

"Okay. Okay I'll call him. He's with the Collier County Sheriff's office, right?"

"Yes."

The sheriff was someone I didn't want to see again. But the sheriff's office had to be a big place. "I'll do it tomorrow."

"Oh Jazz, thanks so much. I think it will help."

After a visit to Cody's trailer and another hour of talking, it was time to go home. I gave her a hug and got into my car. I wasn't sure what I could do for Cassie, but maybe I could find out something.

As I reached the end of her dirt road, I stopped and adjusted my rear-view mirror to reapply some lipstick. Time to look good for my man. In the mirror I noticed a dark-colored car that had been parked a few houses from Cassie. It did a quick u-turn and sped toward me. But when it saw

I stopped, it slowly came up behind me. I mean very slowly, like it didn't want to get too near me. I made the turn onto the main road toward Naples. So did the other car. For a second I thought "Am I being followed?" No, the world does not always revolve around me. I mean who would be following me in Naples? I stepped on the gas and headed back to the condo.

Chapter II

Late the next day I was on my way to the sheriff's office. I had called in the morning. At first I didn't say anything about being a reporter. I told the person who answered that I was interested in the status of the missing person's case on Cody Mullins. A few transfers and I wound up talking to Detective Folgers who had been assigned the case. He wanted to know why I was calling. Was I a relative?

"I know his girlfriend Cassie," I said.

"Then Cassie should be the one talking to me," Folgers said. "And I told her I would call her if I had any information."

This was going nowhere. "I'm a newspaper reporter," I blurted out. Now why did I say that? Now it became official and I wasn't officially on any story.

"Then you should talk to our public information office. I can't talk to the press."

"I'm not doing a story – yet. But I think there are some things that maybe could help you. Could I meet with you?"

The detective let out a discernible sigh. You could almost hear his thoughts. He had so many cases. This Cody Mullins was a drifter. He had only been in Naples eight months, worked part time on a cattle ranch, probably a cokehead, or a drunk off on a binge. But a reporter with information?

"What paper?" he asked.

"Excuse me?"

"What paper do you work for?"

"The *New York Tribune*."

"And you're doing a story *here* in Naples Florida?"

"I told you I'm not doing a story yet. I'm just trying to get some facts straight. Cassie told me some things – I really would like to meet with you."

Folgers let out another sigh. No way to get out of this. He would have to see me.

"Okay. Can you come down here later today?"

"Sure, what time?"

"4 o'clock?"

"That's fine. Could you tell me where to go?"

Not a good line. He probably wanted to say "I'd love to tell you where to go." But instead he said "I'm in the county complex off of Airport Road. Do you know where it is?"

I did. I had been down to the county buildings several times with Wit.

"Yes I do. I'll see you later. Thank you."

For the next few hours I wrote, or at least tried to. Sometimes the writing goes well and at other times, well, this was one of those days. By 2:00 p.m. I turned off the computer and went down to take a swim. That's one of the wonderful things about writing in Southwest Florida. The weather is fantastic. You work, then you can take an hour off and go walk the beach, swim, bike, maybe even play tennis. Eventually I might play tennis. I would become an athlete. Not an official athlete, but at least I could do something athletic. My body seems to be doing fine with my metabolism, and maybe all the sex. But you've got to keep at it.

Today I would swim. I had the condo pool to myself. After a few laps of a combination Rin Tin Tin and Michael Phelps, I had enough exercise. I toweled off and went back up to the condo. After a quick shower, I was ready to go to the sheriff's office. But first I had to walk Willie.

"Time to go outside, Willie." He raced for the door. Down to the lobby again, this time on the service elevator, and we headed out to a small patch of land designated the "Dog Walking" area. It was so small it was more a dog plopping area. You had to watch where you stepped. People were supposed to clean up after their pets, and I had my little baggy or more appropriately a big baggy with me. But some people didn't bother. So often it was like walking through a minefield that the property manager had to clean up each night.

As we returned to the building, the president of the condo board, Howard Millstone, ran toward us.

"Miss Billings!" he shouted.

Willie pulled on the leash to greet him. Willie loves everybody. Mr. Millstone obviously does not love Willie. He glared at the dog.

"Don't forget our meeting in two weeks," he said.

"Oh I have it on my calendar." I gave him a big smile. He started to say more but I rushed past with a "See you."

Back in the service elevator, I looked at Willie. "Our days are numbered, boy."

An hour later I was parking my car in the garage near the police building. It's a free garage. I'm impressed. Nothing in New York is free.

The detective division was on the second floor of a large building that houses Collier's police. Detective Folgers sat at a desk in a corner. Wearing big black reading glasses, he was busy studying a report as I approached him. Like many detectives I've met, he was about 50, slightly overweight, and wearing a gray suit that needed dry cleaning. But that's where the similarity ended. Detective Folgers's hair was dyed jet black and slicked back like John Travolta in *Grease*. Did he think that made him look younger? I thought it made him look like a reject from the TV show *The Sopranos*.

"I'm A.J. Billings."

He took off the glasses and looked up. "Yeah, I Googled you." He motioned for me to sit down. "You're pretty famous in New York. What are you doing here?"

"I have a – a friend here. I'm working on a book."

"About Cody Mullins?"

"No. Not about Cody. Do you have anything new on him?"

"Nothing. Nobody's seen him."

"Or his horse. Don't you find it strange that his horse has disappeared?"

"You want me to do a missing horse case too?"

"But where would he and his horse go in the middle of the night?"

"Who says they left in the middle of the night?"

This was not going well. "He didn't go to work the next day."

"So? Maybe he decided to take the day off. Maybe he had a fight with his girlfriend and decided to go back to Texas or somewhere. Maybe he put his horse in his trailer and took off."

"His horse trailer is still here."

The detective didn't miss a beat. "He could have borrowed someone else's."

"And what car would he have used to pull it? His truck is still with the mechanic. Cassie checked."

"Okay, so we've got a missing person and a missing horse. If we find them, I'll let you and Cassie know."

"But aren't you doing something to find him?"

"Like what else? We talked to his friends, his neighbors, where he works. All we know is that he's not around here. We don't know if he's somewhere else. You have any more information?"

I had to shake my head. "No."

"Well then, I've got other cases to work on. Nice meeting you." He put on his glasses and looked back down at the papers on his desk.

I had been dismissed. I didn't really have anything to tell Cassie. But at least I tried. I walked back to the elevator. As I got in and turned around, I saw the sheriff coming around the corner. No! Bad timing. I hit the door's "close" button hard, then hit it again. I stared at it, willing the door to close. I would not look up. Close, close! Finally it did. Hopefully he didn't see me.

Chapter 12

Why is that New York reporter here? Although he loved to flirt with her and get her all pissed off at him, the sheriff didn't have time for that now. He turned in the other direction and stared at the wall until the elevator door closed. Then he walked over to the young desk sergeant handling reception. The officer sat up at attention when he saw Sheriff Walker standing before him.

"That woman who just got in the elevator," the sheriff said, "why was she here?"

"She had a meeting with Detective Folgers," the sergeant answered.

"Why?"

"I don't know sir. She asked for him specifically. He told me to send her back."

"If she ever comes here again, she sees no one until she talks to me. You understand?"

"Yes sir."

"And get Folgers on the phone. Tell him to come to my office – now!"

Chapter 13

The next morning I called Cassie at the nursery where she worked. When I told her the meeting with Folgers didn't go well, she seemed even more upset.

"Jazz I feel like someone's watching me. I went to the motor vehicles office yesterday to renew my license and I saw this car behind me when I left my house and it was behind me when I left motor vehicles."

I didn't know what to say. It was probably a coincidence, but what about the car I saw? We were both probably paranoid, but I knew that wasn't what Cassie wanted to hear. "You should tell Detective Folgers," I said.

"He won't believe me."

"You should tell him anyway. Have you told your roommate?"

"She's up north with her sick mother. She doesn't know when she's coming back."

"Well the next time you go out, if you see that car again, you call me. We'll go tell Folgers together."

"Oh thank you, Jazz. You must think I'm crazy. I'm sorry to bother you with all this."

In the background, I heard someone call her name. "I have to get back to work," she said. "I'll talk to you soon."

"Okay, call me if you need me." Poor Cassie. What would I do if Wit suddenly disappeared?

But he was still very much around. That night we went to dinner at the latest "in" restaurant on Third Street. Downtown Naples has all these trendy shops and expensive restaurants. What's interesting is that the city's retail areas are split between two roads – Fifth Avenue and Third Street. They are about a mile apart. In between is a residential area with condos and homes. To go from one part of the city to the other, you have to drive. The other thing that makes Naples' downtown different from most is that the Gulf of Mexico is only a short walk from either shopping district.

Before dinner we strolled – I love that word– to the pier near Third Street to watch the sunset. It didn't disappoint. As the giant red ball hit the water, everybody clapped. From houses nearby you could hear conch shells and horns blowing. In Florida, when nature delivers, it gets an ovation.

The following night Wit and I were scheduled to attend a campaign event on Marco Island. Because I was working at the condo, which is north of Marco, and he was at a meeting in Everglades City, south of Marco, I said I would meet him at the event. He asked me to stop on my way there and pick up some documents from Carson's office at the county complex.

Carson was at a meeting, so I was in and out of the building in just a few minutes. As I walked back toward the parking garage, a woman raced by so fast she almost knocked me over. I stepped aside and was ready to give her a piece of her mind when I saw who it was.

"Beth?" It was Beth my reporter friend. But she kept running toward the garage.

"BETH!"

She stopped and turned. "Jazz, I keep running into you. Now literally." She hurried back to me. "Sorry to be so abrupt, but wow, I have got the biggest story. I have to go." She gave me a quick hug and started to walk away.

"Oh Beth, don't do that to me. Can't you give me a hint what it's about?"

She stopped and looked at me. I could tell she was weighing things. Here I was, a reporter who has broken some big stories, and there she was, about to break a major story on her own. She had to share it.

"Jazz if I tell you, you can't say anything to anybody until it's in the paper tomorrow, you promise?"

"Of course."

"No really promise. Not Whitman, nobody."

"Okay, you have my word."

"Well, I've been on the medical examiner's case waiting for the results of the autopsy on the commissioner's daughter, Cara Wicklow. It's taken them days for the toxicology reports. So basically I camped out here. I made friends with someone who works here. I'm not going to tell you who. But finally it's paid off. They are going to release the results officially tomorrow. But I got them today. Jazz, this is big!"

My heart sank. More sadness for Carson, Did Cara overdose? Was she a druggie? I almost didn't want to know, but still I said "What?"

"Cara didn't commit suicide."

I wasn't sure what that meant. "I don't understand."

"She didn't commit suicide. Cara Wicklow, daughter of the Chairman of the Collier County Commission, was murdered."

Chapter 14

It was one of the most difficult secrets to keep. But I promised Beth I wouldn't say anything and someday I might need Beth to do the same for me. So I didn't tell Wit. Not that there was much time to tell him. After the campaign appearance and a strategy meeting that followed, he didn't get home until 11:30. I was already asleep when he arrived. When he saw the paper the next morning, he was beside himself. He came to the bed and sat on my side. I groggily moved over.

"Jazz, are you asleep?"

I tried to focus. "What time is it? Is everything okay?"

"It's 7:00. There's something in the paper. Are you awake?"

I sat up. "Yes, what is it?"

"Cara's autopsy came in. It wasn't suicide. It was a homicide."

I feigned shock. "Oh that's terrible."

"I'm supposed to have a breakfast meeting with Carson this morning if he doesn't cancel. This is going to destroy him."

"Wit, I'm so sorry. He'll be so upset."

"I know, I know." He started to get up then turned and took my face in his hands. He gave me a tender kiss and said "I don't want sadness in our lives."

I wanted to say something to hold on to that moment, but he jumped up and said "I've got to go. I'll call you later."

"Bye," I said. "I love you." He was gone.

Might as well get up and start the work day. I had all day to write. But my writing had stalled. The Vanishing A-list was vanishing before my eyes. I could always write about people, and I know I'm good at that. But this book meant writing about myself and what I had been through last year. Reliving the pain, the shock of what I saw, I just kept going round and round on how to let it out on the page. I stopped going to a therapist after a few months. Maybe I needed to start that up again. I hated relying on someone else. Still my book was going nowhere with the way I was.

What if I just put it aside for a while? I really did miss reporting and finding out things. Like who killed Cara Wicklow? Now that was a story I could get into. Cara's life as a twin, and then her murder would make interesting reading, and for me writing. Who would the suspects be? I was sure the editors at The Trib would be interested. I was even more sure my editor Joe would love for me to do it. But what would Wit say? The election was only a month away. I was supposed to be in Naples for him. Well, how could a feature piece about a murder of a teenager, a friend of the family, upset him? He would want to know what happened to her, wouldn't he? Maybe I could find out things and help the investigation. Maybe it would help Carson too.

I decided to call Joe and run the story idea by him. But as I picked up the phone, there was a voice on the other end. "Agatha Jasmine, you have not called me in days!" It was my mother. The stomach churning started.

My mother calls me by my full name because my southern born mother selected my two first names. Agatha was for the rich aunt "who will think most kindly of you when she dies." Only Agatha thought more kindly of her cat, Sidney. So the cat inherited all the money along with the handler who took care of him.

Jasmine was for the flower. Raised in Georgia, my mother, Delilah Cordelia Billings, loved the smell of jasmine. Only I grew up in New York where my father was from. Southerners love naming their daughters with two names. I could have dealt with Mary Lou or Betty Sue. But Agatha Jasmine? You can imagine what my classmates said. Thankfully my father called me Jazz and my friends did too. When I started working, I began using A.J. and that's what the professional world knows me as. But for mother, it will forever be Agatha Jasmine.

"Why haven't you called me, Agatha Jasmine? You know I worry when I don't hear from you."

"It's been busy here mother. Wit's campaigning and I've been writing."

"A daughter should call her mother. I want to go over the party arrangements. A woman doesn't turn 60 every day you know. And I am anxious to have James come here. We really haven't had a chance to get to know each other like we should."

Uh-oh, the party! I had forgotten about my mother's birthday party. Wit and I promised to go up to Decatur, Georgia for it. What bad timing.

"Could we talk about this tomorrow? I'm really into my writing right now." Okay I lie to my mother. No surprise there.

"Very well dear. I wouldn't want to keep you from your *career*." I could feel the sarcasm through the phone lines. "Do you know if Wit's mother will be coming? I sent her an invitation but for some reason I haven't heard from her."

The chances of Wit's mother attending my mother's birthday party made winning the Powerball lottery a shoo-in. Snobby Doris Whitman was not happy with anything about me, including my family. But this was not the time to discuss all that with Mother. "She's probably not coming," I said. "She's very busy with her charities. She has a big fundraiser the same weekend." Another lie. "But Wit and I will be there. I'll call you tomorrow and we can talk about it, okay?"

"Oh Agatha Jasmine. You say you will call and you never do. I always have to call you."

"That's because you call almost every day. You never give me a chance to call you."

"All right I will wait. I will not call you until you call me. This is a test of your caring for your mother. Don't let me down."

Just what I needed, more pressure in my life. "Okay mother I will call you tomorrow. I promise. I love you."

"Me too. Bye bye love."

"Bye bye happiness," I said to myself as I did every time my mother ended the conversation that way.

My mother says I always put my career first. Maybe this time I would. The thought of doing a story on the Wicklow twin and her murder energized me. Yes, it was time to get back to being a reporter. I picked up the phone and called Joe.

He was excited to hear from me and about the possibility of my reporting again. He told me many of my New York colleagues and friends were worried that I was never going to get back to my old self. So it was good to hear me excited about a story on this teenager murdered in Florida.

"What do you think?" I asked. "Would the higher-ups be interested?"

"Is the Pope Catholic?" he answered. "They would be happy if you wrote a column about home repair. You never realize that after your Pulitzer in feature reporting and then last year's investigative work on the celebrity kidnappings, you're now considered one of the top reporters in the nation. You've been on television and in the tabloid magazines. Just about everybody knows your name, even if they don't know you by sight. You could write your own ticket at The Trib. Why don't you understand how important you are to this paper?"

I didn't know how to answer. So I didn't. He went on, "I'll run this by our new managing editor. But there's not going to be a problem. Do you need any press credentials for down there? How do you want to do this piece? As a freelancer? Do you want me to see about getting you back on full-time payroll?"

I was currently on an unpaid leave of absence. The paper kept my medical benefits going but no salary. Joe said I probably could have that too if I asked. But since the book publisher gave me a large advance, money wasn't something I was thinking about at the moment.

Wait a minute, the book advance. I didn't want to return it. So I would have to keep writing the book too. But that was okay. I felt energized about everything.

"No, I don't want to be back as a full-timer. I need more time. I have to finish the book. This story is just something that I want to do right now. So yes, maybe some kind of a set fee for this. And probably I will need my press credentials updated. Can I have a photo taken down here and sent up there?"

"I'll find out. Jazz, it's good to have you back. I'll talk to everybody here then get back to you. We can talk then about what kind of a piece it's going to be. I'll alert national about it too. Boy, everybody is going to be thrilled about this."

Well not everybody, I thought as I hung up. I still had to tell Wit.

Chapter 15

As my instincts told me, Wit was not happy that I was going back to reporting, even when I told him it was to be a feature about a family's loss – about a twin without a twin. I played down the murder part and any investigation. I made it sound like a woman's magazine article. Regardless, he was not thrilled. But I realized I was.

I love being a reporter. I made a preliminary list of the places and events to research and who I needed to interview. Chasen Wicklow was at the top of the list. A story about a murdered twin would be nothing without the cooperation of the surviving twin. And there would be interviews with Cara's friends who I met at the funeral. I knew I had to visit Triesen's and speak to the administrators and students. The school intrigued me.

I could talk to Beth about the murder investigation. But I really wanted to stay away from that for the moment. That was easier said than done. I couldn't stop thinking about who would kill the daughter of the chairman of the county commission. Was the murder related to his job?

Of course I had to speak to Carson too. And it turned out he was first. I ran into him as I went to pick up some dry-cleaning. He was campaigning outside a supermarket two stores away. Busy shaking the manicured hands of Naples citizens, he put out his hand to shake mine before he realized it was me. "Oh Jazz, how are you?"

I told him I needed to speak to him privately when he had a chance. He said "The chance is now." He turned to his aide and told him that was enough for the day.

"My heart's not in this campaign," he said as he took my arm and we started to walk. I saw empty chairs in front of a little restaurant and suggested we sit there. He ordered a coffee. I ordered lemonade.

"How are you really doing?" I asked him.

"Just terrible. My advisors say I have to go on with this election. It's too important to the community. But I feel as if part of my heart has been cut out. First I thought she killed herself. That was hard enough. Now to know somebody else ended her life. I don't want to think about it. But it's all I think about. "

I wasn't sure how he would react when I told him I was going to do an article on Cara. Would he be like Wit and say leave it alone? No, Carson couldn't have been happier. "Oh Jazz that's great," he said. "Cara's story needs to be told. And it may help find who killed her. Anything you need from me –"

"I need the autopsy report."

"It's yours," he answered. "I'll get you a copy."

A day later he was true to his word. An aide delivered a copy of the complete autopsy. Much of it seemed another language. But I did figure out that Cara died from a lethal drug in her system. There was a puncture mark on her neck where it had been injected. She did not die from carbon monoxide. Obviously the car suicide was staged. And one fact leaped from the pages. The autopsy showed that within 24 hours of her death, Cara had sex. With whom could answer a lot of questions.

Who would know who that person was? Her friends, perhaps. I texted Sarah and Krista, the two Triesen girls I met at the funeral, and asked to see them. They agreed to meet the following Wednesday. Before I talked to them, I had to interview Chasen. Chasen was the one to ask everything.

The next day I called the Wicklow home. The housekeeper answered.

"You want Chasen? She's out shopping," she said. "I can give you her cellphone number."

Shopping? It was 10:00 a.m. on a school day. Chasen was 17. Why wasn't she at the Community School, the private school she attended? Wait. Wit said she was now being home-schooled. Maybe she had an hour off. Still, it was strange. Chasen was the studious twin.

The teenager answered on the third ring.

"Who is this?" she asked. A strange salutation.

"Hi. It's A.J. Billings."

"Oh hi. Your name didn't come up on caller I.D. I almost didn't answer. I was wondering when you were going to call me."

"You were?" I was taken aback.

"I know you're doing a story and you talked to my Dad. I would think you would want to talk to me about my sister."

"Oh I do, I just didn't want to bother you right away. I know this has been very difficult for you."

"Nobody knows how hard this has been for me."

"Well I would like to learn Chasen. Could we meet?"

"I'm at the Waterside Shops. Why don't you come here?"

"Now?"

"I thought you wanted to meet."

"I'll be there in 15 minutes. Where will I find you?"

"I'll wait for you in the courtyard near Gucci's. We can sit and talk."

"Okay, fine. I'll be there soon."

When a subject says he or she will talk, you take them up on it. But it didn't give me much time to prepare questions. I would just have to go with it. Chasen had to know things no one else did. She certainly was the key to my article. And she might be the key to Cara's murder.

Chapter 16

An outdoor retail complex, The Waterside Shops in North Naples is filled with upscale stores – and shoppers. As I parked my little Ford in the parking garage, designer-dressed women hurried to their Jaguars and Lexuses, their arms laden with shopping bags from stores like Saks Fifth Avenue, Kate Spade New York and Louis Vuitton.

Chasen sat at an outside table. Her blonde hair was casually pulled back in a loose ponytail, wispy strands falling on her cheeks. She wore a form-fitting white T-shirt, beige cropped pants and Manolo Blahnick sandals. Large Armani sunglasses hid her eyes and much of her face. Still you could tell this was one beautiful girl. She was reading a text message on her cellphone when I arrived.

"Is this okay?" she asked, her eyes focused on the phone, her left index finger pointing to the table and seats.

It was too early for anybody else to be seated outside. We were alone.

"This is fine," I said. "How are you?"

"I'm existing." She dumped her phone in a large shoulder bag draped over the back of her chair.

"You're not going to school anymore. Does that work, you being home-schooled?"

"I really don't want to see anyone right now. I can't take all the stares, the pity."

"Pity?"

Chasen didn't answer. A mother with a baby in a stroller passed by. Chasen watched them, then turned back and took off her sunglasses. "See these eyes?" she asked. "Cara and I used to say we saw the world through one set of eyes. Now there really is only one set of eyes. I feel like I'm not a whole person. I don't think anybody understands the connection of identical twins. Although we haven't been super close the last year or so, we always knew we were there for each other. Now there's nobody for me." She looked away again and I saw tears well in her eyes.

I reached for the teenager's hand. I really didn't know what to say. There was so much pain in this girl. "I'm sorry" was all I could get out. For a few seconds we held hands and said nothing. Then Chasen took her hand away.

"Everybody says they're sorry," she said. "Except for who murdered my sister."

It was an opening. "Do you want to talk about that?"

"What is there to say? I don't know who did it."

"Do you know why?"

"If I say I don't know who did it, doesn't that mean I don't know why?"

"Not necessarily, maybe you have some ideas."

"I don't want to talk about this."

"Okay. Tell me about – ah – ah - your name." What a stupid question. But I really hadn't prepared anything. I would have to go with it. So I said again "Tell me about the name Chasen. It's an interesting name."

The question seemed to make her relax. "I was supposed to be Courtney. Chasen was being saved for a son. It was my mother's maiden name. My mother was Katherine Chasen of *thee* Chasens."

I didn't know who "*thee*" Chasens were. I would have to Google them later.

"She was an only child, so she thought naming her son after her father would make him happy. Since his first name was Elbert, that wasn't going to happen. But then my mother had complications after I came out – that was 15 minutes after Cara – bad complications, and I guess my mother knew she was in trouble. She asked Dad to name the second girl Chasen so the Chasen name would continue. That's how I became Chasen."

"And Cara?"

"Dad loved the song 'Cara Mia Mine.' It was a song from the 60's or 70's. My mother wanted to please him, I guess. So that's where Cara came from."

I noticed Chasen always said "my mother" never Mom or Mommy. She never had a chance to call her that. My relationship with my mother is a different story. She wouldn't let me call her anything but Mother. "In the South we are respectful," my mother said. Right, but I grew up in New York where a four-year-old saying "Mother" sounded like someone with a bug up their nose.

I would have loved to say Mom. I bet Chasen would have too. "It must have been very hard never knowing your mother," I said.

A big sigh. And another look of such sadness. She looked as if she was going to cry. But then that hardness came back. "We never lacked for mothers. Besides our nannies, we had two stepmothers. Anna - number one stepmother- we liked her. But number two - maniac Mara – she was a real –"

"Mara?" I interrupted. "It wasn't Mara Parkin was it?"

"You know her?"

"I met her recently."

"Well she was our Mommy dearest. The stories I could tell you. We couldn't stand her, especially Cara. They were always fighting. Everybody knew they hated each other. Fortunately Mara's been out of our lives for a while. I was surprised that she came back to Naples. She's lived in Washington for years."

Mara Parkin, their stepmother? Why hadn't Wit told me? Obviously there was a lot to the lives of the Wicklow twins I didn't know about.

"Here's what I would like to do," I said. "I want to write about your sister and her life, and what sharing that life meant to you. I want to know all about her. I think you are the most important person to tell me that. I'd like to sit down with you and talk about your lives together, and her life alone. I think people need to know about Cara and what a loss to everybody her death was. Will you help me with that?"

Chasen didn't say anything. She looked at me for a long time. Then she slowly nodded. "You know I think you are the one to tell this story – Cara's story. I like it. Yes, I will help you. But if you do this, you have to tell everything, and that means some dark secrets. There are things in Cara's life that – some I'll tell you. But some I won't. Let's see how good a reporter you are."

Chapter 17

"I need an office." I didn't really want to have this conversation with Wit, but there was no way I could continue to work at the small desk in a corner of our bedroom. With writing the book and researching the Wicklow story, papers and clippings were piled up everywhere. Besides, I needed to work at all hours of the day. I couldn't write when Wit was lying on the bed watching TV. He was too near, too tempting to touch. It was hard to think of work when he was that close. I had never lived with a man before. Being able to have sex whenever you wanted, as often as you wanted – well, it was addictive.

He looked up from the congressional briefing papers and took off his reading glasses. "Do you want a space in my district office?"

"No, I can't be in a congressional office. I need to rent a space somewhere."

"What about Willie?"

"He can be left alone. He was all the time I worked in New York."

"Not really. Your neighbor Carrie took care of him a lot."

He had a point. Caroline Farley, my upstairs neighbor, had been my best friend and built-in dog sitter when I lived in the Brooklyn apartment. But Carrie moved back to her home state of Ohio to live with her mother. Carrie found out that her husband's late nights of working included working on the voluptuous body of a female co-worker. So Carrie took her son

Jamie and headed for the hills – Cayuga Hills in northern Ohio. I missed her. Our contact was now less frequent. I should call her. I should call Cassie too and see how she was holding up. Why was I such a poor friend?

"You're right," I said to Wit. Carrie used to walk Willie and feed him when I was out late working on a story. Maybe I could get a pet sitter to come in. Or maybe I could rent a small place somewhere and bring him along.

"You know Barbara Wesley's apartment is vacant on the floor below us," Wit said. "She's a good friend of my mother's. I'm sure she would let you use it until she sells it."

Any friend of Wit's mother would probably not be a friend of mine. Doris Whitman had big plans for her only son. Hooking up with a New York reporter was not what she had in mind. She made that very plain when we first met. A year later, the ice still hadn't thawed.

"Tell me about Barbara Wesley," I said.

"Barbara moved into Bentley Village, an independent and assisted living community, after she broke her hip and never fully recovered. She's trying to sell her condo but the market's so bad it just sits there. I'm sure we could pay her something and you could bring in a desk, get a phone line and some internet access. Isn't that all you need?"

"Along with maybe a file cabinet. And *I* would pay her, not you. "

"Okay, I'll call her."

Two days later I had an office a floor below Wit's condo.

In the morning I would bring Willie down to it and set up. That meant using the service elevator, which unfortunately meant running into President Millstone and his dog, Minnie the Maltese. Minnie didn't seem at all upset to see Willie. But not her owner. "Two apartments?" he said as I explained where I was going. "It's bad enough one apartment with that dog. But two? There will be many questions for you next week."

As he talked, I kept a vice grip on Willie's collar. He couldn't even turn his head. But Minnie didn't mind Willie's lack of motion. She was doing enough for both, jumping all over his rear end. "Get your dog away from mine!" Mr. Millstone shouted. He tried to grab Minnie to pick her up but she kept jumping around.

"Your dog is attacking *my* dog!" I shouted back. Fortunately the elevator door opened and I dragged Willie out.

"This is *unacceptable!*" Mr. Millstone screamed as the elevator door closed.

"Screw you!" I thought but didn't say. After all, I was the congressman's "lady" friend. But I sure didn't feel like a lady as I pulled Willie into my new office-apartment.

Chapter 18

I was still upset an hour later when I talked to Joe in New York. I call him almost every day to let him know what I'm working on.

"I'm going to Ave Maria today," I said.

"Ave Maria? What is that?"

"It's a new town in Florida. It was founded by Catholics."

"A Catholic town? That sounds crazy. What if we had a Jewish town? Bar Mitzahville. Whatever happened to places like Mountain Valley?"

"Well there are no mountains in Florida except for landfills. Ava Maria has an interesting history. It was started by Tom Monahan, the founder of Domino's pizza."

Joe laughed at that, but it was true. Monahan, who made millions from his pizza company, is a devout Catholic. He had visions of a town that would have a flourishing Catholic university and a large cathedral. It was all coming to fruition.

"I've got to visit the Triesen Academy which is near there," I said. "And some of the students don't want to meet me right at the school. So we're going to meet in Ave Maria. It's a few miles away. I guess we'll have lunch there."

"Maybe a pizza?"

"Don't be sarcastic. I think it's important I talk to the girls after I see the school. I have an appointment with the head mistress. She didn't sound very happy to meet with me when we talked on the phone."

"Any idea when you might have the first piece ready?"

"Soon."

We had decided Cara's story would be a four-part series. The first article would be a summary of why the series was being done. It would tell about Cara's murder, her leaving behind a grieving twin, and the upcoming election of the twins' father. The second would be a piece on the twins' lives growing up in wealthy Naples and their separate schooling. Third would be the murder and what facts had come out. And last would be a wrap-up article with any new information on the murder, and how Carson, as both father and candidate, and Chasen were surviving the loss of Cara.

Joe said it all had to be published before the November election. That was the important tie-in since Carson was running for office at the same time he was grieving the loss of a child. I had just a few weeks to get it done. That meant putting aside working on the book.

When I told Wit the timetable, he was not pleased. He was trying to focus on the election. He wanted my support for that. Plus in the middle of all we had to do, there was the visit to my mother and her birthday party. My mother! Darn, I was supposed to call her. I had promised to call her. It had been days since I said I would call her. But I couldn't do it right now. I was off to see a very exclusive, and, I would soon discover, a very strange school.

Chapter 19

Triesen's student body was only one shape – thin and female.

The girls of Triesen looked like fashion models. They were required to wear uniforms, but the tailored navy blue jackets and short green and blue plaid skirts looked more Ralph Lauren than P.S. 41. *"Gossip Girl" in the tropics,* I wrote in my notepad.

This was a school without school busses. Mercedes vans and limousines shuttled students where they needed to go. Not that there were many school related outings to go to. There were no sports teams or clubs. The students were there for one purpose, to change attitudes. I could see the ad in a magazine for wealthy people. "Where can you send that difficult daughter?" God forbid she should have to attend public school. For a price, a very high price, Triesen would take her and hopefully change her into the obedient child that jet- setting parents craved.

Carson told me Cara had gotten into trouble in ninth grade. And her troubles continued. Three years later she was still at Triesen, one of about 30 girls scheduled to make Triesen their alma mater. That was not the norm. The school was set up to be a revolving door. Bring them in, straighten them out and ship them back. "We are a school for special young women," the headmistress, Miss Halder, said on the phone. "They have strayed from the course their parents want for them. It's our job to steer them back."

When I drove up to the school I was surprised by the architecture. School buildings always seem the same, either the suburban long one-story buildings, or the old colonial-looking structures with ivy on the walls. In New York, I had been to private schools that had been mansions, the former homes of Vanderbilts and other distinguished families. Triesen had never been home to anyone. It was built to temporarily, and luxuriously, house the delinquent female offspring of the wealthiest in the country.

From the outside it looked like a cross between Southfork, the homestead on the TV show "Dallas," and a Spanish hacienda. A private road led to a building that seemed to go on forever. On each side of the road were pastures fenced in by white fences. Horses grazed on luscious green grass on the right. Scattered orange trees sprouted in a manicured field on the left.

At the end of the long road, a circular driveway swept past a huge front porch. I parked near the middle of the porch. As I started to get out of my car, a man in work clothes came running over. "You can't park here. Don't you see the sign?"

I looked for a "no parking" sign but saw none. "Where?" I asked.

The man pointed to a small sign at the end of the driveway.

"What does it say?" I asked.

The man snorted. "It says 'Visitors park in the lot behind the barn.'"

"Well I didn't see that. I'm sorry. I'll move my car. Where is the barn?"

The man again pointed, this time to a stable that looked like it belonged at Churchill Downs. Then he quickly disappeared as fast as he had appeared.

I moved the car to the lot where I was directed. Mine was the only car there. Off to the right I saw another parking area reserved for students and faculty. It looked like a BMW dealership.

The lobby of the school reminded me of an expensive hotel in seaside Mexico. The walls were dark, huge ceiling fans buzzed overhead, and the floor was tiled in a deep orange terra cotta. To the right I could see a long hallway and a staircase leading up to a second floor. A girl in a school uniform came rushing down the stairs and raced by. As she passed, she gave me a curious look.

In the middle of the lobby was a gold sign saying "Reception" and an arrow pointing to a small wall window, like in a doctor's office. I walked over and peered in.

Seated behind a rosewood desk was a very stylish woman with a page boy of gray hair. "Can I help you?" she asked, with not a hint of a smile.

"I'm A.J Billings. I have an appointment to see Headmistress Halder."

"I'll ring her office," the woman said. "It may be a few minutes."

As there was no place to sit, I returned to the main part of the lobby. A few more students ran by and stared. Didn't anyone walk around here? Or smile? I took out my pad and started jotting down some observations. I noticed a bulletin board set up on the far side of the lobby. The frame was exquisite, like a painting. I walked over to it. Just a few pieces of papers were posted. I started to read one, the school menu. Chilean sea bass was the entrée of the day.

"Something interesting there?" A very tall woman peered down on me. I tilted my head up to look at her. "I'm Emily Halder," she said. Dressed in a dark black suit with a purple blouse, the woman was extremely thin, almost birdlike. She reminded me of something from Harry Potter. But then so did the atmosphere of this school.

"Please follow me," she said. We walked to the head mistress's office and not a word was said until we got there.

"Commissioner Wicklow has asked me to answer any questions you might have. We don't normally talk to the press." She sat behind her desk and motioned for me to sit in the chair in front of it.

"Thank you for seeing me." I noticed the chair I was sitting in was very hard and very upright, probably to make students realize why they were in it. "I'd like to know more about Triesen. How would you describe it?"

"We are a school for special young women."

"How so?"

"They are smart young women who need direction. We provide that."

I underlined "direction" in the notes I was taking. I would come back to that later.

"How many students at Triesen?"

"135." The answer was quick and not expanded on.

"What grade levels?"

"9 through 12. However, many girls stay only for a year or so to get their grades up. Then they go back to their homes."

"How many live at the school?"

"All stay here during the week. About a third go home on the weekends."

"So you have a lot of girls from Florida?"

"Why do you say that?"

"To be able to get home on the weekends."

She shook her head as if to say "Do I have to explain this?"

"Many of our students' families have their own planes," she said, "and Naples Airport isn't far away."

Right. Definitely a different world here. "Could you tell me about school activities?"

"There are no school activities."

"But there must be something the girls do, to exercise for example."

"We have a spa and a personal trainer. We have an indoor pool. There's an exercise room with equipment. Our girls keep fit. Their appearance is very important to them."

"But what do they do after classes?"

"They study, Miss Billings. This is a school."

"Then they all must be very good students."

"They become that, or they leave."

"But you said they leave when they do become good students. So they leave for both reasons. I can see how you have a transient student body. How many actually graduate from Triesen?"

"Our graduating class usually numbers about 35."

"How many are there in Cara's senior class?"

"33 – well 32 now."

"Cara's death must have been a real shock here. Can you tell me about Cara and –"

"The commissioner asked that I answer questions about the school. There isn't much I would be allowed to tell you about an individual student."

"But Carson Wicklow said he sent you a letter giving you permission to talk to me about Cara."

"That is with our lawyers."

"Well in general terms, was she a good student?"

"I'm sure her father talked to you about her grades."

"I'd like your opinion."

"She was a good student when she applied herself. Cara was rebellious."

"In what way?"

"She lacked discipline. She challenged her teachers too much."

"Was she disciplined for it?"

"We don't have to do much disciplining here. The girls understand if they are expelled from Triesen – well it is really their last chance to succeed in life."

"What if they don't care about succeeding?"

"Then we don't take them. Our entrance requirements include a meeting with a psychiatrist."

"Is that person on staff?"

"That person is affiliated with our school."

"I'd like his or her name."

"He is Dr. Nubler. He practices in Naples. But he wouldn't be able to tell you anything. Doctor- patient privilege extends to our students."

A school psychiatrist? Interesting. I wrote down "Dr. Nubler" and put an asterisk next to it. Someone else I needed to talk to. But I didn't want to seem too interested in him in front of the now scowling headmistress.

"Could you tell me about the girls' rooms? I'd like to see Cara's."

"Yes, I know, Mr. Wicklow put that in his letter. I will take you there." She stood up. The interview was over. For now, I thought. For now.

We headed down the long corridor to the right of the lobby. The building seemed to go on forever. Looking out the windows, I saw another wing. The building was in the shape of a U. In between the two sections, a courtyard with exotic trees and ornate wrought-iron benches created a park setting. It really looked like a resort.

While the front made the building appear one story, the wings in back were two stories high. "The girls' rooms are on the second floor," the headmistress said.

We headed up the tiled stairs to the dormitory wing. It was like no dormitory I had ever seen. I felt like I was in a boutique hotel as I peeked into several rooms. Large beds, covered by designer comforters, faced modern flat screen TVs.

"How many girls in a room?"

Again that look. If she could have rolled her eyes she would have. "Most of our girls prefer singles," the headmistress said. "Ninety percent of our rooms are for one occupant."

Because these students aren't use to sharing anything, I thought, especially their privacy.

As we walked toward Cara's room, a door on the left opened. Out came Sarah. I smiled and started to say hello. But seeing Miss Halder, Sarah put her head down and raced past us.

Well I would find out what that was about in an hour or so. Miss Halder put the key in the last door on the right and gestured for me to go in first.

It was a corner room. A queen-sized bed with a blue and white striped Ralph Lauren comforter faced yet another huge television screen. A small desk sat in front of a large window. The window's view was hidden behind white wood shutters. I opened one of the shutters and looked out on a nice view of the field with horses.

To the left of the desk was a small closet. Empty. Nothing in the dresser, either. This was a lovely room but totally impersonal. There was nothing of Cara's – no clothes, no pictures.

"Where are all of Cara's things?" I asked.

"We boxed them and delivered them to the family yesterday."

Was that on my account? I felt like I was in a motel room that just had been vacated. What was Cara's life like here? Was she happy? How could you be happy when you were shipped off from your family, a family that lived only 30 miles away? What a strange existence.

There wasn't anything here that could tell me about Cara. "I'd like to see the rest of the school," I said. "Your spa intrigues me."

Miss Halder locked the door and we headed back down the hall, our shoes clicking on the terra cotta tile.

Chapter 20

Triesen's spa resembled a Canyon Ranch fitness resort. There was a massage area, a large Jacuzzi, and a room for who knows what kind of treatments. In a large heated pool, several girls swam laps. Behind them, a wall of glass offered a view of a modern dining room. A door connected to it, so I headed that way with Miss Halder following me.

It was lunchtime. At chrome and glass tables set for four or six, students picked at their meals. One girl stabbed at a lone shrimp sitting atop a mound of greenery. Everyone was as skinny as runway models. Was there a size requirement for attending Triesen's? How much anorexia and bulimia was in this school?

I tried making eye contact with someone, anyone, but they all looked first at Miss Halder then down at their food. Thank goodness I had Sarah and Krista to talk to. But would they talk?

"I'd like to come back in a few days," I said to the headmistress as we returned to the lobby.

"Why?"

"I'm sure I'll have more questions as I continue my research."

"If this is going to be about Cara's death, the school has nothing to say about that."

"But I'm writing many things about Cara. She went to this school for three years. Her life was here. So I will be back. I'll call to let you know when."

"Miss Billings, Triesen has thrived with no publicity. I hope the article you are working on will not adversely affect our – ah, our – position."

"I understand your position, Miss Halder. I'm just trying to find out about Cara."

"Well Triesen won't give you the answers."

We were by the front door. "I'll be back," I said. "And I'll probably need to spend hours here."

Miss Halder seemed agitated, as if wrestling with something she wanted to say. Finally she did. "Triesen really shouldn't be an important part of your story, Miss Billings. The fact is Cara's association here was going to end even if she hadn't died."

"I don't understand."

"Well I might as well tell you. The police know. I told Detective Folgers. He's part of the murder investigation. I haven't had a chance to talk to Mr. Wicklow about it yet. He has so much going on. But at this point I don't think it matters, and if it helps get your mind off this fixation with Triesen...

"Well I told you Cara always stretched the rules, challenged me. She had no mother you know. I think that caused her not to accept any woman in charge. She was always testing me. Finally she went too far. She knew I would not tolerate fornication in these halls."

I couldn't help smiling. It was such an amazing statement. Fornication? What was she talking about? But I stopped myself quickly. Miss Halder was going to tell me something. I needed to listen.

"Fornication? What happened?"

"You should talk to the boy she was with the day before she died. I had to have him removed from this campus. No males are permitted in the girls' rooms. They are not allowed anywhere except in our receiving area.

But that day, it was lunchtime. One of my students told me there was a boy in Cara's room. I went there and there they were, on the bed– like rabbits."

"Having sex?"

"I said like rabbits. What do you think rabbits do?"

"Who was he?"

"He's the son of that developer, Ross Davids. His name is Reese Davids."

"What happened after you found them? What did Cara say?"

"Well for the first time she didn't say anything. I told her this was it. I had enough. Triesen's had enough. I would be calling her father the next day. I was expelling her. And then she did something so – so –"

"What?"

"She burst out laughing. I told her basically that her life was over and she just laughed at me!"

Chapter 21

I had so much to ask Cara's friends. But when I arrived at the restaurant in Ave Maria they weren't there. I sat down and ordered iced tea.

What an amazing place the Catholic town of Ave Maria is. The modern cathedral is the center piece of the village square. It's nothing like traditional European cathedrals with stained glass windows and that gothic look. The interior of this cathedral looks like a building under construction, with austere steel girders.

Who goes to this church so far away from the city of Naples? Who lives in this town? Are they all Catholic? Where do they work? A story on Ave Maria would be interesting to do. I was thinking more and more of story ideas. After the book was finished, maybe I would return to full-time reporting – if there was a newspaper to write for. The crisis in the economy was destroying the industry that Dad and I made our careers in. My father had been a pressman at The Trib, although my mother told everyone he was an editor. Delilah often embellished. But my father didn't care. He was devoted to us. He died when I was a student at Northwestern. He never saw my success. But our time together was the happiest of my childhood memories. For all the craziness with a southern-belle mother, we really had a close family. Dad would have been devastated if something happened to me or my mother. And look at Carson Wicklow. He had lost a daughter and two wives. His first wife dies in childbirth delivering his only two children. Then his second wife, I learned, dies in a car crash. And then his teenage daughter, his troubled teen-age daughter, is murdered. How do you go on from things like that? And I liked this man. He seemed such a gentle soul. He reminded me of "Gone with the Wind's" Ashley Wilkes, that blonde wispy man from another time. Not at all what you would expect from a politician. They were usually so – what? Callous? Conniving? But stereotypes never really work. Hey, I was in love with a politician.

Lost in my thoughts, I didn't realize Sarah and Krista had arrived. Still in their school uniforms, they looked right at home in this Catholic town. I motioned for them to sit down.

"Sorry we're late," Sarah said, grabbing the chair next to me. "She was watching everybody, Miss Halder that is, especially after you came there. We had to wait until the afternoon classes started. We're supposed to be looking for subjects for our photography class. Of course our teacher meant we should look on campus. We borrowed Hayden's car and raced over here."

"Have I met Hayden?"

"No, I don't think so, she's a sorority sister and –"

"Sarah!" Kristen shouted at her and gave a "don't say another word" look.

"A sorority sister?" I said. "I didn't know there were sororities at Triesen's."

"It's not really a sorority," Krista quickly added. "We just kid about being sisters in trouble. So what did you want to ask us?"

"Would you like something to eat or drink first?"

"We don't have time for that," Krista said.

"Okay. I want to talk about Triesen. But first you have to tell me about Cara and her boyfriend, Reese Davids. He's Ross Davids' son, right?"

"Cara doesn't have a boyfriend," Krista said. "Or she didn't have. She hooked up with guys, but she didn't see anyone exclusively. Why are you asking about Reese Davids?"

"Because Miss Halder caught him in Cara's room."

"WHEN?" both girls screamed at once.

"The day before she died."

"We didn't know that," Sarah said. "And we knew just about everything with Cara. She told us everything."

"No Sarah," Krista said. "She didn't tell us everything. We told her everything. Cara was our leader."

Sarah was still trying to figure out the Reese connection. "He was always around when we went to Naples," she said. "But she never said she was interested in him. What changed her mind? They were in her room? Like having sex?"

I smiled. "'Like rabbits,' Miss Halder said."

"Cara and Reese! That doesn't make sense." Sarah just couldn't believe it.

"She must have had a reason," Krista said. "She always had a reason. She knew what she was doing with Miss Halder. I couldn't believe how far she went with her. You do not cross Miss Halder."

"What did she do with Miss Halder?" I asked. "Why is everyone so scared of her?"

The teenagers looked at each other. Sarah spoke first. "If we tell you things, you don't have to use our names, do you?"

"I'm only using you now for background material. Since you're minors, to use your names or quote you, I would have to get the permission of your parents."

"That would never happen," Krista said.

"How old is a minor?" Sarah asked.

"Under 18 in most states."

"I just had a birthday. I'm 18 now. I was out of school for a year. I don't want to talk about that. But I'm not a minor, right? Krista is 17."

"Then I probably can quote at least you Sarah. If you are uncomfortable, you can always say you are talking to me off the record. That means I don't use your name or quote you. But it's important that we get as much on the record as possible. If it would endanger you in anyway, you could be a source and I wouldn't have to use your name with your quote. But I'd have to get permission from my editors and they'd have to know how vital it is to the story."

Sarah looked at Krista quizzically then smiled as if a light bulb went on in her brain. "How about we tell you something and then we decide whether you can use our names?"

"It doesn't work like that. But I will protect you. You have my word on that."

"Okay," Sarah said. "I'm going to tell you something, but this should not be with my name. It would get me in a lot of trouble." She leaned forward. "Everybody is scared of Miss Halder because she owns us."

"What do you mean?"

"If we get kicked out of Triesen, we lose our inheritances and our trust funds. Our parents signed documents that they would disinherit us if we have to leave Triesen on less than good terms."

"What? That has to be illegal."

"We thought so too, but our parents say it isn't. They told us they have the right to decide what they do with their money and they all decided to accept the terms of the school. Miss Halder told them it's the only way to get us to do what needs to be done. Maybe she's right. It's sure kept me in line with studying and keeping on the good side of Miss Halder."

"But it didn't keep Cara."

Sarah again looked at Krista. Krista answered. "Cara always said her father would never permanently cut her out of his will, even if he signed something like that."

"So all the girls at Triesen have been in trouble enough that their parents would disown them if they don't do well there?"

"We are the problem children," Sarah said.

"Now that's a quote I'd like to use Sarah."

"Okay."

"Tell me about your problems."

"Should we tell her about our problems?" Sarah said, looking at Krista.

"No," the other girl answered quickly.

"Well, what about Cara's problems?" I asked Krista. Krista was obviously the dominant one here.

"Cara was never really happy. I guess you know why she was first sent to Triesen."

"You tell me your version."

"She hit her stepmother. From what I hear it was like a knockout punch. This was right before ninth grade started. The stepmother's name was Mara and they hated each other. They were always fighting. After the punch, Cara's father decided Triesen was the answer. This was before we came. She stayed here for ninth grade. Then she started tenth grade back in Naples. But after a few weeks I guess things weren't any better at home and there was that scandal and they sent her here again. After that, she was satisfied to just stay here."

"Do you know what the scandal was?"

"It was about sex. Cara liked sex. She always told us it was our power over males. She said love really has nothing to do with sex. But maybe that once, she did put the two together. It's just who he was."

"Who?"

"One of the landscapers at her house. I mean he could barely speak English. I think she did it to shock her stepmother and I guess her father too. But the guy was devoted to her. He would give her little bouquets of flowers he picked from gardens. He had been studying to be a doctor back in Columbia or Cuba or one of those places. But then he sneaked into this country and he couldn't find a job, so he worked for the landscaper. She started feeling something for him. Mara came home one day and found them in the pool – naked. That must have been really something. They shipped Cara back here. And the guy got deported back to wherever he came from."

This must be what Chasen referred to as Cara's dark secrets. I had to keep these girls talking.

"Tell me more about Triesen. How long have you both been there? How do you spend your days? Your nights?"

"This is my first year," Sarah said. "Krista's been here two years. There really isn't much to do. So we invent our own fun. It was Cara who started— "

Krista cut her off. "Enough Sarah. We've talked enough. We've got to get back to school."

Sarah didn't want it to end. "We could meet another time. I'll call you on your cellphone, okay?"

"Sure. I'd like that, anytime Sarah." I needed to bond with Sarah. But Krista almost pulled her out of her chair. "We've got to go – *now*, Sarah."

"Bye," Sarah said as they headed for the door.

"Thank you!" I yelled. By the time I put away my notebook and pen and got my stuff together, they were down the street. I headed for the side street where I parked my car. But then I realized I probably should go to the bathroom before heading back to Naples. It was a 45 minute trip. As I started back to the restaurant, I saw the girls in front of a dress shop. They were arguing. Three middle-aged women had stopped near them, right between me and the girls, so they couldn't see me. I walked closer pretending to look in store windows.

"You have such a mouth!" Krista shouted. "How could you mention the sorority? What is wrong with you?"

The older women still served as a buffer. Please don't move, I silently begged.

"But I didn't tell her everything," Sarah whined. Krista threw up her hands and started to walk away, but Sarah grabbed her arm. "I didn't tell her a lot of things. I didn't tell her about the ceremonies. I didn't tell her we were still doing them."

"Well make sure you don't." Krista pushed Sarah's hand away and walked off. Sarah followed her.

I kept looking in a store window, but I wasn't seeing anything. A sorority? Ceremonies? What was that all about? Cara's secrets didn't seem to end.

Chapter 22

Wit was home when I got back from Ave Maria. "I thought I'd take some time off," he said. "Maybe we could take Willie to the dog beach."

It had been days since our relationship was uppermost in his mind. Now my mind was immersed in my story. But Wit, the man of my dreams, was reaching out to me. Priorities. I had to set my priorities the right way.

"I'd love that. How are you? Is something wrong?"

"No. I just thought we haven't spent much time together. I'm not used to an election like this. I've never had a serious opponent. It's bad timing with you here for this one. I want to be with you. Be patient on this, okay? I really want this – us – to work out."

"Oh Wit, I do too." I sat next to him on the sofa. "Kiss me."

"Gentle or hard?"

"Both."

We didn't make it to the bedroom. Our clothes were off and we were on the floor. Willie came over. He had seen this many times. But it was still interesting.

I was in another world with the touching and the wetness. Then suddenly it all stopped.

"Willie, NO!" Wit yelled.

What? I was trying to come back to the moment. I started caressing Wit's bare buttocks. I felt a wet nose.

"Willie, get out of here!" Wit batted the dog away.

"What's wrong?" I was now alert.

"He's sniffing and licking me. What is with your dog?"

"I think he's jealous. Willie go lie down." I pointed to his favorite spot under the big window overlooking the Gulf. Dutifully Willie went and collapsed there. He looked at me with pleading eyes.

"Sorry Willie, we're busy." I turned back to Wit. "Now what was he licking?"

An hour later we were at the dog beach by Lovers Key. A few miles north of Bonita Beach, there is a state park called Lovers Key. Adjacent to it is a small bay beach that's been set aside for people to play with their dogs. Wit and I brought chairs and sat at the water's edge while Willie frolicked in the surf. Dogs were racing back and forth, on the sand, in the water, out of the water. Willie was in heaven. A teenage boy started throwing a Frisbee into the water for his Golden Retriever. Willie and a German Shepherd went racing for it. "Willie, no!" I yelled. But he ignored me. Willie retrieved the Frisbee and brought it back to the boy, the other dogs chasing behind. "It's okay," the boy yelled to me. "They can all go for it."

I dozed off until I heard a rustling sound near me. A man and woman were setting up chairs as they unleashed their dog, a sleek silver-colored Weimaraner. The dog hesitantly walked down to the waters edge where the other dogs jumped in the surf. "Helga's shy," the woman said to me.

"She's a beautiful dog," I said. I looked at my watch. Wit had an event that night.

"We should go soon," I said, touching his hand. "Willie!" I called. "Come here."

Willie was still chasing the Frisbee which he had gotten to first again. With the plastic toy hanging from his mouth he turned to see where I was.

And then it happened. I thought later it was like the TV commercial, the one where the man and woman notice each other in a field and start running toward each other. Willie was looking at me, the Frisbee dangling, when he noticed Helga standing ankle deep in the water. Do dogs have ankles? Well the water was about that deep. The two dogs actually stared at each other. Willie dropped the Frisbee and went over to her. They began sniffing each other. I couldn't believe it. I could almost feel the sexual tension between them. "Wit look," I said, "I think Willie is falling in love." Willie's tail started wagging like a windshield wiper in a Florida downpour. Helga's little stub of a tail was doing the same. They pranced around each other. She licked his ear.

"I have never seen her respond to another dog like that," the woman said. Willie was jumping to the left and right in front of Helga. Then he turned toward the water as if to say "follow me." And Helga did. They ran into the water splashing alongside each other.

"I think our dog has found a friend," the man said. "Perhaps we should introduce ourselves. I am Luis Obermann and this is my wife Marguite."

"I'm Jazz Billings and this is Wit, ah James Whitman." The men waved to each other from their sand chairs.

"They really seem to be getting along. Has your female been fixed?" I asked.

"No," Marguite said. "We've been thinking of showing her. She's only two. We're not even sure she can have puppies. The vet says she has a problem. She's not in heat if you are wondering."

"Willie hasn't been fixed either. He was a show dog. He's an American and Canadian Champion — Champion Willie by the Sea. He's been bred, and his offspring have done well in the ring. I don't show him anymore. I suppose I should think about getting him fixed. The ladies love him."

It was obvious this one lady dog loved him too. She was following him everywhere.

"Willie, come here, we need to go," Wit called. I yelled too. "Willie, come!" He ignored me. "NOW!"

Reluctantly he left the water and headed over to us. Helga followed right behind.

It was time for a quick towel dry. But first the dreaded shake. Water sprayed all over me as Willie shook his entire body. He quickly calmed down, however, because Willie loves the towel drying. He wiggled and rubbed against the beach towel. Then I put the leash on him. "Well I hope we see you and Helga again," I said to the couple.

"We come here every Wednesday," Luis said.

"We'll try to come too sometime. Nice meeting you." I pulled Willie toward the parking lot. He kept straining to look back at Helga.

"Willie come on."

We got in the car but Willie didn't do his usual lie down on the back seat. He sat and stared out the window. Helga had started to bark. At least I thought it was Helga, and the way Willie was acting, it sure seemed to be Helga. He started barking too and then let out almost a howl.

"Were we this bad when we first met?" I asked Wit.

"I don't remember howling at you," he said. "But I sure wanted to get into your pants. It will be easier for Willie."

"What do you mean?" I asked.

"Helga doesn't have any pants."

Chapter 23

The next day I researched other private schools for girls, and their policies compared to Triesen's. If I was going to do a story on Cara and her last few years, Triesen would be very important. I also couldn't get over the feeling that the school, and whatever went on there, might have something to do with Cara's death. A sorority? Secret ceremonies? I had to find out about that.

Perhaps Dr. Nubler, the school's psychiatrist, would have information. When I called his office, his secretary told me he was on vacation and he wouldn't be back until the following week. I made an appointment to see him with the excuse that I was writing a feature story on teenage girls and their contact with mental health professionals. Would he talk to me about Cara? I wasn't sure.

People were speculating that her death had something to do with the election. The timing of the close race and the murder of one of the candidate's daughter made many believe the commission seat was responsible. Either Cara knew something that was going on, or her death would force Carson to withdraw. He had talked about that possibility with me. But I wasn't so sure the campaign was the reason she was killed.

I wanted to focus on Triesen. Cara spent the most time there. And it was such an odd place. What was this about the parents disinheriting their children if the girls didn't succeed there? How unusual was that? I asked

Carson if it was true. He said yes, he signed such a document. But he knew it could be rescinded and he never planned to disinherit Cara. He just hoped it would motivate her.

Had any parents followed through on disinheriting? I planned on asking Miss Halder that, but she was stonewalling me. Twice I called to set up another interview and she didn't return the calls. I would have to go around her, which meant talking to more of the students. But how?

The opportunity came with a small announcement in the sports section of the Naples newspaper. Triesen girls were trying to organize a tennis team. If successful, it would be their first interscholastic team. I wondered how Miss Halder felt about that. The Triesen students were hosting a "just for fun" invitational at the Imperial Tennis Club in North Naples. Teams from local high schools were invited. The incentive to participate was that each player would receive a gift bag filled with merchandise from local stores like Dillard's and Nordstrom. The goodie bags were being paid for by the Triesen tennis team. No surprise there. The girls had learned from their parents. When in doubt, buy them out.

Several high school teams agreed to play. According to the article, the tennis matches were scheduled for the next afternoon and the tournament was open to the public. This would be my opportunity to meet more Triesen students.

Tennis made me think of Cassie. I wondered how she was doing. Why not invite her to go with me to the tennis matches? She needed to get her mind off things.

But when I phoned her, she was very abrupt. "Can't talk now, Jazz. I'm busy."

"I was just calling to see how you are and how you are dealing with Cody gone."

"I haven't given up on him, if that's what you mean."

"No, sorry Cassie, that's not what I mean. I just wondered how you were holding up."

"I'm so tired of everybody telling me I should move on. I know something happened to him, so I've been doing some digging on my own. Like an investigative reporter, like you are. I've heard a few things. But I don't want you to be involved anymore. You have your life. But I'm going to keep digging."

"Well just be careful. If someone did do something to Cody, they're not going to be happy with you snooping around. You should leave it to the police. "

"The police don't do anything. And they warn me not to do anything on my own. But if I don't do it, no one will. I want you to stay out of it, though, okay?"

"Sure. I called to try to get your mind off things. I'm going to a girls tennis match tomorrow. I thought you might want to join me."

"I couldn't take off from work."

"It doesn't start until 4:00."

"No, I working until 5:30 and I can't leave early. We're getting new flowers in. I have to sort them. Sorry, my boss is looking at me. Got to go. Thanks for calling Jazz, really thanks. I'll call you soon." She was gone.

Cassie seemed to be doing fine without me. Now I wouldn't feel so guilty focusing on Cara's story.

The following day I drove to the Imperial tennis courts, which are located off 41 in a community called Imperial Golf Estates. It's a mix of homes and condos overlooking a golf course and little lakes. Much of Southwest Florida features that landscape.

In the parking lot, top of the line Mercedes and BMW's prevailed. The Triesen "buses" had arrived.

Out on the courts, twosomes of girls in brightly colored outfits were slamming yellow balls at each other. These girls could really play. I took up a position on the bleacher-like steps in front of the small clubhouse.

On court number one, two girls from Triesen's battled it out in a doubles match against Naples High School. Triesen had chosen outfits of red Ralph Lauren polo shirts and short white tennis skirts. No school name appeared anywhere. If the team didn't work out, the outfits could still be worn.

Only a few spectators sat near me, so I focused on the match. The Triesen girls were good but seemed no competition for Naples High. The first set went by fast with a score of 6 to 1 in favor of Naples. A few rows in front of me, two girls sat down. It was obvious they were Triesen supporters because they clapped anytime the Triesen girls scored. I moved down behind them.

"Hi, sorry to bother you, but do you go to Triesen?"

"Yes, we do," said a girl with a blonde ponytail that stuck out the back of a red baseball cap. The front of the cap said "Aspen."

"I wonder if I could talk to you for a few minutes. My name is A.J. Billings and I'm doing a story on Cara Wicklow. Did you know her?"

"Everyone knew Cara," the blonde said, answering me but watching the court. One of the Triesen players hit an overhead smash and won the point. "Way to go, Hayden!" the blonde yelled. Then she turned to me.

"What do you want to know about Cara?"

"What type of person she was, what people thought of her."

"I liked Cara. She had the room next to mine. She could be sarcastic but she was fun."

"What did she do that was fun?"

"She was always on Miss Halder. Once she had us all stand up and sing "God Bless America" when Miss Halder began a lecture. Miss Halder didn't know whether to yell at us or sing along." The blonde and the other girl laughed at the memory.

"What did Miss Halder think of Cara's sorority?"

The girls abruptly stopped laughing. "I don't know what you're talking about," the girl with the ponytail said.

I decided to stretch the truth. "I've heard from several people about a sorority and the special ceremonies that take place."

"I don't know what you're talking about," she said again, but she wasn't looking at me. She was looking behind me. I turned to see why. Krista was now seated behind us.

I leaned into the girl and whispered "I'm trying to find out what happened to Cara. Don't you want to help?"

The girl would have none of it. "I don't know anything!" she said very loudly. "I've got to go watch another match." She got up and left. The other girl followed her.

I hadn't asked the girl her name because it can be a turn off to people when you start interviewing them. I learned you get them to open up first, then you get their names. But it didn't matter. This girl was not opening up, period.

Krista moved down and sat next to me.

"I didn't know you liked tennis," she said.

"I've tried to play; I'm not very good."

"Then why are you here?"

"To see Triesen's new team. Do you play tennis?"

"No, some of my friends are playing."

"Like the girl who just left, what's her name?"

Krista ignored my question. "Let's go Hayden," she yelled to the tall lean blonde who was about to serve. With nothing else to say we watched the match. Triesen was making a charge for the lead. The score in the second set was 3-3. Sensing an upset, the bleachers started filling with girls. But which ones were Triesen's? It was hard to tell. This was not a school where students wore sweatshirts with the school name on them, or painted their faces in school colors. I had to find girls to talk to. And I had a feeling Krista was not going to leave my side.

"Got to use the ladies room," I said. I needed to find someone without Krista near.

I went into the bathroom and when I came out, the crowd was cheering for a winning shot from a Naples player. I used the noise to slip away from the bleachers and head out to one of the courts where there wasn't a big crowd. There had to be someone from Triesen who would open up. If only Sarah was there. But I hadn't seen her and I didn't want to ask Krista about her.

On the far court a singles match was going on. Watching it was a girl in a red and white tennis outfit. A wet towel hung around her neck, and her dark hair was plastered back from sweat. Obviously she recently finished a match. I sat down in the chair next to her.

"How'd you do?" I asked.

"Not good," she said, "but thanks for asking."

"You're a student at Triesen?"

"I just started. I'm a freshman."

"Did you know Cara Wicklow?"

"Just by sight. She was one of those seniors you don't approach. They approach you."

"Do you know about their sorority?"

"No, is there one?"

"I'm trying to find out."

"Lila would know. She's a senior. She's playing singles on the next court."

"Thanks."

I got up and headed over to that court. The girls there were shaking hands. I looked at the score. The Triesen girl had lost both sets, but the match was close at 6-4,7-5. The player in the red and white outfit collapsed in a chair under the canopy.

"Are you Lila?" I asked.

"Yes." The teenager looked at me curiously. "Do I know you?"

"No, but what a close match. You did very well."

"Thanks. It was tough. But she's a very good player. I'm happy I held in there."

I took out my reporter pad. "Mind if I ask you a few questions?"

"No, not at all. We would be glad for the publicity. We're hoping this team takes off."

She thought I was a sports reporter. Well we'd see where that goes. "What's your name?"

"Lila Monrote."

"Where do you live?"

"I'm from Alexandria, Virginia."

"Wow, you're a long way from home. Why Triesen?"

"Don't you want to talk abut tennis?"

"Of course. How many members on the team?"

"We have just 8 now."

"Who's your best player?"

"I would say Hayden Langley."

"Where is she from?"

"Hayden's from Palm Beach."

"Did you know Cara Wicklow? I heard she was a good player."

"Cara? Yes I knew Cara, but she wasn't a tennis player. Where did you hear that?"

"I think one of her sorority sisters told me."

"Sorority sister? Did someone call themselves that to you?"

"I heard Cara was in a sorority. Are you in it?"

"We say we're sisters and we call our group Phi Sigma, or P.S., but it's not official or anything."

"So you're in it, this sorority, Phi Sigma?"

She looked uncomfortable. "We're all just friends in P.S. We do things together."

"But I heard there were sorority ceremonies."

"Ceremonies?" she looked shocked. "Who's been talking to you? We do things together. We have a drinking game. We play it sometimes. Maybe that's what you mean by a ceremony."

Maybe that's what I did mean. Maybe there was nothing to talk about, except underage drinking at Triesen's. I was sure Miss Halder would love to talk about that.

"Thanks," I said and started to walk away.

"Hey Miss Billings, you left this." Lila held up my pen. I came back and got it.

"Thanks," I said again. I was probably making something out of nothing. I walked away from the court. And then it hit me. "Miss Billings?" How did she know my name? I never said it. I intentionally didn't say it because she thought I was a sports reporter. I stopped and looked back to where the girl had been sitting. She wasn't there. She had run over to the next court and the group of girls gathered there. In the middle was my old friend Krista. They were talking excitedly, and loudly. I heard one girl say "Tonight? Really?" Then Lila looked in my direction. She pointed toward me. Krista turned to see what had gotten her attention. When she saw it was me – well, if looks could kill. I turned and walked away.

This Lila knew my name. That meant Krista told others about me. It was going to be hard to get anyone to talk. And I needed someone to talk. Because whatever secrets the girls at Triesen's were hiding, something big was going to happen. And it was going to happen tonight.

Part II

THE CEREMONY

❧❦

Chapter 24

They stood in a circle. This had always been Krista's favorite part, never knowing whose turn it was, whose life had changed. Cara had been the only one who knew, except of course the girl who did it and would soon reveal all to her sorority sisters.

Now Cara was no longer with them. So it was Krista who knew, and they would be shocked tonight, just as she was when she was told the mission had been accomplished.

All the girls looked so virginal in their flowing white negligees, the gowns bought in the bridal department at Saks. That too had been Cara's idea. She loved the idea of the appearance of virgins and what that stood for, when what these gowns stood for was the exact opposite. But then that was true of the candle ceremony as well. In most college sororities, passing a candle and then someone blowing it out meant finding out who received a fraternity pin. In this circle of teenage girls gathered in a Naples condo, it meant something entirely different.

"We will start," Krista said. There was instant silence. One of the girls started recording on her smartphone.

Flute music drifted through the room. The recorded sound actually sent chills down some of the girls' spines. Hayden Langley lit the long white candle. She passed it to her left. Slowly each girl took it and even more slowly passed it on. It had to go around the entire room once before someone could blow it out.

Tonight 13 girls stood in the circle. Cara had been the 14th. The candle made the first pass. Tension filled the room. Sarah could feel her heart pounding. She looked at Krista standing across from her and smiled. Krista smiled back. Obedient Sarah. But Sarah loved to talk. And this was certainly not anything to talk about. She would have to watch Sarah as Cara used to.

Nobody was sure the sorority would survive after Cara's death. When her death was ruled a homicide, several girls thought Cara was killed because of the sorority and its initiations. Lila Monrote said we better stop right now. But Krista knew Cara would want it to go on. So after the funeral she brought them together and gave all the arguments why they should continue. Nothing was different with their families. Their parents still despised them. Why else would they send them to this wealthy girl's jail? The girls needed to take power, to hold something over their parents' heads like their mothers and fathers had done to them. And more important, everybody who pledged to participate hadn't done so yet. The sorority wouldn't be a true sisterhood until every girl went through the initiation. There were still four left. The ceremony had to go on. And so tonight it was.

The candle was passed to Sarah. She looked one more time at Krista then passed it on to Hayden. Hayden went to pass it, then brought it back. She took a deep breath and blew out the candle. A cheer went up. "It's Hayden."

"Not Hayden? You're a virgin!" a girl shouted.

"Not anymore!" someone shouted back.

"Oh who is it, Hayden?"

Krista went over to the table and turned on a small lamp. The living room was still in shadows.

"Sit down girls. Hayden is going to tell us her story."

Chapter 25

"It happened three nights ago," Hayden said. "Krista gave me one name and I chose two others. Krista approved them too." The girls looked at Krista with newfound respect.

Hayden continued. "I have never been so scared. I didn't think any of the names would work. But I called the first on the list and got his secretary. She wanted to know why I wanted to speak to him. I told her it was for a term paper I was doing at school. I mentioned who my father was. That did it. He knows my father. Everybody knows my father. He agreed to meet me in his office at the end of the day. I did as Cara taught us. I didn't wear any underwear. He couldn't stop staring at my nipples through my blouse. It was gross. And then I said I was uncomfortable in the chair so I moved over to the couch. I crossed my legs. He saw I had no panties on. It was as if a pervert button went off in his brain. He moved over to the couch and sat down beside me. I think we could have done it then. But rules are rules and I wanted the most points. I knew I had to get him to the condo. I had to wear the nightgown. I had to get the souvenir. And I was going to get a video!"

"A video? *You* made a video?" Sarah gasped.

"No interrupting Sarah," Krista said. "You know the rules too."

"When he put his arm around the back of the couch I didn't move away," Hayden said. "I took out my notebook and I leaned toward him and I did what Krista said worked for her. I dropped it in his lap and when I picked it up, my hand stayed there. There was a huge bulge. It got even bigger when I – this is really embarrassing. I don't know if I can do this."

"Hayden you know how this works." Krista said. "The initiation doesn't finish until you give us specific details."

"Okay, I started rubbing, you know, the bulge, and the hand that he had around the back of the couch came down and touched my breast. He kind of rolled his thumb over my nipple. I started to feel something. I thought this is amazing. He's so old, and yet my body is responding. Then he kissed me and he smelled like an old man with cigar breath, like my uncle, and that was really hard because I wanted to pull away. He started to unbutton my blouse. And I said 'No, not here. Someone could see us.' He said 'Where, when?' I said 'I don't know.' I acted like a thought just came to me. I said 'One of my friend's aunts has a condo here in Naples. Nobody's in it.' He asked 'Do you have the key?' I said 'I can get the key.' And then he looked at me like he suddenly realized 'what am I doing?' and he pulled back. He said 'Why me? I'm old enough to be your father." And I said 'That's why. I've always wanted to screw Daddy.'"

Everybody laughed. "You're so clever, Hayden," a junior named Priscilla said.

"I wish I could take credit. But I got that from Krista, too. I asked her what I should say if he asked me why I wanted to do it."

Again eyes went to Krista. She just smiled. She wasn't going to tell the younger girls the line originally came from Cara. Cara used it for her initiation and told Krista.

"So what did he say then?" Sarah asked.

"He laughed and said 'Your father is one of the most powerful men on Wall Street. I have friends who lost money with him. I'd like to screw him too."

They all laughed. Hayden relaxed.

"Then he got on the phone and called his secretary. He asked her what was on his schedule the next night. She said he had a meeting with the mayor. He told her to switch it to the afternoon. And she said she would. So we made plans to meet here. I got to the condo early, and I put on all the soft lighting the way I was told, and I set up the surprise. I put the negligee on the bed. I didn't think I should meet him at the door in it. But I didn't wear any underwear again. That seemed to work the last time."

She let out a deep breath and looked at all the faces hanging on her every word. It was going to be harder now. For a second she felt sick. She could not tell them what happened next. Maybe she could go through it fast. "And then we did it, okay?" She started to sit down.

Krista stopped her. "Hayden, you are scoring high points. But you need to finish. Details, remember?"

Hayden looked at her sorority sisters – her new friends, probably now her only friends. "You know I begged my father not to send me to this school," she said. "I wanted to spend my senior year in Palm Beach. But he wanted to be alone with his *third* new wife. This one's only five years older than me. She hates having me around. I hate her. So I wrote some things about her on the internet, nasty things. She deserved them. But she told my father it was either her or me. He chose her and I was sent here. That's why I did this."

"And you're doing very well telling us about it," Krista said, "so continue."

Hayden took another deep breath and went on. "When he came into the condo, it was like 'Maybe this isn't such a good idea.' He said 'What are they teaching you at Triesen's?' I said 'This.' I pulled him to me and kissed him. I used a lot of tongue. But he still pulled away a little. So I took his hand and put it under my shirt right on my breast."

Krista was impressed. Who knew virginal Hayden had this in her? Cara would have loved this story. Sorry Cara. It's my show now.

"Then I said I had a special surprise for him and I was going to get it. I said 'there's liquor in the cabinet if you want any.' I went in and put on the negligee. He had a vodka in his hand when I came back out. He really smiled when he saw this white nightgown." She touched the front of the gown, smoothing it out.

"He took a big swig of his drink, then grabbed me and put his hand between my legs. He was rough and I didn't feel sexy or anything. But I helped him take his pants off and led him to the bedroom. There's wasn't much before it happened. He pulled my nightgown off, pushed my legs apart and just looked at me. He touched my breasts and said 'they're small, but they're firm. Lovely teenage breasts.' Then he pinched a nipple, really hard, and started sucking it. I stared at the ceiling. I just wanted it to be over."

Krista looked at the other girls in the room. They were spellbound. She nodded encouragingly for Hayden to go on.

"Then he was on top of me. I felt it go in. It wasn't that big. And it went so fast. I thought for a second why haven't I done this with someone I like? I thought it would hurt so much, you know, but it didn't. It was over in about a minute. He didn't come inside me. Oh I forgot. He asked if I was on the pill. I said yes, but I'm not sure he believed me. So just before he came, he pulled out and shot it all over my stomach.

"That's about it. Oh, there was some blood on the sheet. He got real upset when he saw that. He said 'You are a virgin!' I said 'So what?'"

Several girls nodded approvingly. "He told me to clean myself up. Then he turned away and put on his pants. I couldn't wait for him to get out of there. But I knew I still needed to get something from him. I saw his jacket on the floor and I picked it up. That's when I took it."

"Took what?" Sarah asked.

"This." Hayden went over to a table and opened an envelope. In it was a small gold pin.

Krista joined her by the table. "I think it's time we learned who is the latest powerful man to be seduced by a sister of P.S., or as we really call it, the Power Sex sorority."

For the first time that night, Hayden genuinely smiled. She held up the pin. It was shaped like an elephant. "It's for the Republican Party," she said. "The man who took my virginity is Mack Solan, the chairman of the Collier County Republican Party."

There was silence in the room. "Wow!" one girl finally whispered. Then Lila stood up. "And I did it with a big-time Democrat from the East Coast," she said. "We're an equal opportunity fucking sorority."

Everybody burst into laughter and started talking at once. "Sisters, this is Hayden's night," Krista shouted. They all quieted down.

"Good," Krista said. "Now let's watch the video."

Chapter 26

To find out more about Cara's life, I needed to speak to Reese Davids who was now a freshman at Dartmouth College. He must have been home for the weekend when he was with Cara at Triesen's. I called the university switchboard, but they wouldn't release his dorm information or tell me how to reach him. So I contacted the school's media relations person. After telling her who I was, I asked her to give him the message that it was important he call me. It was about Cara Wicklow.

I waited two days. He didn't return the call. I called back the media relations person. She told me she personally had given him the message.

Reese was one of the last people to see Cara alive. She kept their relationship secret. Why? The autopsy showed she had sex before she died. That had to be with Reese. How close were they? Cara's story wouldn't be complete without talking to him.

Joe had been badgering me to come to New York to meet the new managing editor. Why not combine a trip to the city with one to the New Hampshire college? I could do it all in two or three days. I called Joe and told him I would get a flight out the next day. Wit was so busy with events he wouldn't miss me. Or so I thought.

"Now you're going to New Hampshire," he said, "to see a boy who probably had a one night stand with Cara. What kind of tribute to Cara is this story?"

"I never said it was a tribute. I don't write tributes. I write articles that deal in facts. And their relationship is an important fact. And technically it wasn't a one night stand, it happened at lunchtime." I waited for him to smile. He didn't.

"You said you were doing a feature story. You said it would be in between working on the book. But you're working on this 24 hours a day. And now you announce you're going to New York tomorrow?"

"You know my career is important to me. I'm not a person who can just go to fundraisers and luncheons every day." The day before I had accompanied him to a Junior League lunch where he had been the guest speaker. I knew he would immediately think of that, so I quickly added "Not that I won't support you and be there when you need me. But I don't think you need me to go to all these things, do you?"

"No, I suppose I don't need you to go to any of them!" He got up from the couch. "Have a nice time in New York." He was almost to the bedroom when the phone rang. "Yes?" he shouted into the phone. And then his tone changed.

"Oh hi, Mara. What's up?"

I could almost hear that elegant sounding voice on the other end.

"Yes, I'm going –" Pause. "Really? Yeah, I know it's on Sanibel." Pause. "Well, why don't you go with me? I'll drive. I need to take the Corvette out." Pause. Laugh. Another laugh.

I looked skyward. Ha, ha, oh she's so funny.

Wit was still smiling. "No she's not going. She has to go out of town on business." Pause. "No, It's no bother. I could use the company. Do you want to come here first?"

Come here first? What for?

"Okay, I'll pick you up at the Waldorf Astoria," he said to her, "around 6:00." Big smile. "Right. See you then." He hung up and walked into the bedroom.

The Waldorf Astoria hotel is a New York landmark. Naples having a Waldorf is like Des Moines having an Eiffel Tower. It's funny to me. But funny was not how I felt right then.

I followed him into the bedroom. "Why are you so upset? Don't you want to talk about this?"

"What's to talk about? You're going to New York. I'm going to Sanibel for a dinner event with Mara. I hope we both have a good time."

He went into the bathroom and slammed the door.

Chapter 27

Southwest Regional Airport in Fort Myers has several nonstops to New York. I chose Jet Blue's. I like watching the satellite TV on the plane. But on the flight I took, the televisions weren't working. "You will all get vouchers for your inconvenience," the flight attendant announced. Too bad we don't get vouchers for all the inconveniences in life.

Wit and I were hardly speaking when I left. The kiss goodbye was perfunctory. I needed to make this a quick trip. I decided to go to the paper, meet with Joe and the new managing editor, then take a Delta shuttle to Boston. I wasn't happy about leaving Wit for very long after our argument, especially with the claws of Mara hovering over him. Plus there was Willie. Wit said he would take care of him, but I didn't want that to go on too long. This had to be quick. My plan was to stay overnight in Boston, rent a car the next morning and drive to Dartmouth. Then I would return to Boston, stay overnight again and take an early Jet Blue flight back to Fort Myers. That meant only two nights away from Wit and Willie.

It was going to be strange being back in the newsroom. So much had happened since my last time there a year ago. Besides things in my personal life, there was the crisis in the newspaper business. Talk was the paper might be in financial trouble. Who would have thought the *New York Tribune*, an institution in New York, would be in such a perilous state?

Joe gave me a big hug when I arrived at his office. "How is my star reporter?"

It had been a joke—me and Brenda Starr, the old comic strip character. But now even Brenda Starr was gone. "I'm doing okay, Joe, How are things here?"

"Well you can imagine. Everybody's doing double duty. They've even got me overseeing some copy editing on the national desk. But let's not talk about that. I set up the meeting for you with head-honcho Buiner at noon."

I looked at my watch. It was 11:45. "I'm sorry I cut it so close."

"No problem, I thought we could go to lunch after, like old times."

"That would be nice." So many memories here. I looked across the room at the cubicle that only last year had been my office. A man was hunched over his computer. I didn't even know who he was.

Joe saw me look. "That's David Meminger. He's the new hot shot national columnist. His days are probably numbered. There won't be many columnists soon. Papers can't afford them. Come on, let's go see Buiner."

We headed down the corridor toward the large office in the corner. A woman sat at a desk in front of it." A.J. so good to see you." It was the former secretary for the national editor.

"Mary, how are you?" I said. "You're working for Wallace Buiner now?"

"Yes, they moved me here." She leaned forward. "It's been a challenge."

The door to the office opened and a small man emerged. With his thin frame and beady eyes, he reminded me of a weasel. He wore a dark gray oxford shirt with the sleeves rolled up and a matching gray tie. On seeing Joe and I, he rushed back into his office, rolled down his sleeves and put on his gray jacket. Then he came out again to officially greet us.

"A.J. Billings. It's nice to finally meet our star reporter."

I looked at Joe. Was Buiner in on the joke? Joe gave me a "no-way" look.

"Thank you. It's nice to meet you too."

"Come in, come in. Let's talk about your role here at the paper."

Role? I was working on one freelance article. "I'm not sure of any role. I'm really just trying to get my feet wet again."

"Yes, yes, I know," he said, closing the door. "Joe briefed me about the articles. How are they coming?" He sat behind his desk. We sat in front of it.

"Well there may be some interesting twists. I'm working on that."

"Mancox was talking about you the other day. He's very excited you might be coming back full-time. He wanted to see you today but he had to go out of town."

Charles Mancox is the publisher of The Tribune. He and I respect each other but are not close in any way. "I think we're being premature about me coming back full-time," I said. "I'm still on a leave of absence for at least five more months."

"I know, but give it serious thought. We need something to get circulation up. Your sex story was incredible last year."

Joe winced. I couldn't believe that wording had come from the managing editor.

"I'm not sure I would classify it as a sex story," I said.

"Of course, of course. It was more than that. Thought you'd get the Pulitzer for it. I'd love for you to get another one. Maybe for this story."

"I don't think it's going to be anything worthy of a Pulitzer."

"Oh you're too modest. Well I just want you to know that I want you back. I need you back. And I want you to report directly to me on this story. We'll see if we can't make it Pulitzer worthy."

I looked at Joe. What was going on here?

"I have always reported to Joe."

"Yes, well, he's busy with other things here. And he'll still be available to you as your copy editor. But I want you to bounce things off me. I like the idea of this story, a rich good-looking teenager murdered in Naples. That's like Palm Beach or Malibu isn't it? What celebrities live in Naples?"

"Judge Judy." That was the first person I could think of, but she certainly had nothing to do with the story.

Buiner kept going. "I'll get you your own photographer down there, lots of shots of those sexy young friends of the murdered girl. And she's got a twin sister, great shots."

I didn't know what to say. This was The Trib, the stately Trib. He sounded like an editor for the National Enquirer. Unconsciously, I grimaced.

"Okay A.J., I can see I've probably come on a bit strong for you. But I'm going to make this paper the must-read of New York. And you are going to be right there with me. I'd like an outline of what you're working on by next week, okay?"

Enough already. "That's not how I work. This series of articles on Cara Wicklow is not a book. I don't do outlines. Joe and I decided there would be four parts and –"

"Look, with all due respect to Joe, you and I are going to be working on this now. Sure bounce things off of Joe. Right Joe? I know you have this relationship with him. If it makes you feel better, send the stuff to Joe. He'll get it to me. Would that work better for you?"

"I don't know. I'm kind of – it's not how I worked here before."

"Look just write your pieces. Do what you need to do. Give them to Joe. You won't even know I'm involved to start, okay? Now Joe says you're going to New Hampshire to interview a kid up there at Dartmouth. Fine, fine, do it. We'll talk every once in a while until you're ready to send something in. But I really need it all in a few weeks. Any problem with that?"

"No, I can certainly have the first article finished soon."

"Okay, great. I've got a lunch date. Otherwise I would take you to lunch. Maybe next time. Good to meet you A.J., we're going to do great things together." He stood up. The meeting was over.

We walked back to Joe's office in silence. "Don't say anything until we get to lunch," he said. I was too shocked to say anything anyway.

At lunch Joe tried to pacify me. It would all work out, he said. It could still be the way it was. And when he hugged me goodbye he told me to forget about Buiner. He would take care of everything.

But I wasn't so sure.

An hour later I was still thinking about it as I sat on the shuttle waiting for the rest of the people to board. The seat next to me was empty. It was one of the few that were. I had been on so many planes with so many seatmates. Hopefully this time there wouldn't be one. The door was closing. Yes, yes, thank you. I would be alone. Oh no, the flight attendant was letting on one more passenger. Eyes focused in her direction, not because she was last, but because she was a knockout. She was about my age, but beautiful, with a mound of lush blonde hair casually piled on top of her head. With a little black beauty mark on her cheek, she looked like the late Anna Nicole Smith, but without the extra large boobs and the too thin body. This body seemed perfect. She was smiling at everyone as she headed down the aisle. And like a magnet, everyone smiled back at her.

"There's an empty seat about halfway down," the flight attendant called to her. The man across the aisle was practically drooling. He poked my arm. "How about switching with me?" He wanted to sit next to Miss Universe. *Please.* Get a grip, I thought.

Now the beautiful female was next to me.

"Is this seat taken?"

"No." I stood to let her in.

"Sorry, I'm always late." She collapsed into the seat next to me, fastened her seat belt, and almost immediately the plane backed away from the gate.

For some reason I felt like talking. "Are you going to Boston on business?"

"No, pleasure. How about you?"

"Business, but not in Boston. I'm heading for New Hampshire."

"Really? I'm going to Vermont. Just for a day or two. Business in New Hampshire? What do you do?"

"I'm a writer."

"Oh I've always loved writing. I majored in English Lit in college. But I never got to use it. The lit part that is. I guess I use English everyday, don't I?"

We both laughed.

"What kind of writing?"

"First tell me what you do."

"Well…" she paused. And then that smile again. It was infectious.

I smiled back. "Tell me."

"I'm a DEA agent."

"A federal agent? Drug enforcement?"

"Yes, although I'm on leave from the agency right now. I'm on another assignment. Okay back to you. What do you write?"

"I'm a newspaper reporter. Well I was a newspaper reporter. I'm on leave right now while I write a book. But I am working on an article for the paper. So it's confusing. I guess I'm trying to do both right now."

"This is so interesting. Where are you based?"

"I'm in Florida right now. My paper's in New York. But I want to know about your career too. Do you carry a gun?"

"Oh yeah." She patted her purse.

How could anybody so beautiful be a gun-toting federal agent? But of course it made sense because she could get anybody to talk to her. Like me. "Where are you an agent?"

"Usually in New York. But they've got me working in Florida now which is nice because my mother lives down there, on the West Coast in a place called Bonita Springs."

"I'm in Naples, That's just south of Bonita!"

"Oh I know Naples. I go there with my mother. She likes that downtown area. It's kind of like the Hamptons, isn't it? My mom lives in a development called Pelican Landing, although I guess they don't call it a development. They call it a community, right? Have you heard of it?"

"Yes, one of the editors at my newspaper retired there."

"We've got so much to talk about," the blonde said. "Let's have a drink."

The flight attendant was approaching with the cart. I ordered a wine. So did she.

"Too bad it's not a closet drink," she said.

"I don't understand."

"You've never heard of a closet drink?"

"No."

"You know how in Naples, before going out to dinner, people have a drink at home? Well some women call it their closet drink, because they go into their huge closets to pick out what they are going to wear, and they bring their drink in with them. They sip while they look at all their dresses and shoes."

"You've got to be kidding."

"No, my mother has a friend who always has her closet drink."

"Well that would be a problem for me, because first I'd have to have a closet big enough to walk into. Then I'd have to have enough clothes to fill it."

My seatmate laughed. "Me too. Now tell me about your books. Have I read any that you've written? Wait, I don't even know your name."

"I'm Jazz Billings and this is my first book. I write under my initials, A.J. Billings. What's your name?"

It was like a ping pong game. We kept batting questions at each other.

"Tess MacInteer. Jazz, huh? There's got to be a story there."

"With Tess too."

The talking continued as did the bonding. The plane hit turbulence but we barely noticed. I told her about how I got my name, and about my work, and Wit. Then it was Tess – short-for-Teresa's – turn. She had been borrowed from the DEA by Homeland Security. She was working on terrorism threats, especially in Miami. She had been in New York to meet with her supervisor. Now she was going to Boston because that's where her fiancé Bob worked. He was a DEA agent too. She was going to spend the night with him, then they were going to Vermont to the Hero Islands near Burlington because she heard that was a perfect place to get married. She was trying to find a real romantic destination for her wedding. They had already visited Martha's Vineyard and Montauk Point. The engagement was taking longer than Bob wanted because Tess wanted the wedding to be just right.

Opening her purse, she took out a green velvet jewelry box. Inside was an exquisite diamond engagement ring, with about a two carat stone set on a simple platinum band. She put the ring on her finger. "I don't wear it at work. What do you think?" she raised her left hand toward my face.

I grabbed the hand to get a closer look. "Oh it's beautiful. Now show me your gun."

We laughed again.

"Are you serious?" Tess asked.

"Yes, I think I am. I don't know a thing about guns, but I can't believe you're packing. They let you do that on a plane? Do the flight attendants know?"

"Oh yeah." She opened her purse again and let me peek inside. There sat a big black monster of a gun.

"What is it?" I asked

"It's a Sig Sauer. I prefer them."

"You're a good shot?"

"I'm a very good shot."

"Have you used it on a person?"

"Yes."

"Whoa, let's change the subject."

"I like you Jazz Billings. Are you going to Dartmouth tonight?"

"No, I have a room at the Boston Marriott. I'll go to the school tomorrow."

"Well then let's go out to dinner tonight. I'd love you to meet Bob."

"I'd like that."

But when we arrived at Logan Airport, Tess got a text message. Bob had left for Philadelphia on a special assignment. He'd be gone two days.

"It happens all the time," Tess said. "Now I'm on my own."

"No you're not," I replied.

Sometimes people meet and they know they will be friends forever. I felt that way about Tess. Our dinner raced by as she talked about Bob and I talked about my relationship with Wit.

I told her how great the sex was living with a man. She told me how great the sex was not living with a man. I went on about Willie, and my life in New York. And finally I told her what happened last year with the kidnappings and how I thought I was going to die. We were quiet after that.

"I really want us to be friends," Tess said. "I haven't had time for a real friend in so long. I'm in Miami. We could get together. I could come over to the west coast and stay with my mother. And you have to meet Bob."

We were the last ones to leave the restaurant. It was a short walk back to my hotel.

"I have a great idea, "Tess said. "I'll go with you to New Hampshire tomorrow. Then you come with me to Vermont to look for a place to get married. Who knows, you and Wit might marry there someday. You were going to spend tomorrow night in Boston, spend it in Vermont instead. You could leave from Burlington on Jet Blue. You'd only be gone a few more hours. Then you could go back to Florida and that awful heat."

I had told her how I missed the changing seasons. An extra day in New England? That would be nice.

"I can just walk around the campus while you interview this kid," Tess went on. "Then we can head off to Burlington. What do you say?"

Why not? I rarely did anything on the spur of the moment. Maybe it was time to start.

"It's a deal. I've got the rental car booked, so I can drive. Where should I pick you up?"

"It's too confusing for you to find Bob's. I'll just meet you at the hotel. What time do you want to leave?"

"They say it takes about 2 and ½ hours to get there. How about we leave at 9:30? I know which dorm he lives in. I'm going to try to track him down there. But he plays soccer and there's a practice at 3:00. So if I can't find him before then, I'll go to the field."

"Fine, I'll be in the lobby at 9:30. This is going to be so great!"

In a few minutes we were back at the Marriott. We hugged goodbye and Tess got into one of the cabs waiting by the front door. The doorman held the car door a little longer than necessary. He was dazzled by her. Tess didn't notice. "Bye Jazz!" she shouted as the taxi started to move. "Our adventure starts tomorrow."

"Bye!" I shouted back. Yes an adventure. I'm spending the next few days with someone I've only known for five hours. And she's carrying a loaded gun.

Chapter 28

What a day to be driving in New England. The temperature was about 65. With the bright blue sky, brilliant sunshine and the orange and red leaves on the trees, it looked like a painting.

"Oh how I've missed this," I said. But Tess wasn't listening. She was on her cellphone.

"I checked him out two days ago," she was telling someone. "He is not our guy."

The other person obviously disagreed.

"No, I'm telling you it's a waste of time. We've got to move on the warehouse. They could pack up in the middle of the night."

Another pause, and then a shake of the head. "Sam, I'm going to be gone for at least two days. You can go over what I've already done and waste those two days, or you can go to the warehouse and interview the guy who hired a terrorist to drive a semi."

She listened again. "Fine, Fine. You decide. Call me when it's over."

No infectious smile now from lovely Tess. She ended the call and stared out the passenger window. I doubted she was focused on the scenery.

"Want to talk about it?"

"Can't, national security. National security idiots. I work with idiots."

"I know the feeling. I've got a new managing editor. He thinks he is God's gift to reporters. I could tell you some stories about the newspaper business."

"Tell me one. Get my mind off this."

So I started talking and soon we were back in our conversational ping pong. We went from work to love, current and past. Tess had been married before. It lasted only a year. He was a body builder and fitness trainer. They must have been some couple to look at.

Time flew and soon we were in Hanover driving by some of the buildings of Dartmouth College. It was 12:30. "Want to have lunch?" Tess asked.

"No, I won't be hungry until I finish this. You can find some place to eat if you want. I'll meet you back here in front of the dorm in an hour. Otherwise I'll call you on my cellphone."

There was no reception desk in the dorm, only a small foyer with a few lounge chairs. A male student sat in one using his computer.

"Hi, I'm trying to find someone," I said to him. "Reese Davids."

"Reese? He's in room 304. Don't know if he's there now. Not many people here now. It's lunchtime."

"Have any idea where he might go to lunch?"

"He could go into town or to the student center. But he could be in his room too." He motioned toward the stairs.

I took the hint. I figured 304 would be on the third floor. I was puffing by the time I got there. No signs offered directions like 300- 308 to the right, or 310-320 to the left. So I went to the right first, past the elevator. Elevator! Duh. I was still out of breath. I passed 321 then 323. I was going the wrong way. I headed back toward the stairs and down the other corridor. 304 was at the far end. I knocked. No answer. I knocked again.

"They're not in there," a voice called from the other side of the hall. I walked over to the room the voice came from. A pale-looking girl with her brown hair weaved into a single long braid sat on the bed. Obviously this was a coed floor. It was different when I was at Northwestern. But male and female floors, and sometime suites, are what today's college life is all about.

"They both went out about 10 minutes ago," the girl said.

"Reese and his roommate?"

"Yeah, Reese and Cooper."

Reese and Cooper, it sounded like a candy bar. "Do you know where they went?'

"They were going to lunch. They asked me if I wanted to go. But I've got to prepare for my chemistry class at 2:00."

"Do you know where they went to lunch?"

"The student center, I think."

"Do you know Reese well?"

"Who are you?"

"Sorry. I need to talk to him. I'm a friend of a friend of his from Naples. It's important."

"You're from Florida?"

"Yes, I came up just to talk to him."

"Hey then it must be important. I hear it's beautiful where he lives. I'm from Chicago."

"I went to Northwestern. I love Chicago. What's your name?"

"Bonnie Wickes. My brother Dave goes to Northwestern. He's going to graduate this year."

"It's nice to meet you, Bonnie. I'm A.J. Billings. This is a beautiful campus. Do you freshmen all pal around together?"

"Some do, some don't. Reese and Cooper always include me. That's really nice of them. I opted for a single because I want to try to finish in three years. So studying is very important to me."

"Have you gotten to know Reese well? Does he talk about back home and what's happening there?"

"Sort of. I know he was pretty upset when his friend died. Is that what this is about?"

"Yes. Has he said much about Cara?"

"Is that the girl who died? He was pretty shaken up about it. He was calling home all the time."

"Did he tell you how long she was his girlfriend?"

"Girlfriend? What are you talking about? This Cara wasn't his girlfriend." She laughed.

"Why are you laughing?"

"Because Reese isn't into girls. Don't you know? He's gay."

Chapter 29

Reese was gay? What was going on? My thoughts were a jumble as I walked to the student center. Miss Halder said he and Cara were going at it like rabbits. Sarah said Reese was always around Cara. Maybe he was bisexual. What would that mean to Cara's story? I would probably keep the sex part out, at least I hoped to. Who knew what would happen with this new editor?

If Reese was gay, what were he and Cara up to? What was going on in her dorm room? I had many questions to ask Reese Davids once I found him.

The only way I would know him was from his high school yearbook photograph. But real life can be a lot different than a picture. In the student center, lots of young guys looked like him, or what I imagined he now looked like. I should have asked Bonnie what he was wearing, but I was supposed to know him so that wouldn't have worked.

The center was a blur of faces as hundreds of college students ate and talked. How was I going to find him? Nobody stood out. Whoops, except for one beautiful blonde sitting alone by the window. Tess. She saw me and waved.

"I decided to eat," she said as I sat down across from her. "I'm always hungry. Want some?" She pushed a plate of French fries toward me. Another plate was filled with an overflowing tuna salad sandwich on rye, coleslaw and pickles on the side. It was a meal I would love to eat. But right now I had to find Reese.

"Reese may be here with his roommate. But I'm not sure I can pick him out."

"I think that might be easy," Tess said. "What will you give me if I find him?"

"I'll buy you dinner."

"A good dinner? Not McDonald's or something?"

"A dinner in the Vermont restaurant of your choice."

"Okay that's a deal. He's sitting at the table by the beverage dispenser."

"What? How do you know?" I turned in the direction she was pointing.

"Easy," Tess said. "He's the only one in the room wearing a Naples, Florida T-shirt."

I looked at a boy in a brown T-shirt. Sure enough. There were the words "Naples" and "Florida" staring at me. And he certainly looked like the picture from the yearbook.

"You are great," I said as I left her and headed for Reese's table.

Reese and another guy, must be Cooper, were busy talking.

"Hi. Are you Reese Davids?"

"Yes," he said with a questioning look.

"I'm A.J. Billings. I need to talk to you."

"About what?"

"I think we need to talk in private."

"About what?"

"Cara."

Reese turned pale. "Who are you? You're not the police. I already talked to the police."

"I told you, I'm A.J. Billings. Could we go outside for a minute?"

He weighed that suggestion.

Cooper took the initiative. "I'm finished Reese. You stay here at the table. I'll go back to the dorm."

"You don't have to leave," Reese said.

"It's okay. See you back there." He nodded at me and left.

I sat down.

"Okay, tell me what this is all about," Reese said.

"I'm a reporter. I'm doing a feature story about the Wicklow twins. Carson Wicklow has given me his full support. He really wants to know what happened to Cara."

"We'd all like to know that. But why do you want to talk to me?"

"Because you were one of the last people to see her alive. I thought you could tell me about her and what happened that day."

"It was you who called me, wasn't it?"

"I left a message here at the school. You didn't return the call."

"Because I don't want to get involved in this. I can't believe you came all the way here."

"Reese, you are involved in this whether you want to be or not, and some things I don't understand."

"Like what?"

"Are you gay, Reese?"

He didn't answer, just stared at me.

"I don't know if you are open about that or not. I can protect your privacy. I just need to know. It's important."

"I can't believe you're asking me that. What kind of a publication are you writing for?"

I had to think about that for a second. Who knew what Buiner would turn the paper into? But I went with what I believed in. "It's the *New York Tribune*. I don't have any intention of putting that in the article. It's just something I need to find out so I can put some parts of the puzzle together."

He let out a deep sigh. "If I talk to you, you can't use any of what I say in your article. Is that agreed?"

Whatever happened to interviewing people on the record? But Reese had a right to his privacy. "Regarding your personal life, yes, it's agreed, unless someone goes on record with the same information and it's important to the murder investigation."

"People don't know about me in Naples. My father would – well maybe it's time that I'm honest. I haven't been open about being gay. At least I wasn't in Florida. Here it's different. Here I can be myself. Back there, my father was big into pretending that I was his All-American athlete son, the heterosexual big man on campus type. None of that was me."

"Did Cara know?"

"Cara knows everything." He sighed. "Cara knew everything."

"But I've been told that you and Cara were—what would be the term— hot and heavy the day she died."

"I don't want to talk about that."

"You must have talked to the police about that."

"Not about being gay. They didn't ask that. Nobody's asked that. You said you would protect my privacy on that."

"And I will, if I can. I promise. But if you are gay, are you also bisexual?"

"No."

"Then I don't understand. Were you or were you not having sex with Cara in her room at Triesen's?"

"It depends on what you mean by sex."

"Are we going to have a semantics quiz, Reese? Okay, INTERCOURSE!"

I shouted the last word so loud surrounding tables of students were now staring at me.

Reese didn't seem to notice. "It was Cara's idea. She said it was worth trying. I always liked Cara. My father said over and over 'pick someone. You can have anyone with my money and your looks. So pick someone. Go after one of the Wicklow twins. Chasen would be good.' But it was always Cara who I was drawn to. She was as tortured about life as I was."

"What do you mean? What tortured her?"

"She wasn't happy with the person she was. Or really the person people thought she was. She came off as this self-assured bitch. But there were times she was as insecure as the rest of us."

"So what happened that day at Triesen's?"

"We were at a party the night before and she suddenly said 'how about us hooking up?' I never talked to her about being gay. I was pretty discreet, only hooking up with guys from Port Charlotte or Tampa, nowhere near home. I should have been honest with her right then. But she said 'I've always wanted you Reese, be with me.' I thought maybe I can do this. So I said 'Okay let's go over to Miami or something and get a room.' And she said no, she wanted to do it at Triesen in her room. That would be more exciting. And she told me to come over at lunchtime the next day. I was home to see my dentist, to get a crown worked on. I had to get back to school by the end of the weekend, so the timing worked. But I was really reluctant about going to her school. She was adamant, though. I don't know why. And I thought this is it, got to try. So I said okay and the next day I sneaked in.

"We took off our clothes and got in bed. She was like helping me and telling me to keep moving. But it was not working. Then suddenly she whispered to me 'I know you're gay but we can do this. Think that I'm some gorgeous guy like I don't know who, Lance Bass?' I was shocked that she knew and I tried to stop, but she kept kissing me. I mean she was like in a frenzy, and then all of a sudden this hand grabbed me and pulled me off her. It was the headmistress. It happened so fast. That Miss Halder yelled at me to get my clothes on and get out of there. And I did. I just raced out of the room. I felt bad later and I tried reaching Cara to find out what happened but she didn't answer her cellphone. I called and called. I had to go back to school without talking to her. Then I found out she died. I wanted to go to Naples for the funeral. My father said to stay here. I couldn't believe she killed herself. But she was in such a strange mood that day. That's all I know."

"Then the police came to question you?"

"No, they never came here. A detective named Folgers called me. He asked how long I had been seeing Cara and he asked about that day at Triesen. He said I might have to come back to Naples sometime to talk."

I couldn't think of any more questions. The puzzle had even more parts. Cara told him it must be at Triesen's, and it had to be at lunchtime. So Cara must have set up Miss Halder to discover them. But why? And more confusing, the autopsy said Cara had semen inside her within 24 hours of being murdered. I assumed it was Reese's. He was pretty emphatic that it hadn't gone that far. So if it wasn't Reese, the big question, perhaps the key question was, who did Cara have sex with? And was that the person who killed her?

Chapter 30

"Intercourse?" Tess was still laughing as we drove toward Vermont. "That had to be the loudest intercourse ever heard at Dartmouth. The loudest intercourse. Hey I made a joke, didn't I?"

I had to smile. "That interview was really confusing," I said. "I expected Reese to have a lot of the answers. Instead he raised more questions. I assume the police already know these things, don't you think?"

I had told Tess a lot about the case. After all she was in law enforcement. Maybe she could help.

"Well they know he was with Cara," Tess said. "So they would have taken DNA from him or requested it. You don't know how much Reese is telling you. Maybe he lawyered up."

"Well he sure didn't seem to be lawyering up with me. And he didn't say anything about DNA testing."

"Maybe he wanted you to think some things that may not be true. I tend to be cynical. It helps in my job. Oh, change of subjects, I made a reservation in the Marriott Residence Inn near Burlington. It's got a two-bedroom suite we can have, plus they have great breakfasts. I hope you weren't thinking about staying in some cute Vermont B and B."

"A Residence Inn is fine. I do Marriotts all the time. We'll save the cute inns for when we're with our men. Speaking of which, I should call Wit and let him know where I am."

I had called him from Boston and told him I was taking an extra day in Vermont. He said he missed me, Willie was fine, and it was good that I was taking some time for myself. Still, I didn't like the distance in his voice. I decided I would start showering him with attention. I called his office. Jennifer said he had gone to a meeting in Miami with Mara Parkin. She'd give him the message that I called.

So much for showering with attention. I could feel myself getting angry. Mara again. Was she after the congressman's power, or the congressman? And most important, how did he feel about her?

"Beautiful, isn't it?" Tess asked. The view from the car was like a travelogue. Orange- gold leaves framed a hilly landscape as we entered the state of Vermont. Tess couldn't stop raving about it. "This is really something isn't it? I was thinking of getting married in May. But a fall wedding here would be wonderful."

Any wedding date might be something. Could Wit and I make it permanent? Not with these fights. Ever since we met, we have had these little sparring episodes. I know most of them are my fault, because of my insecurity. I do love him. But then I always wonder does he love me the same?

More thoughts of Wit came the next day when we went to the Hero Islands to see the Grande Isle Lake House. It's used mostly for weddings, but it wasn't like any catering hall I had ever seen. The quaint building consisted of a large dining area for parties and charming rooms where guests could stay. As I stood on its beautiful lawn overlooking Lake Champlain and the Green Mountains, I started fantasizing about Wit and I saying our vows there.

Tess was doing the same. "I think this is it," she said. "What do you think?"

"It's wonderful. I love these islands. I didn't know anything about them. They're like Long Island was back in the 1950's before the

Hamptons became the chic place to go. I would really like to come back here with Wit."

"Maybe for my wedding," Tess said. "You will have to come to my wedding. Hey, you could be in my wedding!" She grabbed my hand and squeezed it. I impulsively hugged her.

"You will be such a beautiful bride!"

"You would be too."

"No, I always wanted to look like someone like you. You're like a young Marilyn Monroe."

"Well you're like a young – ah, Courteney Cox, or some freckled brunette person."

"Thanks – I think. And thanks for suggesting I come here with you. I'd like to get married here myself. Wouldn't it be nice to have marriage and kids? A white picket fence? We don't have to work, do we?"

"Are you kidding? You and I live for work. We can have it all. Why do you think you have to choose?"

"I don't know. I just haven't met any woman who had it all and succeeded."

"We can be the first, and second!"

We laughed. But Wit and work? Right now that wasn't balancing well at all.

Chapter 31

The glow of the islands and my new friendship with Tess stayed with me all the way back to Florida. I was scheduled to arrive in Naples by late afternoon. Tess was due in Miami later. She promised to contact me soon. In fact a text message was waiting when I landed and turned on my phone.

"Hey new best friend, miss you already. Good luck on the story. Let me know if I can help. Off to make the world safe for democracy. T."

I also expected to find a message from Wit, but nothing. There was, however, one voice message. And boy did it get my reporter juices stirring.

"Hi this is Sarah, from Triesen. I need to talk to you, but not on the phone. It's important. I don't want it to be anywhere near school when we talk. It's got to be private. Can I come to you? I can borrow a car. You can text me back, or leave a message on my cell. That's 239-555-3089. It's really important that I speak to you before tonight."

I checked when the call came in. Ten in the morning! How had I missed it? I looked at my watch. It was almost four o'clock. I didn't want to call her back while I was still on the plane. I had to get off – now. Slowly the people in front were moving. A little old lady needed help getting her bag down from the storage compartment. A man slowly assisted her. And then the little old lady, ever so slowly, pulled out the handle and started rolling the bag down the aisle. It was as if she was in slow motion. Come on come on, I silently urged her.

Finally, we were off the plane. I raced to the concourse and found a small alcove near the restrooms. What did Sarah want? I couldn't wait to find out. I took out my phone to dial her number, then froze. Walking toward me was Wit! He had come to meet me. But no, he wasn't alone. A woman was walking slightly behind him. He stopped to wait for her, and she looped her arm in his. It was Mara. She said something that made him laugh and he couldn't have looked happier. I felt sick.

Chapter 32

They must have taken a plane from Miami and just gotten back. For a moment I thought of not even letting him see me. But he looked my way and his face turned into a big smile. "Jazz! Hey, hi!" He rushed over and hugged and kissed me, a nice kiss, a missing you kiss. Well maybe things aren't always what they seem.

"I didn't know you were getting back right now."

"I left a message with Jennifer."

"I didn't get it. You remember Mara. We just got back from Miami. Do you have any bags? Do we need to go to the baggage claim?"

"No I did carry-on."

"It's good to have you back with me." He gave me another hug.

I felt the weight of the entire state of New York lift off my shoulders. He wasn't being distant. The Grand Isle mansion came floating before my eyes. Maybe a wedding after all. Maybe kids to go along with my dog child. Wait a minute. If Wit was in Miami, who was watching Willie?

"What about Willie? Who's taking care of him?"

"I got Fritz the handyman to feed him and walk him. Willie's doing fine. He'll be glad to have you back. We're going to Carson's for dinner tonight. I didn't realize you'd be here. You can come too, right?"

Who were the "we" going? "I'm sorry, who's going to Carson's?"

"Mara and me. But of course you'll go too, now."

"If you're not too tired," Mara piped in.

Okay. Time to try another tactic. Be super nice to Mara. Kill her with kindness. And right now I did feel like killing her with something.

"Oh I'm fine. I think I can make it a few more hours."

Wit started telling me about how Mara had gotten a private jet to take them to Miami and they flew back on an American Airlines' commuter plane.

"We went through this incredible thunderstorm –"

I was barely listening. I was too busy trying to watch their body language. Stop it, I screamed at myself.

In front of the terminal, Jed from the congressional office waited with Wit's car.

Wit jumped into the passenger seat signaling Jed to do the driving. That put Mara in the back with me.

"So how was your trip to New England?" she asked. "I understand you're doing a story on Cara. Did you see Reese?"

How did she know all this? Was Wit telling people what I was working on?

"Reese?" I asked.

"Well yes. Reese Davids is at Dartmouth. Everybody knows that. I thought you probably saw him up there."

"Right." I was not going to answer this nosy woman's questions. Boy was I going to let Wit have it for telling her what I was working on.

"When I was Cara and Chasen's stepmother," Mara went on, "Ross Davids and I used to joke that we would get one of the twins and Reese engaged. It would be such a powerful union. But Carson would say 'leave them alone.' Carson never thought in terms of what was best for the future. And look what it got him. He let Cara run wild and now she's dead."

"Tell me about the girls when they were young."

"Oh could I tell you —" Her phone rang. She looked at the number.

"Sorry, I have to take this." She turned her body, like that was going to give her privacy? In a whispery voice she said "Hi, I'm in a car with Congressman Whitman."

I tried, oh so subtlety, to hear what was being said on the other end. But it was muffled. I could tell it was a man's voice but not what he was saying.

"Yes, I will work on that. I'll call you later with the details." Another listen, then "Yes, okay, I will talk to you later. Bye."

Business? An employee? Maybe an employer. "You must be very busy," I said.

"You have no idea. James, are we stopping by your office?"

"No, we'll go right to Carson's. That's okay with you, right Jazz?"

"I was hoping to change my clothes."

"You look fine. Carson's got a debate tonight. And I've got to go to another fundraiser. You want to come with me to that?"

"I don't think so. I probably should do some work after dinner." Work? What was it I needed to do about work? The news about Reese had to be digested and I had to go over the notes on that. But there was something else. Something really important. Sarah! Damn. I had forgotten to call back Sarah. She said it had to be before tonight. Was I too late?

Chapter 33

As soon as I got out of the car at Carson's, I said I had to make a phone call. Mara offered her phone. "No I'm fine with mine," I told her. "I'll meet you all inside in just a minute."

Wit looked at me questioningly. "Business," I said brusquely, still upset that Mara knew about Reese.

I dialed Sarah's number. It was 5:30. Was it too late? She answered on the second ring.

"Sarah, it's A.J. Billings I was on a flight. I didn't get your message until –"

"I can't talk now," she said.

"Can I call you tomorrow? Can we get together?"

"I can't talk now." Click. Sarah was gone.

Had I blown a big lead? Darn. Timing was so important in getting information. But there was nothing I could do about it now.

In the house, everybody was gathered in the "great room" as they call family rooms in Florida. And great it was, probably the size of most of my Brooklyn apartment. It was cocktail time. Carson and Mara sipped wine. Wit was pouring himself a scotch and asked what I would like. I said Scotch would be fine for me too. He practically choked. I never drink scotch. But I was so upset about Sarah. And where was Chasen?

"Is Chasen going to be eating with us?" I asked.

"She told me she would," Carson said. "She's probably in her room. She rarely comes out of there. I'm worried about her. I want her to see someone, a psychologist or somebody, but she refuses. Maybe you could go and see if she'd join us, Jazz. She does talk to you."

Not enough, I thought. I had only spoken briefly to Chasen twice since starting the article. Maybe tonight would be different. "Where's her room?"

"Down the hall to the left. It's the last room."

The door was closed. I knocked gently.

"Who is it?" came a wispy voice.

"It's A.J. Billings. I'm going to have dinner here tonight. Your father was hoping you would come out and join us now."

The door slowly opened. Chasen looked if she had been sleeping. Her hair was disheveled. She had on sweats and a rumpled T-shirt. Still she was stunning.

"You're having dinner here? Just the three of us?" Chasen asked.

"No, Wit is here and Mara Parkin."

"Mara? What is she doing here? I am not going to eat dinner with her." She walked back to her bed and plopped down. I followed her into the room, anxious to see how it looked.

"Mara and Wit were on a business trip," I said. "I think your father would really like for you to join us. He's worried about you."

"He should worry more about himself."

"What does that mean?"

Chasen didn't answer. She changed the subject. "How's Cara's story going?"

An opening. I jumped on it. "I still have so many questions. Did you know she was seeing Reese Davids?"

Chasen looked startled. "Reese? What's with Reese?"

"What do you know about Reese?"

"He always was friendly. What do you know about Reese and Cara?"

"I was just up at Dartmouth talking to him. He saw Cara the day before she died."

"You went to Dartmouth? Really? What did he say?"

I sat down on the bed. "How about you first tell me what you know about Reese and Cara?"

"I don't know anything about them. I told you, Cara and I didn't share secrets the last year or so."

"But you haven't told me what caused the rift?"

"What does it matter? I don't have a sister anymore."

"Everything matters now. And maybe it would help to talk about it."

She stared at my face. Finally she said "Maybe it would. The fight? It was about a boy. Cara didn't know I really cared about him. So she hooked up with him. She hooked up with a lot of people. But he was very special to me. I was so hurt. I told her she betrayed me. She was sorry about it. She said I was the only one in her life who really cared about her, and that she really was sorry, and that she would never do it again. But he was my first real boyfriend, and after they hooked up he followed her around like a little dog. I could never look at him the same way. I hated her for that. And I told her. We never really spoke much after. She spent more time with her friends at Triesen's, you know, Tweedledee and Tweedledum. We never got a chance to forgive each other."

"Tweedledee and Tweedledum?"

"Krista and Sarah. Cara was always giving people names. Dad was "Popsie. I was Miss Chaste. Her headmistress was the Wicked Witch and Mara – Mara was the Dragon Lady. Mara was so mean to Cara. If Cara was still alive Mara would never be let into this house. I tried to make them get along. I even told Cara to forgive Mara. I told her forgiveness would make it better for all of us."

"Touching Chasen." Mara stood in the doorway. "Touching that you should talk about forgiveness. Cara never wanted forgiveness. She used people. She used you. But that is finally over. Your father is waiting dinner on you." She turned and left.

"I hate that woman," Chasen said.

"I hate her too," I said, before realizing it was out. Chasen looked at me shocked. I smiled. "Now get dressed and let's go out there and show her what Cara wanted to show her, that she can't affect any of us. "

Chasen grinned. "That," she said, "is a very good idea."

Chapter 34

Why had Billings the reporter waited so long to call? Sarah wanted to tell her everything so she would help.. Now it was too late. She had to do it. Her life would be unbearable if Krista got more upset with her. She never had been good at making friends. Cara and Krista accepted her when few others had. Most people found her too willing to please, boring almost. Over and over her mother told her she was a follower. She did whatever her peers asked. That's why she had gotten into trouble. That's why she started with the drugs, and why her parents sent her to Florida instead of letting her come home after rehab. They never visited her in rehab. She was the only one there who had no family call or visit. She would never forgive them for that. One phone call? How much time did it take to make one phone call?

She disliked her mother, but she especially hated her father. He treated her like a trophy to be brought out and admired when she was good. Her nanny, Sally, had been her real parent. Sally had been there for comfort when she cried, or when she wanted to be held.

When she got too old for nannies, there was no one to give her real love. Her father's business meant he traveled all over the world. Her mother usually accompanied him. Having Sarah had been a mistake, her father once told a confidante. He didn't know she was listening. "I wasn't meant to be a parent," he said to his friend. "I feel guilty leaving her, but uncomfortable when I'm with her. Yes, she's lovely to look at, but she clings so. Where is that independence her mother has?"

The schools she went to always had cliques and she never fit in. People treated her as if she was stupid. And she wasn't stupid. She was just – well she was just never loved enough.

She tried to find acceptance. Her parents had a summer home in the Hamptons. She got involved with a drug crowd there. At least they liked being with her. And the drugs they gave her made her feel better. She didn't mind buying things for them. They seemed to like her even more after that. Everything was good until she was arrested for drug possession. Her parents' lawyer got her off with the stipulation she would go into rehab. But her parents wondered what to do with her after that? All their friends knew about "Sarah's drug problem." She was an embarrassment.

So her parents decided to find a private school where nobody knew the family. Triesen Academy fit the bill. At Triesen's every student had some type of problem. And now her parents were in no rush for her to return home. She tried to be a model student and get good grades so they would let her come home. But they ignored her calls. Her father's secretary would tell her they were traveling. She knew her parents weren't traveling. She saw their photos online at various charity events in her hometown of New York.

Cara seemed to understand the loneliness. It was Cara who accepted her at Triesen's. When she heard Cara started a secret sorority, she begged to be included. Cara hesitated. Sarah was so childlike, she told Krista. Could she handle the initiation? Maybe they could make an exception. Krista was emphatic. If she was to be a sister, she had to do what all the other sisters did.

While Cara was alive, Sarah always stayed way down on the list. Each month she thought she would be called in and told it was her turn. But it didn't happen. Secretly she was relieved. She really didn't know if she could do it. Then Cara died and Krista was in charge. After Hayden's ceremony, Krista called her into her room.

"Sarah, you will be initiated next," she was told. "You pick two men. I will give you the third name. You must succeed with one of them."

Knowing that someday it might be her turn, Sarah had been looking. It had to be some man in South Florida because she wasn't supposed to go home until Thanksgiving, if even then. It had to be some older man who lived or worked nearby. The school would drive her as far as Miami if she made up some excuse about a doctor's appointment or something like that. But the Naples- Bonita area seemed better because the girls at Triesen had gotten a reputation. The men felt safer knowing that if they were caught it would be the word of a local outstanding citizen against a troubled teen-ager from out of state.

So Sarah's names were local. She selected the head of a construction company and a state official from Fort Myers. The politician was her first choice. She had seen a picture of him; he had a nice smile. Then there was the third name, the one Krista chose. Her heart raced. She could never approach him. Hopefully she wouldn't have to.

How was she going to accomplish this? Her first thought was she couldn't. What should she do? And then the solution came to her. If she told A.J. Billings about the sorority and what the girls had to do to be initiated, Billings would print it in the newspaper and the ceremonies would stop. She wouldn't have to approach anyone. But Billings wasn't there when she called her, and tonight was the night Krista said she would drive her to an event where the politician was speaking. She had to go. She had to try to do it.

It wasn't so much the sex part. It was hard for her to turn down anyone who showed interest in her. But having sex with a man as old as her father? Would it be like having sex with her father? She was sick to her stomach when she got into the white BMW Krista borrowed.

"You don't look well," Krista said.

"I don't feel good."

"Grow up, Sarah. You wanted to be part of this. You should have done this months ago."

Sarah didn't respond. It was true. Cara had saved her. Now there was no Cara.

There was little conversation as they headed toward the Hyatt Regency hotel north of Naples. Sarah bought a ticket to the fundraising event there. Krista was to drop her off and go shopping at the nearby Coconut Point center. If Sarah was successful, she was to call Krista and cancel her ride home.

Sarah had never picked up anyone, especially an older man. Her body was shaking as Krista pulled up to the hotel.

"Remember, it doesn't have to happen tonight. You just have to get him interested tonight. It would work better for you at the condo. And you'd get more points."

Points? Who cared about points? Sarah got out of the car without saying a word. She didn't even look back as Krista drove away. A group of women were entering the lobby of the hotel. She followed them in.

They all headed to a registration table. "Do you have a ticket?" a woman asked her.

"I called it in. I charged it on my credit card."

"What's your name?"

"Sarah Van Holben."

"Let me look. Oh yes we have you. You paid for the VIP party too. Here, I'll put this red band on your wrist and then you go down the hall to the left. See that man with the clipboard? He'll let you into the reception."

"Thank you." Her legs still shook. She was never going to be able to do this. Maybe if she called Billings again and told her everything right now, the reporter could get her out of school so she would never have to see Krista or anybody ever again. The man with the clipboard was looking at her as if to say, "yes, what?"

"I have a ticket to go into the reception before dinner." She showed her red wrist band.

"What's your name?"

"Sarah Van Holben."

He checked the list. "Okay. There's not much time left. There's an open bar on the left, but I don't think you're old enough for that."

She walked into a room of dark suits, clinking glasses and loud talk. It was now or never.

Chapter 35

Two days had passed and Sarah wasn't returning my calls. To move the story further, I needed something. I decided to go back into Cara's life, all the way back. There were only two sources for that – Carson and Chasen. An interview with Carson went well but Chasen could add so much more. At the dinner with Mara, Chasen and I exchanged glances like we knew something no one else did. I felt we bonded. I hoped that Chasen would be more receptive to an in depth interview now. And she actually sounded friendly when she agreed to meet.

We were back at the Waterside Shops at the same table.

"So start from the beginning," I said.

"Cara's beginning? I guess that was when my birth killed our mother."

Whoa, deep problems here. "Who took care of you after that?"

"I'm told my Aunt Molly stayed with us until we were about 2. I don't remember that. I know we had a nanny. Her name was Linda. Then my father married Anna. She was really nice."

"What do you remember about Anna?"

"Anna Wozinski." Chasen's face softened. It was the first time I saw her face without strain. This must be the softer Chasen her father always talked about. The girl was even more beautiful when there was no tension in those eyes.

"Anna was a secretary for a builder. She was working there when Daddy met her. He married her really fast. She had long silky dark hair. I remember how I loved to touch it. When we were about three years old, she moved in with us. She stopped working to be a full-time mother. It was like a normal life. She really understood us. 'Cara is my creative child,' she would say. Cara would pick up frogs, then kiss them and say they were going to be her princes. She was always singing and pretending she was a recording star or a movie star. 'Theatrical Cara,' my father called her. She starred in our elementary school play. And she wrote stories and acted them out. She was really creative. Anna was very supportive. It seems so long ago that Cara was free like that. Cara really loved Anna."

"And you?"

"Me? Oh I loved Anna too. I think it's easier for me to love people."

"What did she call you?"

"Her 'caring child.' She told my sister 'Chasen will always be there to support you, to calm you down. She will be your rock. You are the perfect pair.'"

"And then you lost Anna."

"When we were 11. She was killed in an automobile accident at the 41- Pine Ridge Road intersection. She was making a left turn. She had the turn arrow, but a car came speeding through the light and crashed into her. Anna died, and it all changed."

"You've lost two mothers. That's incredibly hard."

"Yes, but I think we would have been okay if Dad hadn't married Mara."

"Mother number three?"

"We *never* called her mother. You hear those stories about wicked stepmothers. She was the modern version of that. She thought we needed more discipline, especially Cara. I told Cara to obey her, it would be easier. But I know that was really hard for her. Mara didn't want to share Daddy with anyone."

For a moment she stopped talking. I waited. The only sound came from a nearby fountain spewing water.

"By the time we were 13," she continued, "it was really bad. She wanted us to dress a certain way, act a certain way. Cara rebelled. She told Dad how bad Mara was, how she was destroying our family. Mara overheard that. After that it was really war. One day I heard Mara yelling at Cara that she was ruining her perfect life with Dad. She screamed that she hated her, that she wished Cara had died at birth not our mother. I came into the room to see if I could stop her yelling. But she just got louder and Cara started yelling back. Then Mara slapped Cara hard across the face. Without thinking, Cara hit her back. Mara fell into a cabinet and broke her nose. Dad walked in and saw Mara all bloody. He yelled at us to stay in the house, and rushed off with Mara to the emergency room. It all happened so fast. None of it was intentional. I tried to tell Dad but he wouldn't listen. Two days later, Cara was sent to Triesen's.

"She couldn't come home then. Thirteen years old and she couldn't even come home for a weekend. Daddy should have done something. He should have said to Mara 'this is my daughter. She deserves to see us at least on the weekends.' I told him that. But he wouldn't listen. A year later, they finally let Cara come home. But by then, she couldn't forgive Daddy. And of course she still hated Mara. They didn't speak to each other. And then Eduardo happened. Do you know about him?"

The landscaper. I nodded.

"That was really sad. He was very special to her. And he was only working for the landscaping company because he couldn't speak English well. He was learning it with Literacy Volunteers and he was hoping to go back to medical school. But nobody would listen to Cara about what a good person he was. So she was sent back to Triesen. And you know, she finally just wanted to stay there. She had it with Mara, Daddy – even me. She said I should have fought harder for her. I tried. But sometimes it's easier not to fight."

"But Mara and your father did break up?"

"Yes, about a year later. Mara didn't want to go. She really has a thing for my father. But he kicked her out. I think he finally realized how she wrecked our family."

"Then why didn't you and Cara make up?"

"It was too late I guess. Sometimes when you want to stop something, to make it go away, it's just too late. You can't go back. I wish I could."

"Let's talk about what happened around the time Cara died. She was coming home that weekend, right?"

My phone rang. Darn. "Sorry," I said to Chasen. I looked at the number. It was Cassie. I would have to get rid of her fast.

"I need to see you, it's important," Cassie said.

"I'm busy right now. Can I call you back?"

"Please. Right away. It's important."

"Okay, in a few minutes." I hung up. "Sorry," I said to Chasen. "My friend's boyfriend is missing. She's pretty upset."

"Missing, like how?"

"It's a strange story. They went out for a ride on his horse one night. After he dropped her off, he was never seen again. Neither was his horse."

"And you know him?"

"No, I know her. I never met him."

"What are the police saying?"

"No leads. I'm not sure they are working too hard on this. But back to Cara around the time she died."

"Dad asked her to come to the fundraiser. He was trying to break through, to make her forgive him. And maybe she was getting tired of all the strain between them because she agreed to come. She was probably getting ready to go to the party when she died."

"Was she dating anyone, I mean besides Reese? I don't want to be graphic but the autopsy showed she had sex with someone within 24 hours of her death."

"Really?" Chasen looked shocked. "The autopsy showed that? Nobody's mentioned that to me. I don't know who it could be. You should find out who it was." She sounded angry. Then her mood softened. "It's all so sad."

"Why sad?"

"I don't know. Trying to piece her life together. Maybe she found some-one."

"None of her friends at school know who it could be. Or at least they won't tell me. But then everybody says she was – what's the official word? Promiscuous?"

"Right. Yeah, well that's true. Cara was promiscuous. All I know about that night is that she had come home from school, changed her clothes and died in the car in the garage. I was waiting for her at the party. You saw me there."

And then I remembered. "You know Chasen, there's something about that night that I always keep meaning to ask you and forget. At the party, I was with you, and the sheriff and Davids started coming toward us as if they needed to talk to you. You abruptly left like you were avoiding them."

"I don't remember that."

"But it happened. What's your relationship with the sheriff and Davids?"

"I don't have a relationship with them. They know my father. I guess I didn't feel like talking to anybody. I thought this interview was about Cara."

"But talking about you is talking about Cara."

"What do you mean?"

"You were twins. I'm sure you felt the same way about a lot of things."

"I told you. We weren't close for the last year or so."

"Chasen, I think there are things you're not revealing. I think you know more about Cara's life than you are telling me."

She stiffened. "It's not my job to tell you things. You're the reporter. You are supposed to find out information on your own. Go to Triesen. Talk to her friends there. If Cara had something to hide, that's where you'll find the answers."

She stood up, said a quick good-bye and hurried off. I was more baffled. What was with these teenagers and their secrets?

Chapter 36

That night would forever be etched in Sarah's mind. She recalled how she retreated next to a wall. She knew nobody at the event. How was she going to get his attention? He was across the room surrounded by a group of people. She went over to the bar and asked for a club soda. Nobody in the room was her age. She felt so out of place. Time went by, then more time.

"Are you a volunteer?" A large man in a wrinkled beige suit approached her.

"Excuse me?"

"Are you a volunteer for our esteemed legislator? Are you working on his campaign?"

"No, but I'd like to. I'd like to meet him."

"Well I can arrange that. I can arrange a lot of things. What's your name?"

"Sarah. Sarah Van Holben."

"I'm Brian Watstone. I'm a committeeman. Come on, let's go over and see what he thinks of you."

Sarah followed him over to the group.

The legislator was surrounded by patronizing followers. Pulling Sarah by the arm, the committeeman pushed her to the front of the circle. She put on what she thought was a seductive smile. The elected official ignored her. Well nobody said this would be easy. She thrust out her hand. "Hi, I'm Sarah." He took the hand, barely giving her a smile. A man on his right was whispering in his ear. The committeeman started to interrupt them when the seas seemed to part. Approaching was a stylish woman who demanded respect. The legislator straightened up like a soldier coming to attention. "Ah my wonderful wife is here. Laurie, I have many people for you to meet." He looked at the crowd. "This is the woman responsible for everything good that has happened to me." He put his arm around her.

Sarah crumbled. It wouldn't work. She had met the wife. Well technically she hadn't really met her. But she saw her and they looked happy. And she had seen such little happiness in married couples. She couldn't, not with him. She would have to go to number two. As she headed to the lobby she tried to think of what to do. She would have to figure out how to meet the construction company owner. It would have to start all over again and she had so little time. How could she do this?

And then by divine intervention it happened. Holding the hotel's front door to let two women enter was Krista's choice, heart stopping number three. She couldn't. So much wrong could come from this. The two women went through the door and he turned, but then he saw her and smiled. This was it. She raced toward him.

She grabbed his arm. She just did it. He smiled again.

"Are you the doorman?" she asked trying a suggestive smile.

"I could be," he said, "for you."

Chapter 37

In the midst of all this work and campaign turmoil, Wit and I had another argument. He said I was "lecturing" him about Mara and my reasons for going to New Hampshire. He didn't tell her and he was sick of my accusations. Accusations? What accusations? Was this law school? I told him we weren't at Harvard, I didn't lecture and I was tired of his accusation that I made accusations.

It kept escalating. We were both on edge and scheduled to attend my mother's 60th birthday party in Georgia. Wit had promised to go for a long weekend. Now he decided he could make it for only one night. He would fly up the morning of the party and return the next day. The election was only three weeks away. My deadline was less than that. I felt really guilty because I decided I would go back with him. My mother would not be pleased.

She hadn't spoken to me for days after I finally remembered to call her. We were talking again, but it was strained. I waited until the day before we were to fly up to tell her about the shortened visit.

"You don't really care about family, do you Agatha Jasmine?" she said.

"Mother, I have been really busy. I'm a bit overwhelmed by all this. And things with Wit–"

I paused. I could hear my voice cracking and I did not want to cry.

There was silence on the other end. My mother has many faults but she can be as protective of me as a lioness with cubs. In a quiet voice, she asked "What's wrong dear?"

Well, that made me tear up even more. "I can't talk about it now. Maybe when I'm there. Be patient with me, Mother, okay?"

"I miss you Agatha Jasmine. Everything will be all right. I will see both of you tomorrow."

"Yes," was all I could get out.

My mother wasn't finished with the conversation. "Oh and don't be alarmed by the number of people in the house. I invited some people from New York to stay with us. But you and James will still have your own rooms."

I smiled. My mother knew we were living together. But in the South, ladies did not talk about that, or even acknowledge it could happen. The way things were going, maybe we would need both of those rooms.

Chapter 38

We took an early morning flight scheduled to arrive in Atlanta at 8:00 a.m. Wit was busy reading the briefing papers his staff gave him about another crisis somewhere. He didn't tell me where. And for the first time I didn't ask. I was rewriting the article on Cara's early years. I was so into it, that as we hit the ground at Atlanta the bump jarred me. I let out a loud "Ahh!"

Wit jumped. "What is it?" He looked concerned.

I was glad to have any type of attention. "Sorry," I said. "I didn't realize we were landing. It startled me."

"You scared me. I thought there was something wrong."

Everything is wrong, I wanted to say. But I simply smiled. It was not going to be easy for him being with my mother and who knew who else. How many people had she invited to this thing?

Two hours later I found out. As we walked into her house in Decatur, it was standing room only, and that was just for breakfast.

After my father died and I graduated from college, my mother decided to return to Georgia. We had lived in a small house on Long Island. She missed the big old houses of the South. With the insurance money, she bought an old plantation house with thick white columns and a large front porch. Then she renovated it "to bring it back to its former beauty." Only my mother's idea of beauty is a bit off the norm. She had the contractors finish the outside of the house in bright yellow aluminum siding. "It will never need painting," she said. It would also never need a GPS to find it. It was the only bright yellow aluminum-sided house in Decatur, maybe in Georgia. The neighbors called it the canary house. I called it Tara gone Tulsa.

Wit had never seen it. I laughed at his expression as he drove the rental car down the long driveway.

"What is that?" he asked as the house came into view. "My God it looks like a giant canary."

"It's aluminum siding," I said "in yellow."

"I didn't know they made aluminum siding in bright yellow."

"It was a special order."

He looked to see if I was joking. I wasn't. We both laughed.

"Welcome to Delilah world," I said.

Who were all these people? It looked like the entire population of Decatur was nodding and smiling as we headed toward the back of the house and the kitchen. I assumed my mother would be there overseeing the cooking. She measures success by the abundance of food served. Maybe it's a Scarlet O'Hara thing. I always remember that scene with the one carrot. Growing up, our refrigerator overflowed with leftovers. "Just in case," my mother would say. What? That the Chinese army was coming to dinner?

As we reached the kitchen, I heard my name shouted.

"Jazz, hey you're here."

I looked around and saw Joe my editor and his wife Marcia.

"Surprise!" he said. "Your mother invited us."

"Is there anyone she didn't invite?" I quickly realized that didn't sound right. "Oh Joe, what a great surprise. So good to see you. And Marcia, how are you? Have you met Wit?"

Marcia put out her hand to greet him.

"Is that my famous daughter and her famous beau?" My mother glided in from the kitchen. She was wearing something flowing. I wasn't sure what it was. But it was floor length, gauzy and a lavender color. Her newly dyed hair, bright yellow—to match the house?—was piled on her head like Brigitte Bardot used to wear it. And her makeup was flawless. It was 10:00 in the morning and she looked like she was going to the Oscars.

"Agatha Jasmine, how are you?" she gave me an air kiss then turned to Wit.

"And James, how good to see you again. We've had so much excitement in the last year, we haven't had a chance to visit." She gave him an air kiss too.

Wit smiled warmly at her. I think he really likes my mother. She is so different than what he grew up with. And they bonded last year when I was missing.

"Mother, who are all these people?"

"Well you know Joe, don't you?"

"Yes, that's one. Marcia is two."

"Well there are neighbors and people from my bridge club, and others. You know how I love people. And I thought I would have a birthday weekend, not just one event. We have a brunch this morning. Then tonight is the big party. Now I will show you to your rooms so you can put your bags down. Where are your bags?" She looked behind us.

"We only have two carry-ons, one for each of us."

"But what about what you are going to wear tonight? I hope you brought something appropriate. How could you fit that into a *carreee-on*?"

"It'll be fine Mother. Why don't you introduce Wit to some of your friends?"

"Oh, yes, how rude of me. Will you excuse us, Joe?"

Joe smiled. He has known my mother longer than he's known me. When my father started working at The Trib, the first person he met was Joe. They were both copy boys. My father later chose to be a pressman. Joe went on to an important editing job. Joe always said my dad could have done anything at the paper, but he wanted a job where he would be home during the afternoon to see his daughter grow up. After Vietnam, my dad changed his priorities. I was glad he did.

In my father's eyes I had few faults. My mother's? Well, she always saw something. "Stand up straight," she whispered as I leaned against the dining room wall. "And pay more attention to James. I'm not sure he's having a good time." A few minutes later she was at it again. "Come and sit with my friends. And stop daydreaming. You always have something else on your mind."

Hours later, the crowd had thinned and Mother was telling those of us left about the sex scandal at River Down, the local assisted living facility. One of the patients was a man of about 90 who "still could do it" as my mother put it. So he did it with every woman he could find. Of course these "loose" women were in their 80's or above, so mother wasn't sure exactly what they did. But almost every night the administrators found this man and a different woman in some cleaning closet or in the therapy room, working on some "real therapy." The staff was concerned the newspapers would get hold of the sex scandal and shut them down. They asked the man's daughter to move him to another facility. She was fighting it. Her father was happy. "And why not?" my mother added. Lawyers were now battling over what to do about the sex at River Down.

While some of Mother's listeners looked uncomfortable, Wit practically choked on laughter.

Eventually there were only the three of us. Mother was plying Wit with croissants and conversation. There was this cruise she wanted to take. She was going to –

My cellphone rang. Caller ID said it was Cassie. I had called her right back that day after interviewing Chasen. The funny thing was she didn't answer. Nor did she respond to my messages the following day. She said it was important, then she didn't return my calls? What was going on? "I've got to take this," I said.

"It's my birthday Agatha Jasmine. Can't we have some family time?"

Family time? We had been at the Delilah show for the last four hours.

"I'll be right back." I walked out on the porch to get better reception and away from my mother's snooping.

"Hi Cassie, how are you? I called you several times. You didn't call back."

"I know Jazz. I'm sorry. I decided you shouldn't be involved. But now I'm scared. There's someone who—I can't talk about it over the phone. In fact I've borrowed this phone from someone at work. I've got news about Cody. I left messages on Detective Folgers' voice mail, but he doesn't call me back. Can we meet somewhere and talk?"

"Cassie, I'm in Georgia with my mother and Wit. We'll be back tomorrow. What's your news?"

"I don't want to say too much over the phone. But someone saw Cody the night he disappeared. I'll tell you everything when I see you. I need to tell someone. What time will you be back?"

"We take an early plane. I should be back in Naples by noon. I'll call you and then come over."

"No, not to my house. Call me on my cellphone. We'll pick a place. I'm sorry to bother you. I know you're busy. I just don't know who to talk to about this. I thought maybe you could go see Folgers with what I tell you. He pays attention to you." She started to cry.

"Oh Cassie. Please don't cry. I'll be there soon. We'll figure this out. I'll see you tomorrow."

There was a weak "bye," and then a hang-up.

Chapter 39

I had been so involved in Cara Wicklow's death, I hadn't thought much about Cody and Cassie. It was that friendship thing again. "I should be a better friend,' I said.

"To who?" Wit had come up behind me.

"Oh Wit," I touched his face. "I become a different person when I'm working and I forget about people and friends, and especially you. I'm so sorry. And then I get with my mother and the stress factor makes me worse."

He hugged me and kept holding me. "I have the same problem with my mother," he said, "although not in the same way. She gives me the silent treatment when she's mad at me."

"Oh my mother does that too." I pulled over a rocking chair. "Sit with me?"

He pulled over another chair and sat down.

"That was Cassie," I said. "She says she's got some news but the detective handling Cody's case won't take her calls. That's funny, isn't it?"

"What's her news?"

"She didn't want to tell me on the phone, something about someone seeing Cody the night he disappeared."

"She should tell the police, not you."

"She's trying. She needs a friend. I'm sorry we're so far away. But we get out of here tomorrow. Has it been bad?"

"Actually, I find you mother quite entertaining."

"That's because she flirts with you. She needs somebody to focus on. After what happened with you-know-who last year she's sworn off men."

My mother had been celibate, at least I think she had, since my father died. But last year, in the midst of all that was happening to me, she met someone. I thought I would have a stepfather, but it didn't work out. Since then we are only allowed to refer to him as you-know-who. "Maybe she will meet someone on her cruise," I said to Wit.

"Your mother asked me when we were getting married."

"No! Oh God, I am so sorry. She is really something." This was terrible. We hadn't really discussed it ourselves. But curiosity got hold of me.

"What did you say?"

"I said we're getting married at Christmas."

"What? Did you really say that?"

"I did. You should have seen her face. Then I told her I was kidding. We hadn't even talked about marriage." He laughed.

I laughed too. But silently I was thinking "what's so funny?"

The party that night was a miniature ball. Mother was dressed to the hilt. I'm not sure what that phrase means. Sounds like a sword stuck up the derriere. Somebody once told me it has to do with the Hilton Hotel. Anyway, my mother says it all the time and it defined her dress. It was a floor length gold gown with actual crinolines underneath it. They were bunched up in the back. Was that supposed to be a bustle? She looked like a fairy Godmother sitting on a pumpkin. It was appropriate because I felt like Cinderella. My black slacks and white silk blouse were not what she had in mind for her gala. But they were easy to pack. And I wore a bright red pasha shawl that dressed it up. Plus, I had on my red Jimmy Choo shoes. The heels are almost 5 inches. I thought I looked chic. So did Wit. But mother?

"Pants? You're wearing pants? Oh Agatha Jasmine. You can't catch a man in pants."

The night seemed to go on forever. There was dinner, a very long dinner. Then we went to the "parlor" for games. Wit actually played Charades. He wasn't half bad.

But my mind kept wandering. I worried about Cassie. She sounded so upset. What did she have to tell me?

I would never find out.

Chapter 40

Cassie didn't answer her cellphone. As soon as the plane touched down I tried calling, and I kept calling for the next hour. Cassie always said her phone was part of her body. She was never without it. She even answered it once while catching a tarpon. And she was expecting my call. Why wasn't she answering?

After unpacking, I decided to drive out to her house. It was on the way to Triesen's and I thought I would make an unannounced visit there.

Her car was out front. "Good, she's gotten back from wherever," I muttered. I knocked on the front door. No answer. I knocked harder. Still no answer. I called her cellphone number. No answer there either. Okay, now I was getting nervous.

I walked around to the side of the house. I remembered a door there leading into the kitchen. I went to knock on it but realized it was slightly ajar. As I opened it, I called out "Cassie? Are you here?" Only silence. Then a few meows.

Cassie's cat came out from under the kitchen table and rubbed against me. "Hi cat. Where's your mistress?" I went to pick it up and almost threw it back down. The cat's paws were covered with blood.

Chapter 41

"Cassie? Cassie? Are you okay?" I started running through the house looking in every room. Not in the living room, not the bathroom. What about the bedroom? The door was closed. I took a deep breath and pushed it open. Oh God. Cassie lay on the bed. Blood was everywhere. I raced over to see if she was still alive. Her head had been battered, her face distorted from being beaten. But she blinked. She was alive.

"Oh Cassie, what happened? I'll get help. I'll call the police." I reached for the cellphone in my pocket. Cassie weakly grabbed my hand. "Po-lice," she whispered, "no, no police."

I could barely hear her. What? What about the police? Cassie was so weak, so trying to talk. Words came out in a breathy whisper. "No police. Jazz, truck — black — Johnny, get Johnny." And then she started to wheeze, and went limp. I felt the life going out of her.

"No Cassie, no! Talk to me, I'll get help. Please, oh stay with me." I dialed 911, holding Cassie's hand as I gave the operator the information. "Hurry. Hurry!" I shouted into the phone. But I knew it was too late. Cassie was gone.

Chapter 42

I couldn't breathe. I kept holding Cassie's hand. What should I do? Wit, maybe Wit could help. Somehow I dialed his office. Jennifer said he was in a meeting. "Tell him it's an emergency," I said.

Wit was on the phone in a few seconds." Are you okay? What is it?"

"Oh Wit – Cassie." My words tumbled out. "She's covered in blood. Her face is beaten in. I called 911. I'm waiting for the police. Oh God, please. I think she's dead. I can't go through this again." Memories of last year and the brutality of what I saw came flashing back.

Wit tried to calm me. "Where are you? I'll get there as soon as I can. Just tell me where you are."

"Cassie's house. Take Immokalee Road out past Oil Well, past—I don't know – to Willow Street. It's on the left. I don't know how many streets."

"It's okay. I'll find it on the GPS. I'll get there soon. Just hold on and don't say anything to the police." He could hear sirens in the background. "Jazz, do you here me? Don't say anything until I get there." He hung up.

Don't say anything? What was he talking about? I felt like I was passing out. I heard banging on the front door. Banging? The door must be locked. I rushed to it and unlocked it. Standing there were two police officers, and hurrying up behind was Bub Walker. They all looked at me, my hands covered with blood.

"Why Miss Billings," Bub said. "I've think we've got a lot to talk about."

Chapter 43

The next few hours were like a nightmare. The sheriff kept asking me what happened. I told him several times how I found Cassie. All sorts of crime units and police officers swarmed around me. The sheriff said I would have to go to police headquarters. I said Wit was coming and I would wait for him. I was told that wasn't my choice. Wit could meet us at headquarters. The sheriff was adamant. I had to go and I had to go now. There was nothing I could do unless I wanted to sit on the floor and refuse to move. So I let him lead me to a police car.

They put me in the back and we drove off. Was I a suspect? How ridiculous. I found her.

But when we got downtown, they took samples of my blood and fingerprints and a DNA swatch from my mouth.

By the time Wit showed up, I felt as if I should confess to something. A detective had been with me forever. He kept asking me over and over what I knew about Cassie. I told him Cassie thought she was being followed. She was nervous. I came to talk to her.

Wit was furious that I had been held there. Later he told me that when he asked about me, no one told him right away where I was. He called Bub, who wouldn't talk to him, and then the Governor's office. When he got to the headquarters I could here him shouting in the hallway. Finally, somehow, he got me out of there. When we got back to the condo, I broke down. He half carried me to the bed and told me to try to rest.

My mind wouldn't stop. Cassie, poor Cassie. I kept seeing her face. Was the rest of my life to be about death and murder?

Wit gave me a sleeping pill, but it did nothing. I couldn't sleep. Who was Johnny? "No Police," Cassie said, and "Johnny knows" or did she say "get Johnny?" I couldn't remember. I didn't tell the sheriff about Johnny. I didn't tell the detective who interviewed me either. He never asked if Cassie said anything to me when she lay dying. I didn't even tell Wit. He would think it insane that I was withholding information. And the more time passed that I didn't tell him, the more I wasn't sure how I could tell him.

The next morning Wit asked if it was all right if he went to the office. There was another emergency about some Washington legislation. I told him to go. I had so much to think about. Who was this Johnny? Who hurt Cassie? Would she be alive if I had been there yesterday morning?

I had to talk to someone about this. I got out of bed and called Joe. He and Marcia were back in New York. I told him everything, including Cassie mentioning a Johnny, and me not telling anyone. Was I withholding evidence? He didn't answer. Of course I was withholding evidence. But he knew how I felt about the sheriff. And Joe also knew how I felt about my reporting. Several times I hadn't told the authorities things until I researched them. How could I find this Johnny? He told me to stop thinking about it and rest more.

For the next two days it was all I could think about. I learned from the funeral home that Cassie's mother, Dee Dee was planning a small private service. They gave me her phone number. Dee Dee Moran said her daughter mentioned me several times and that I was a good friend to her. Right, a good friend – good enough to let her die.

Cassie was to be cremated and then her ashes spread over a spot in the Gulf of Mexico where she loved to fish. A small charter boat had been hired. Along with the minister from the local Baptist church, going on the boat were Cassie's family, and her roommate back from up north. I asked if I could be included. I think her mother was touched that I wanted to go.

The seas were rough so the service was very short. On the ride back to the dock, I stood next to Dee Dee, her flaming red hair a sad reminder of dear Cassie. I told her how sorry I was, and that I wished I could have done more for Cassie and her search for Cody. Dee Dee asked if I had any idea who would beat her daughter like that. I said I didn't know. But I had heard something about a Johnny, maybe a friend of Cody's. Did she know him? She said she never heard of him. But Cassie often talked about people from the local bar where she met Cody. It was called Filly's. Maybe the people there would know something.

The day after the service I went to Filly's. I found the address on the internet. Someone had done a tongue-in-cheek review of the bar's "Fresh from the Swamp" alligator sandwich. When I drove up, the place looked deserted. Only one car was in the dirt parking lot. A Bud beer sign flickered on and off in the window. Was it even open? I pushed on the old wooden front door. It creaked open. It was so dark inside that it took time for my eyes to adjust. The only light came from behind the bar where the liquor bottles on the shelves were lit up.

I could make out the outline of a bartender and two men sitting at the bar, one in the middle and the other at the far end. I sat down near the door. The two men turned and looked at me. The bartender, a large man with gray hair and a pot belly, walked over. You could tell he had seen it all. He put a menu in front of me and said "What do you want?"

"Did you know Cassie Moran?"

"Are you a cop?"

"No, she was a friend of mine. I need to help her. I need to find out who would do that to her. Can you help me?"

He ignored my plea. "You want something to drink?"

When I didn't answer, he turned to walk to the other end of the bar.

"Somebody has to care!" I shouted at him.

He walked back. "Cody cared," he said. "And what happened to him?"

"You knew Cody and Cassie together?"

"Everybody did. They couldn't keep their hands off each other. They were like joined at the hip. They were nice kids."

"Do you have any idea what happened to Cody?"

"Just that he disappeared. Nobody's heard from him. And he never would have left that girl on his own. He lived for that girl." He started wiping the bar in front of me.

"Did they have any friends they socialized with?"

"Didn't really see them with too many people, outside of us here in the bar. And now somebody's beat her to a pulp."

All I could think of was how I found her. I must have looked faint.

"Sorry. You want something to drink? Some water?"

"No, thank you." There was nothing else to say. I got up to leave.

"Good luck," the bartender said, then headed toward the customer at the other end of the bar.

"Thanks." I opened the door to leave.

He turned to the customer. "Hey Johnny, want another beer?"

Chapter 44

He was about twenty-five, dressed in a blue denim work shirt and jeans. The blue denim was almost black from the dirt caked on it. He looked like he hadn't cleaned up in a week. I walked over to him. "Excuse me, is your name Johnny?"

He glanced at me, then looked back at the beer the bartender put in front of him. It was as if I didn't exist.

"I'm a friend of Cassie's," I said to him.

This time he really looked at me. "You knew Cassie?" His words were slurred. How many beers had he had?

"Yes."

"She was a good person. She was always nice to me. I liked her."

"I want to try and help her. I want to find out who killed her."

"You mean who killed them."

"Them?"

"Cody too. The guy who was chasing Cody, he probably killed both of them."

Johnny must have been the one who saw something. "Can you tell me about that guy chasing Cody?"

"What are you a cop? You look like a cop. You don't look like nobody Cassie would be friends with."

"Cassie and I played tennis. We had a lot of fun together."

"Tennis? Who are you? Cassie never played tennis. She liked to fish. I remember she told me she caught a tarpon once, almost pulled her out of the boat." He guzzled down the beer and signaled the bartender for another.

"She wanted to play tennis because she wanted to be like Chrissie Evert. She thought Chrissie Evert was the classiest person she ever saw. She had a picture of Chrissie in her house."

Johnny put down his beer. "I remember. I remember seeing it. She had a party at her parents' house after we graduated from high school. I saw it there. We sat next to each other in homeroom. Cassie Moran and Johnny Moraine."

"Tell me about the guy chasing Cody."

"No, no. I shouldn't have mentioned it. I shouldn't have told her. I drink too much. Don't know what I see."

"Johnny, Cassie died in my arms. Her last words were to find you, to ask you about the black truck."

"Oh boy, she told you huh? They could come after me next."

"What did you see?"

"Not much really, just a truck chasing behind Cody on his horse. But that was the last night anybody saw him, so you got to figure that might be who made him disappear. And that might be who killed Cassie because I told her what I seen, so now he'll be after me – and maybe you."

"Tell me about the truck."

"It was black with a big white stripe on the driver's side."

"Like a police car?"

"The police cars here are white with green on them."

"Did it look like some souped up kid's truck? What kind of stripe?"

"I don't know. I just remember the stripe on the driver's door. I was out in the field. I was drinking that night. Nobody would believe me anyway." He took another gulp of the new beer.

I didn't want to lose him. What other questions could I ask? This might be the only opportunity to talk to him.

"What time did you see this?"

"Late, maybe around midnight. I was walking back to Carl's house. I sleep there when I can't make it to my sister's house. I was on the edge of the pasture when I saw Cody's white horse race by and then a truck behind it."

"Why do you think the person in this truck killed Cassie?"

"They both are gone. Wouldn't it be the same person who killed them both?"

"I don't know."

"I miss Cassie."

"I do too."

"I hope you find who killed her."

"I do too."

We stopped talking, each lost in our own remembrances.

Chapter 45

Well I had found Johnny and he told me about the truck. I couldn't withhold information any more. Besides, I didn't have the resources to search for the truck. The police did. I called Detective Folgers. He sounded almost sympathetic about Cassie, but he didn't think her death and Cody's disappearance were related. However, he said he would find Johnny, talk to him about the truck and get back to me.

He never did.

Instead, two days later the Naples Daily News had an article that ended any more research about the truck. The police had a suspect for Cassie's murder. The story was bigger than the original piece on Cassie's death, which had been only a few paragraphs. All that one said was that a woman name Cassidy Moran had been found beaten to death and the police were investigating. Beth Johnson's byline was on both stories. I called her.

"Don't tell me you have a tie-in to this murder too?" she said.

"Yes, I knew Cassie, and I was the one who found her."

"That's not in the report I saw. You found her? I can't believe it."

Wit must have convinced the sheriff to keep my name out of it. "Who is the suspect, Beth?"

"They're not releasing the name."

"But you know?"

A pause. She knew. "He's involved in another murder too," she said.

"Cody Mullins murder?"

"How do you know about that?"

"It figures that whoever went after Cassie had something to do with Cody disappearing. I just don't know how."

"Well I do. It was a love triangle thing."

"What?"

"The guy was in love with Cassie. He wanted to get Cody out of the way, but after he did that, Cassie rejected him. He got pissed and beat her up. Didn't mean to kill her."

"Where did you get all this?"

"It's in his confession. They haven't released it yet. But I've seen it. You're not the only one who has sources, you know."

Obviously Beth was upset with me. She probably knew I was writing the articles for The Trib. "Are you mad at me?"

"Why? I guess we both are crime reporters covering Naples now. How's your article coming?"

"It's a feature piece, Beth. You're the crime reporter and a great one."

Silence, then "sorry Jazz. It's tough being at a small paper when you've got a big story."

"I know. But it doesn't matter what paper you write for. You always do a great job. And smaller papers win awards too. Did your source tell you who the suspect is?"

"Yes. We'll be publishing his name tomorrow. They're talking about the death penalty for him."

"Wow. Well I know Cassie's family will be happy to find out what happened and who did it. I will be too. Cassie told me she thought she was being followed. I didn't know it was a stalker."

"I guess he's been after her for a long time. They went to high school together."

"Really, it's a local guy?"

"Oh yeah, Johnny was born here."

"Johnny?"

"You can't use that, Jazz!"

"Johnny? Johnny Moraine?"

"Don't tell me you know him too. Yes it's Johnny Moraine. He confessed to killing both Cassie and Cody."

Chapter 46

The Johnny I met didn't seem a killer. But then people can be deceiving. And I've been wrong before. Still, after Beth's article came out, I called Folgers one more time to ask about the truck and to question Johnny's guilt. The detective was very abrupt. He said the confession was solid. Johnny did it because he was in love with Cassie, and Johnny was now on a suicide watch because he was so distraught about it. Case closed. Good-bye. But I didn't hang up. I shouted "What about the horse?" That stopped him.

"What horse?" he asked.

"Cody's horse. He disappeared when Cody did. Cody was last seen riding his horse. Did Johnny explain about the horse?"

"N-o-o," Folgers said slowly, as if he was talking to a child. "He didn't explain about the horse, or your phantom truck. He confessed to beating up Cassie and shooting Cody and throwing his body in some alligator infested swamp. So one more time, why don't you go back to your writing and leave those of us who get paid to do police work to do our jobs? That's it. Over and out. Good bye." This time he was gone.

I called Cassie's mother. She was glad they found the killer. I said something about innocent until proven guilty but she already heard from the police. She said if they were certain Johnny did it, that was enough for her.

It was case closed. And a trial hadn't even been held. But then why would Johnny confess to murder if he didn't do it?

I tried to get back to my research on Cara's life. I couldn't concentrate. Wit found me staring at the computer screen in my office. "Let's go to dog beach with Willie," he suggested.

We spent such little time together, the three of us going out would be like a family outing.

"Can you take time off from the campaign?"

"If you can take time off from your reporting. You want to go out, Willie?"

Willie was under my desk. At the word "Out," he did a back crawl and freed himself from the furniture. Then he raced toward the door.

It was a beautiful day. Aren't they all in Southwest Florida? How many different ways can a TV weather forecaster say "sunny" down here? After settling in our chairs, I dozed off. I awoke to the sound of Willie barking excitedly. Where was I?

Willie was jumping back and forth around another dog. It was Helga, the weimaraner. Her owners were trying to carry their chairs and keep Helga on a leash until they got settled. But Helga was too energized at seeing Willie, and vice versa. The jumping caused Helga's leash to get all tangled around the woman. Finally she just dropped the leash and the two dogs ran off down the sand.

"Hi," I shouted. "Looks like they're still in love."

"Yes, I think she's been pining for him."

I couldn't remember their names. Fortunately they remembered ours. "Jazz and James, yes?" the woman said. "Remember us? I'm Marguite and this is my husband Luis."

"Yes, how are you?" Wit gave a wave. They put their chairs down next to ours. The two dogs were nowhere in sight.

"I need to get that leash off of her," Marguite said.

"I'm sure we'll see them racing back soon." Willie couldn't stay in one place for very long.

We had a nice chat. Well, actually I had a nice chat. Wit's face was buried in some briefing book from his staff. Relax, I wanted to say. We're out in the sun.

It was 15 minutes before we saw Willie and Helga again. All of a sudden they were racing toward us. "Helga here!" Luis shouted.

Helga jolted to a stop a few feet from him. He undid the leash. They took off again toward the water.

It would be nice to run around like that without a care in the world. I realized I was seriously depressed. Cassie's death was such a heavy burden. She wanted to tell me about Johnny. Maybe she wanted to tell me she was scared of him. I'd never know. I should put that behind me. But it was difficult. I kept thinking that maybe I should contact Johnny in jail. What if he didn't do it? It was hard to believe the guy I sat next to in the bar killed Cassie. And if he didn't do it? Who did? Maybe I would call his lawyer in the next few days.

"We better leave soon," Wit said. "I've got that debate tonight."

The debate. I had forgotten about it. I felt like going to a debate like going to the dentist. But Wit and I were a team, right? He rescued me from that horrible sheriff. The least I could do was support him by going to a debate.

"Right, the debate, we've got to leave. Willie!" After a quick goodbye to Luis and Marguite, and a pat on the head of the now exhausted-looking Helga, we headed for the car. Willie collapsed in the back seat. He looked like he was smiling.

Chapter 47

The debate was scheduled for the meeting room of the *Naples Daily News*. A few years ago the paper built a large modern plant in North Naples. Hopefully it gets enough advertising revenue to pay for it.

With both the newspaper and the League of Women Voters sponsoring the debate, it included most of the Collier County races. The candidates' table was almost as crowded as the audience section.

I took a seat in the back. A few people looked at me and whispered to their neighbors. In the front row facing the candidates sat some of their staff, and, no surprise – Mara. She picked a chair right in front of Wit. He smiled at her. She waved back. She also smiled at Wit's opponent. He nodded back to her.

Playing both sides, are we Mara?

Wit's opponent, Stephen Reynor, is a very distinguished looking man in his 40's. Wit says he is just a prop for this new political party, BBP. But I heard him speak at several events and he is no dummy. I made the mistake of telling Wit that and he wasn't pleased. It would be easier for him to think his opponent has no smarts.

Also at the table were the candidates for county appraiser, supervisor of elections, tax collector and Carson's commission seat. Each candidate sat next to their opponent. It was an interesting arrangement. I guess the feeling was let the adversaries get up close and personal. The interviewers sat a smaller table across from them.

After an introduction by the paper's Editorial Page Editor, the Congressional candidates started. They were to be given double the time for their debate as the others, and the debate began with a two minute opening statement. Wit was great, talking about his roots in Florida, his commitment to the area, and what he thought Southwest Florida needed from the federal government. There was loud applause when he finished.

Then Reynor spoke. He didn't talk of his roots, his commitment to the area, or what he thought it needed from the government. He just attacked Wit and everything about him. Wit came from money, he said, and his family was trying to buy the election. Wit really lived in liberal Washington, not in conservative Southwest Florida. He even mentioned the Congressman's new girlfriend, this liberal reporter from New York, who would make sure he didn't stay in Naples and make sure he wasn't conservative. He looked at me. People turned and looked at me too.

Wit's face grew redder and redder. I didn't know what to do. When Reynor finished, Wit asked if he could respond. The league's moderator said there was no response time set aside for opening comments and she immediately went into questions. At every opportunity, Reynor attacked Wit, citing his liberal voting record. Liberal? At times Wit is to the right of Attila the Hun. But Reynor made it seem like Wit's moderate stances were almost socialistic. There were a few more digs at me too. I couldn't believe it.

I barely paid attention to the debate between Carson and his opponent, or to the other races. I was so upset. It was just a terrible night and when it was over, Wit shook a few hands and practically pulled me out of the building. He slammed the car door as I got in.

I didn't know what to say. I rarely had seen him this upset. "He was horrible," I said.

"He was effective," Wit answered.

"You don't think those people believed what he said, do you?"

"I think it made them question some things. I've got to get my campaign manager to do some polling. We've got to see how some of these charges fly."

"Like about me? And your connection to this liberal Commie reporter?"

"Yes, we'll probably put something in about the congressman's personal life."

"You've got to be kidding."

"All's fair in politics, Jazz. Nobody said it was going to be easy."

"But it has been for you. You're just sensitive that there have finally been some charges."

"What is that supposed to mean?"

"I mean I think you may be overreacting. There were what, a couple of hundred people there? Even if they paid attention to that guy, there are tens of thousands who will vote for you because of your record."

"Do you know what a media campaign can do?"

"I would hope so. I work in the media."

"Maybe you shouldn't have come tonight."

"What?"

"Maybe your being there gave him ammunition. I don't want to see people attacking you."

"Maybe you don't want to see yourself being attacked because of me."

"That could be true too."

"Oh screw you!" I couldn't help it. I felt myself fill with fury. I had tried to be so understanding and now – was he ashamed of me? I couldn't stop. "Or better yet, why don't you find somebody to screw who you won't be ashamed of!"

"Maybe I will. Maybe I need to screw somebody who doesn't come with all this baggage."

Baggage? I turned to the window and didn't say anything more.

And we didn't say a word to each other for the rest of the night.

Chapter 48

When I got up the next morning, there was a note on the dining room table. "Have to go to Washington today. We'll talk when I get back."

Oh yeah? I felt like saying "don't come back." I was so mad. After walking Willie and going to my office, I was still mad. But the emotion had my adrenalin going. I vowed not to think about my personal life. And for most of the time, I didn't. I wrote, and wrote.

Wit was gone for two days. I called him once. He never called back. After a good cry, it didn't hurt as much. I was back working full-time. I would stop to walk Willie or make a quick something to eat, then I would spend hours at the computer. The only break I had to take was for the "the dog" meeting with the condo commandos.

Here I was writing about a murder and what that does to a family, and I had to stop and focus on the evils of a dog in a condo? Please! Plus this was Wit's condo and he wasn't even here to discuss it.

The meeting was scheduled for the downstairs card room of the condo building. I thought for a moment of bringing Willie, so the defendant could have his say. But the stuffy board of directors would probably not find that funny. When I walked in, the five member board was waiting. Four elderly men and one not-so-elderly woman sat behind a long folding table, the kind you use at a picnic. President Millstone sat in the middle. In front of the table was a single chair. It looked like a war inter-rogation room.

"You can take that seat," Millstone said, pointing to the chair. I wanted to say something funny, but I just sat down.

"As you know," he said, looking not at me but at several sheets of paper in front of him, "there are several charges we need to discuss."

Charges? Was he serious? "Do I need a lawyer?" I asked. The female board member started to chuckle but quickly stopped when given a stern look from the president.

"You do not need a lawyer, Miss Billings," Mr. Millstone said. "And it would be refreshing if you weren't so sarcastic. You may not think this is serious. But I can assure you to our condo owners it is."

I bit my lip. So much I wanted to say. But I was trying to be good. This was after all Wit's home. Wit, yeah right, who was too busy to call the person who lived there with him.

"First there is the problem with the size of your dog. He is big, very big. Our condo rules say small, very small dogs are allowed." He paused and stared at me over his reading glasses. Did he want me to say something?

I looked at the other board members. They were staring too. Maybe I should answer. I guess the first charge was that Willie was large. "Yes Willie is a big dog,' I said, "but—"

"Please don't interrupt me," Millstone interrupted me. "We do not allow big dogs. We made an exception because we think so highly of our fellow homeowner, Congressman Whitman. We thought you and the dog would only be here a few weeks."

That may still be the case, I thought.

"But now we understand that you have rented another apartment and you and the very large dog go back and forth to it several times a day."

"I use the service elevator," I said.

"Yes, I know. That brings me to charge number three."

Charge three? What happened to charge number two?

"Your dog attacked another dog in the service elevator."

"Are you talking about your little Maltese? She was the instigator. She couldn't get enough of Willie."

"That is outrageous," Millstone said. "Your dog tried to rape my Minnie."

Did he say rape? I do not take kindly to any loose use of the word rape. Few women do.

"Mr. Millstone," I said, speaking oh so slowly. "Please do not *ever* use the word rape in front of me again in such a flippant manner." The female member of the board gave me a nod. "Yes, my dog was interested in your dog, as your dog was in mine. It was unfortunate that they shared that interest in the elevator. And yes, Willie is big and I'm sure he appeared to you as the aggressor. But Willie is a little slow in the romance department. The first bitch he was bred with–" another board member actually gasped. I turned to him. "Bitch is the acceptable term for a female dog. The first time Willie was mated with a bitch" – I just had to say that word again– "the breeder had to use artificial insemination." They all looked at each other like how far will she go? I decided not to tell them that most of Willie's sexual experiences consisted of humping an old green rug. He *loved* that rug. Instead I said "If Willie scares you I apologize. And yes we were only supposed to be here for a few weeks. And it's possible that time will be up soon. Until it is, I need the other apartment to write in."

"Well Miss Billings, unfortunately this is not going to be on your terms. The board has decided to give you notice about having this very large dog. He must leave the premises within a month or we will start legal proceedings against Congressman Whitman. We hope you will go quietly. We wouldn't want this to become a campaign issue."

"Are you saying my dog and I both must leave?"

"Well, we assume you would have to leave if your dog has to leave."

"Not necessarily. But wait, how does any of this become a campaign issue?"

"Howard, perhaps we don't need to go there." The female board member was finally speaking up.

But he would not stop. "Not now, Alice," he said, dismissing her. To me, he said, "You must realize your New York City politics do not sit well here in our conservative Naples."

"How do you know anything about my politics?"

"I know all about you New Yorkers. Acting as if rape is some kind of dirty word. Only feminist liberals would get upset at that."

"I would get upset at that," Alice the board member said.

"Shut up Alice," he said. "I'm talking."

The other board members looked at each other. This was not what they volunteered for. One cleared his throat. "Ah Howard," he said. "That's not necessary. Let's stick to the facts."

I couldn't hold back any more. "You are an asshole!" I shouted at Millstone. "And I'm not going to listen to you anymore. My very large dog with his very small libido and I will get out of this building when we're ready to get out. If you don't like it, sue me."

I jumped out of my seat and started out the room. Millstone yelled after me. "It won't be you we'll sue. It will be the congressman and we'll make sure to do it before the election!"

"Go right ahead!" I shouted back at him. "I can't wait. And I hope the next time your little Minnie tries to seduce a male dog, it's a Great Dane!"

Chapter 49

My reporting was becoming a juggling act. With four articles to do, I would work on one then switch to the other. One day I focused on the murder article, the next the piece on Cara's life in Naples. Then there was her time at Triesen Academy. The school and its students were becoming a big part of my research.

I had found out some of the problems that had put the "problem girls" in Triesen's. For Sarah, it was a drug arrest. I discovered that in public records. Then Chasen told me about other girls. Krista stole jewelry from her mother's friend. That had been hushed up when she was sent to Triesen. As had the libelous comments Hayden Langley posted on the internet about her very young stepmother. Lila Monrote had assaulted someone. Chasen wouldn't say who. Could these girls' lives be turned around? Could Cara's have been?

To answer these questions, I needed to talk to Dr. Nubler, the Triesen psychiatrist. After his office cancelled my scheduled meeting, I kept calling back. His receptionist said he would return my calls. He never did. It was obvious Miss Halder had contacted him. I decided to play a little hard ball. After the receptionist told me for what was probably the fourth time that "he is really too busy today," I told her time was up. He would be in my article whether he wanted to or not, and that his always being unavailable would not look good. An hour later she called back and said he could fit me in at 3:00 p.m.

Dr. Nubler's office was in a cluster of medical buildings in south Naples. Why do doctors all like to congregate together? Is that in case the psychiatrist's patient suffers from insecurity about her looks, and a plastic surgeon is next door? Dr. Nubler's office was adjacent to an ear, nose and throat specialist. I would have to figure out that connection later.

When I said my name, the receptionist gave me a less than friendly look. I was the only one in the waiting room so I took a chair by the television. Fox News was on. Was this to be my penance? Why don't doctors' offices stop showing news channels and put on something educational like the History Channel?

Fifteen minutes went by. How long would I have to wait here? After ten more minutes, the door to the doctor's office finally opened.

"Miss Billings?"

I was not prepared for what I saw. Dr. Nubler was at least 75 pounds overweight and as bald as a cue ball. His pants were too long, his jacket too tight and he literally rolled when he walked. Everybody I met associated with Triesen's had been stylish and thin. Those words would never describe Dr. Nubler.

I followed him into his office and he motioned for me to sit on the black leather couch near his desk.

"I'm not sure what help I can be to you," he said. "Everything is restricted by patient privacy."

"Well let's talk first about your background and your arrangement with Triesen."

After listing colleges and fellowships that seemed to go on and on, he finally came to Triesen. "I consult with the school and their students."

"Don't you also meet with the parents and their daughters *before* the girls are enrolled as students?"

"Yes, I do that, too."

"And what is the purpose of that?"

"It's important that there be a good fit."

"For the school, or the students?"

"Both."

"How long have you been doing this?"

"Three years."

"And has your consultations resulted in girls not going to Triesen's?"

"A few times."

"And what was wrong with those fits?"

"That would be getting into patient privacy."

"But they weren't your patients. You worked for the school evaluating potential students."

I had him there. He paused, trying to think of a reason not to answer. When he couldn't find one, he said "some of these girls were not ready to abide by Triesen's rules."

"Such as?"

"Triesen demands a dedication to studying, not partying. Some of the girls, whose parents are trying to get them into Triesen, live for partying."

"And drugs and alcohol?"

"That goes along with partying."

"And you were able to find out that they would not stop this partying if they went to Triesen."

"I had no problem finding that out. You have no idea how arrogant these rich girls can be."

Ah ha, a crack in Mr. Professional. I decided to show empathy. "I have met many. They are indeed arrogant."

"You have no idea."

"Like how?"

"Patient privacy."

"But there are arrogant girls attending Triesen. How can they be a good fit as you call it?"

"If we prevented all the rich girls who are arrogant from attending Triesen, there would be no student body."

"But it must be difficult working with them. Do you have consultations with them after they become students?"

"Sometimes."

"Cara Wicklow?"

"Yes."

"She wanted to meet with you."

"Miss Halder wanted me to meet with Cara. There were problems between them."

"Were you able to resolve them?"

"Cara was complicated."

"How so?"

"Patient privacy."

"I'm trying to understand her. Would you call her arrogant?"

"I would call her a lost soul."

Wow, we were on the record. He knew that. "Yes," I quickly said. "She had a very difficult life. I've spoken to her sister at great length. The mother issues were very painful for them."

"It is painful if someone acknowledges it is causing pain. Cara was a difficult patient."

"Did you see her many times?"

"No."

"More than once?"

"Yes."

"Did she want to talk to you?"

"No."

"Did she talk to you?"

"Once. A few days before she died."

"Was there anything she said that might help the police find out who her murderer is?"

He paused for a long time and then stood up. What was happening? Was I being dismissed? No, he turned and went to his bookcase where he picked out a book on the top shelf. He came back and handed it to me.

I looked at the title. *Lolita.* I gave him a confused look.

"She gave it to me," he explained. "Look at the inscription."

I opened the book. On the title page in large letters was written **"To Triesen's doc, from Triesen's Lolita."**

I quickly tried to remember what *Lolita* was about. Wasn't it a young girl with an older man? "Did she explain why she was giving you this particular book?"

"Yes."

"Well, what?"

"Patient privacy."

"Have you told the police about this?"

"They never interviewed me."

"But surely they should know. This could help them with the murder investigation. If you can't tell them what she said, you can at least tell them about the book. Why not contact the police?"

"It's not my job to contact the police. I'm not a particular fan of our sheriff."

Well, there was something we agreed on. "Why are you sharing this with me?"

"You asked. Nobody else has."

Chapter 50

Triesen's *Lolita*. I couldn't get that title out of my head. After finishing with Dr. Nubler, I immediately went back to my office and downloaded *Lolita* on my computer. I spent the rest of the day reading it.

Cara had an affair with an older man. That had to be why she gave the book to Dr. Nubler. Did she tell the doctor who it was? He wouldn't say when I asked him. But he did say she talked that day. Was Cara's older man concerned she might tell someone? Did he know she talked to the doctor? I would definitely use Dr. Nubler's comments and the book in one of my articles.

Right now I was in the final editing of the first piece, a set-the-scene. It was a recap of the murder, the timing of it with the upcoming election, and how rare something like this was for the resort town of Naples. I also threw in a few teases about Cara's troubled years leading up to the murder. Buiner, the managing editor, called only once about changes. I told him I *strongly* preferred talking to Joe about the editing. Hearing the edge in my voice, he backed off and left me alone. I was on my cellphone with Joe when the condo's land-line rang.

It was Jed, Wit's district administrator. "Sorry to bother you Jazz," he said. "But you got a call here."

"Who from?"

"A woman named Marguite Obermann. She said she met you and the congressman at the beach and she needed to talk to you."

Marguite? Yes, she owned Helga, Willie's dog friend. "What's her number?"

He gave it to me. I thanked him, got back on the phone with Joe and promptly forgot all about Marguite.

The article was due to run in two days in The Trib's large Sunday paper. I was feeling the insecurity and excitement I always felt before a big piece came out. Did I get it right? Would it be received well, especially by Carson and Chasen? And what about Wit? We had made up again but there was still tension.

It wasn't until 8:00 at night that I remembered Marguite. I dialed her number and she answered on the first ring.

"I am sorry to bother you," she said. "But I have something to tell you. I'm not sure how you will take it. I wasn't sure how I felt about it at first."

"Is everything all right?" I couldn't imagine what she had to tell me.

"It's about Helga."

"Oh, is she all right? She's not sick, is she?"

"She can't keep any food down. She is losing weight and that is not good."

"Have you taken her to the vet?"

"Yes."

"Does he know what's wrong?"

"Yes."

Why was this woman calling me about Helga? "What is it Marguite?"

"Helga is pregnant."

"Oh that's wonderful!" Whoops. Who's the father, not Willie?

"I don't think I told you but we tried to breed Helga and nothing happened. The vet decided she was infertile. So we never really worried about her with other dogs."

"You think Willie is the father?"

"I know your Willie is the father. Helga is very shy and private. Willie is the only dog she's had contact with."

"Wow, I don't know what to say. Are you angry about this?"

"Well I was at first. What kind of mix would these puppies be? But then I started thinking this may be the only chance Helga has to be a mother. And you know Luis and I don't have children, so this will make me a grandmother. So I am all right with it. And I thought I should tell you. You are going to be a grandmother too."

"Well if you are okay with it, I think it's wonderful. I wish I could tell Willie. He knows a lot of words, but conception is not one of them. 'Willie,' I said to the black lump lying next to my bed. 'You're going to be a daddy!'" Hearing his name Willie looked up and wagged his tail. I felt a pang. He is such a good dog. "When is she due?" I asked Marguite.

"In about 5 weeks."

"Oh this is so much fun. Please let me know if I can do anything. I would love to see the puppies when they come. Maybe I could even keep one." Put that in your pipe, Millstone condo commando.

"I will call you. We are not taking Helga to the beach anymore, not in her condition. So we probably won't see you for a while."

"Well please, if you want to get together or anything, just call me." I gave her my cellphone number, and after quick "say hellos" to each other's male partner, the conversation was over.

This was news. I had to tell someone. Wit was at a political rally in Fort Myers. I had begged off, telling him I needed to finish the article. Well there was only one other person to call.

"Hey guess what? You're going to be a great grandmother!" There was silence at the other end. Then finally my mother said, "I think I'm going to faint. I can't speak. Agatha Jasmine we have to plan the wedding right away."

"The wedding?" Then it hit me. Delilah Cordelia Billings had missed the "great" part. She thought I was going to have a baby!

Chapter 51

Mother and Wit showed some excitement about Willie's impending fatherhood. But a few days later Wit was more interested in the certified letter that arrived from his condo board, laying out "charges" against Willie. He was enraged that another issue had surfaced about me. Me? It wasn't my fault that Willie was large. Wit said we would talk about it when he had time.

I let it go because I had more important things on my mind. The first article had come out, and the reaction was big. The local media picked up on it, as did several television networks. All over Collier County, people were talking about The *New York Tribune* doing a series on the Cara Wicklow murder.

Carson said the first piece was fine and he was anxious to see the next one. That was due to be published in three days. I hadn't quite finished it. It had become a bio of Cara's brief life – she and her twin trying to cope with the deaths of both a mother and stepmother, their growing up in Naples, and what Cara's life had been like after she was sent to Triesen. A lot of the article was about Triesen. I knew Miss Halder would just love that. But the school fascinated me and I still had this feeling that Cara's death was somehow related to what she did there.

Miss Halder and Sarah continued to ignore my phone calls. I decided to go to the school and see if I could talk to anyone. On the way driving there, I passed the turn for Cassie's street. A wave of sadness swept over me. I couldn't help thinking I didn't do enough for Cassie. I should have supported her more, maybe helped her find out who was following her.

Then Filly's came into sight. Two rundown cars were parked out front. The Bud sign blinked on and off as it had when I stopped there and met Johnny. I wondered what the bartender thought of Johnny murdering Cassie. On an impulse I jammed on my brakes and made a sharp turn into the parking lot. Maybe just a word with the bartender.

He looked up in surprise as I walked in. At the far end of the bar, a man and a woman were talking. He served them drinks then slowly walked toward me.

"Do you remember me?" I asked.

"Yeah, you said you were Cassie's friend. You talked to Johnny."

I sat down.

"Do you want something to drink?"

"I really just wanted to see what you thought about Johnny confessing to her murder."

"I think it's crap."

"But the police have the confession."

"You mean the sheriff has the confession. I heard it was him who got it."

"I didn't know that. You don't think Johnny did it?"

"He loved that girl like a sister. He would never beat her up. And kill Cody? They were friends. It's crap."

"Well hopefully at the trial we can learn more facts."

"The trial? What planet are you from? There ain't gonna be a trial. They'll ship him off somewhere." He looked behind me as the front door opened and two men came in. Their dusty jeans and work shirts were spotted with white plaster, probably construction workers on their lunch break. "Two beers," one said as they took a table by the window.

"Got to work," the bartender said to me. "If you want to be a friend to Cassie, you should try to find out what's happening with Johnny. Billy, one of the regulars here, he went to visit him and they wouldn't let anybody near him." He turned and poured two beers from the tap then brought them over to the table. I couldn't think of anything else to say. So I got up, waved good bye, and walked out.

Maybe I did need to try to see Johnny, or at least talk to his lawyer. But how many things could I get involved in? "If you want to be a friend to Cassie," the bartender said. Yes, I wanted to help Cassie. I sat in the car and dialed Folgers's number. The phone rang a long time before he answered.

"It's A.J. Billings."

I could hear a deep exhale. Then he said "How do you find out these things?"

"Excuse me?"

"I only heard ten minutes ago."

"You heard what?"

"Now you are not going to play innocent on me. Somebody told you about Johnny killing himself and you want me to investigate that too, right?"

"Detective Folgers, I don't know what you are talking about."

"You're not calling about Johnny's suicide?"

"Johnny is in jail. How could he kill himself?"

"Tied the sheets together and hung himself. Guess he couldn't take killing that girl."

"Will there be an investigation?"

"You see. You always want to play detective. Of course there will be an official investigation. But there is nothing to investigate. The kid couldn't live with what he did."

"I was calling to ask what would be the procedure for me to see him."

"Well we don't have to talk about that now, do we?"

Johnny dead? I couldn't believe it. "Don't you find all this a bit too convenient?" I asked. "The police don't find out anything about Cody's disappearance. Then Cassie keeps asking questions and she dies. Johnny is arrested for both their deaths, then he dies. And I heard the sheriff got the confession."

"Are you a mystery writer?"

"What?"

"Sounds like you're writing some cheap mystery novel. This is real life Miss Billings. People get murdered and the people who do it sometimes can't live with that. So they kill themselves. Now stop bothering me!"

This time I hung up first.

And then Folgers hung up, and called the sheriff.

Chapter 52

When I got to Triesen's, the receptionist with the gray pageboy and the "I'm better than you" attitude said Miss Halder was unavailable. I said I would wait. I walked over to the bulletin board to see if anything new was on it. In the reflection of the glass I could see the receptionist pick up her phone. When she finished the call, she came out from behind her little cubby hole.

"Miss Billings, I misspoke. Miss Halder went to an outside meeting."

"So now you're saying she's not here?"

"That's correct. I don't know when she'll be back."

"Who's in charge when she's not here?"

"Well, no one. She's the one in charge."

"Do you have a dean of students?"

"I'm really not authorized to talk to you about the staff. Perhaps you could come back when Miss Halder is here."

"And if I say I'm not going to leave and I'm going to walk around and look for the dean of students or a teacher or someone, what will you do then? Will you call security?"

The self assured façade vanished. "Please Miss Billings. Things around here have been very tense. Everybody's concerned about what you are going to write about the school. It's expected that I can handle you and get rid of you. I'll owe you if you will leave now and not make a scene."

"What's your name?"

"Joyce Jacin."

"How long have you worked here, Joyce?"

"Since the school opened. Please Miss Billings I need this job. I'll get Miss Halder to call you. I'll think of something. Would you please leave?"

I didn't want someone to lose their job over something that probably was not going to pan out anyway. Plus having Joyce as an ally might come in handy. "Okay I'll leave. But I have questions Miss Halder needs to answer. If she doesn't, I will just have to make assumptions."

"I understand. Thank you so much."

I headed for the front door. As I opened it, in walked Sarah. She looked shocked to see me.

"What are you doing here?" she asked.

I pulled her aside. "I came to see Miss Halder. But Sarah I tried to get back to you after you called. You haven't returned any of my phone calls."

"I can't talk to you here."

"Sarah what's going on? What was so important?"

"I can't talk here. I'm with Krista." The front door opened again and Krista walked in. Seeing Sarah and I together, she quickly said "We have a class Sarah. We're going to be late."

"On my way. See you there." Sarah disappeared down the hallway to the right.

That left Krista and I staring at each other. Joyce Jacin hovered behind us.

"Weren't you leaving?" Joyce asked.

I ignored her. "Would you like to talk to me Krista?" I said. No harm in trying.

"I'm late to class." The teenager rushed toward the same hallway as Sarah.

Another dead end. "Goodbye Joyce," I said. "Don't forget your promise." She nodded as I walked out the front door.

Chapter 53

One more day before article two was to be published, and still no call back from Miss Halder. So much for Joyce Jacin's promise. But I had some good material. I had talked about Triesen's policies with private school administrators from other well known academies. They never heard of disinheriting students. They voiced major concerns with the way the school was being run. And two parents of Triesen girls talked to me. Carson, of course, but I also spoke to Lila Monrote's mother. She thought the threat of disinheriting was the only answer for her daughter. On the advice of Miss Halder, she hadn't seen or spoken to Lila since the teenager started at the school in September. The headmistress advised that policy for all parents. Not everyone adhered to it, Mrs. Monrote said, adding "Some parents are weaker than others. They sneak in a call or visit with their girls."

A leading child psychiatrist thought the practices at Triesen's were basically "child abuse." No doubt all this would cause quite a stir at the school.

My third installment focused on the murder investigation with the autopsy findings, police interviews and Dr. Nubler's bombshell about the Lolita book and the speculation about Cara's involvement with an older man. That article was almost done unless something new broke. My final piece would tie up the loose ends. I was still working on that too.

In fact I was working all the time. I missed several debates and fundraisers for Wit and other Republican candidates. Well, I was working, wasn't I?

But the friction with Wit was getting worse. The pollsters kept saying his race was close. He couldn't believe it. He was spending more time on the campaign trail and less time with me. He was angry that I wasn't supporting him by going to the events. Then I reminded him he didn't always want me at the events. There was less fun, less kidding in our relationship. We would argue and then make passionate love. It was getting very stressful. I found myself spending more time in my work apartment. I was wrapped up in my story but I didn't feel like I had an ending for it.

And then the phone call came.

"Is this A.J. Billings?"

"Yes."

"This is Reese Davids. Remember, from Dartmouth?"

"Yes, Reese, I remember. How are you? What's up?"

"I saw the article you did about Cara. And I know you are going to do more. Is there anything new on who might have killed her?"

"No. I check with the police every few days, but they say there is nothing new. Nobody can find a suspect. You're not one by the way. Your DNA didn't match whoever had sex with Cara before she died. I was surprised that when we met you didn't tell me you had given a DNA sample."

"I didn't know how much to tell you. Sorry. My father arranged for me to give the sample up here with the Hanover police. But I need to tell you something. I should have told you when I first saw you, but —"

"What is it Reese?"

"Do you know about Cara's sorority?"

"I know she was part of one, but I haven't researched it much."

"Well, you should. It could be why she was killed."

"I don't understand."

"Do you know the name of Cara's sorority?"

"Yes it's P.S., for Phi Sigma."

"That's not what P.S. really stands for."

"Hopefully you are going to tell me." I got out my notepad.

"P.S. stands for power sex. The girls Cara picked for her sorority had to go through a very unusual initiation." He stopped talking. I waited. There was only silence.

"What? Reese *tell* me."

"To be part of P.S., the sorority sisters had to have sex with some prominent man, then they had to describe what happened at an initiation ceremony. Not all of them have gone through it. Cara and others had. And Cara did it more than once."

Triesen's Lolita! The sex with an older man was part of the sorority ceremony. "Do you know who these men are? How did you find out about this?"

"Cara told me. She started to have second thoughts about it."

"Do you know who Cara had sex with?"

"I know one."

"Who?"

A long pause.

"My father."

Chapter 54

Finally a break through. Reese explained why he called me. After a big fight with his father, he confessed to him that he was gay and proud of it. His father was furious. He asked his son why couldn't he find a good woman like he had – like his mother. His mother? Reese thought of the lies she had to live with.

"I had enough," he told me. "I shouted at my father about what a hypocrite he was – talking about the immorality of being a homosexual, yet he was having sex with underage girls. That shut him up for a second. Of course he denied it, yelling that I was out of my mind. But I told him Cara told me everything. He got threatening then, telling me if I knew what was good for my future – any future, I should forget about this. But I can't. I have to talk to someone. I don't want to go to the police. I thought maybe since you were writing about Cara, you could put the sorority initiations in one of your articles. Then my father would know that others know, not just me. I've got to tell you. He scares me. Who knows what he's capable of doing?"

What a revelation. I was still holding the phone minutes after we finished our conversation.

On my desk was a chart I had made with possible reasons why Cara was murdered and who might have done it. Most of it consisted of ramblings. I picked it up and erased some of my old theories. Now there were suspects, like the men she slept with. They would want her quiet. Davids was one. I put him at the top of the list. But who were the others? There were the sorority sisters, the power sex sisters. They wouldn't want anyone knowing what they were doing. There was even the staff at Triesen's. Miss Halder didn't want bad publicity. Bad publicity? How about your students being involved in a sex ring?

I had to confront the girls. But first I had to talk to Chasen. How could Chasen not know what Cara and the sorority were doing? She must know. This was one of Cara's dark secrets she warned me about.

I called and Chasen suggested we meet at the Mercato shopping center near Vanderbilt Beach. It had some happening bars like the Blue Martini. But this was daytime and I needed answers. We sat at an outdoor table by The Pub restaurant. Since it was lunch time, we ordered salads and a couple of iced teas. I could barely eat. I was so excited about what I found out.

"What's wrong?" Chasen asked. "You look like you're going to jump out of your chair."

"I've got some – well first tell me about the sorority."

"What?"

"Cara's sorority at Triesen's."

"I don't know much about it."

"I know you know everything, Chasen." A lie was worth a try.

"Whatever I know, what does it matter now?"

"Oh but it could. What happened there could be the reason she was killed."

"Don't you think I've thought of that? I decided it can't be anything at school."

"Tell me about the sorority."

"How much do you know?"

"Pretend I don't know anything."

"You were supposed to get these things from Cara's friends. Aren't you interviewing them?"

"They haven't given me much."

"What kind of reporter are you?"

"Chasen please tell me what you know. There's a murderer out there. Don't you want him found?"

She looked away. It seemed a long time. When she looked back I didn't know which way she would go, to talk or not to talk. I had a fifty-fifty shot. I'm not sure which way I would have bet. Probably that she wouldn't say anything. I would have been wrong.

"Cara wanted to show how hypocritical these powerful people around here are."

I didn't say anything. Silently I was pleading keep going, keep going.

"Cara's friend Sarah told me that Cara formed a sorority and that it had some secret initiations and it was dangerous. I asked Cara about it. She said 'Don't even think about this Miss Chaste. This is not anything you should, or even could, get involved in.' I guess she was trying to protect me. The next time I saw Sarah I asked her again and she said it had to do with sex but Cara told her not to talk to me about it anymore. That's it. How did you find out about it? From Sarah too?"

"No, Reese Davids."

"Reese? He told you? You're still talking to him?"

"Yes. He's scared about something, and Cara had confided in him."

"What's he scared of? How much did he tell you?"

"I can't go into that Chasen."

"But maybe if you tell me what he said, I can think of something about it that Cara said."

"It has to do with his father."

"Cara didn't like his father."

"What did she say about him?"

"She said he thought he owned people. He thought he owned Reese and she'd – she'd like to prove he didn't own anybody."

"Do you know if they had any contact?"

"Who? Mr. Davids and Cara?"

"Yes."

"Well that would be strange wouldn't it? Cara and Mr. Davids?"

"Yes that would be strange, and perhaps very dangerous."

Chapter 55

Chasen left me with the strong advice to talk once more with the girls at Triesen's. When I got back to my office I wrote down some questions. I would start easy. Who were the members of the sorority? How were they picked? Then I would get into the big subject – the initiations. Who did they have sex with? What did they know about Cara's affairs? Was affair even the right word?

I called Sarah but there was no answer. I left a voice message and a text message.

I am still more comfortable talking to a person than texting. You can sense emotions when you speak to people. I certainly sensed a strong emotion when I reached Krista by phone.

"Hi, it's A.J. Billings. I need to talk to you."

"I am very busy!" she practically shouted. 'You've got to stop bothering me. We're studying for a big exam."

"This is important and it will only take a short time. Can we meet?"

"No, I can't get away. But hold on."

I could hear her say to someone "I've got to take this. I'll be back in a minute."

There was a low rumbling of background noise as Krista and the phone moved to another place. "Okay, I'm in my room. What do you want to talk about?"

"The sorority."

Silence, then – "I told you before it's nothing. It's a joke that we made up, a sorority because we're in school and schools have sororities."

"Krista, I know all about it. I know about power sex."

A long silence. Then finally, "Who have you been talking to? Did Sarah say something to you?"

"I can't reveal sources. What I want right now is to talk to you about it."

"This is just fantasy stuff. It's not real. Sarah has this imagination."

"It wasn't Sarah who talked to me, okay? People know about this sorority. I need to talk to you and the girls in it."

"I have nothing to say. I've got to go." Click.

Well, that went nowhere. I needed to get to Sarah, and soon.

Krista was thinking the same thing as she rushed back into Hayden's room. "We've got to find Sarah to make sure she doesn't talk. That reporter knows about the sorority."

"What?" Hayden said. "Is this about what happened to Cara?"

"Who cares about Cara?" Krista said. "It's now about what happens to us."

Chapter 56

Sarah didn't answer her cellphone or respond to any of the text messages. Where was she? Both Krista and Jazz wondered.

At that moment she was wishing she was anywhere but where she was – parked in a car with a man the same age as her father. And he was groping her, and putting his tongue practically down her throat, and she couldn't stand it. She could not do this. She had to get out.

"Stop it, stop it!" she shouted, pushing him away. The man jumped back like someone tasered him.

"What's the matter? You asked for this. You wanted this. What's wrong with you?"

"I can't do this. Please drive me back." She started buttoning her blouse.

"You're crazy, you know that?" He zipped up his pants and pushed her away. "You better not say anything to anyone. I'll tell them you're crazy."

Maybe I am, Sarah thought. She spent days trying to set this up. And now she couldn't go through with it. "I won't say anything," she whimpered, then started to cry.

"I had to get a wacko." He started the engine and practically floored the gas pedal to get out of there. In a few minutes they were back at the parking lot next to North Naples Community Hospital where she told him to meet her. "Get out," he said. "And stay away from me."

She opened the door and was barely out of the car before it roared away. What to do now? She had ruined it. She knew she couldn't do this with an older man. This was too much like being with her father. And there were the memories she tried to smother in her brain for so many years. This brought them all back – her father coming into her bedroom, whispering to her, touching her. She started to shake. She had to call the school to come and get her. She had told them she had a doctor's appointment. She could say the doctor had an emergency and the appointment had been cancelled.

She took out her phone and noticed the messages. "Urgent, call me!" Another, "Call me right now! Important." The same type of messages, from two very different people – Krista and Billings, the reporter.

Who should she call first? The decision was easy.

Chapter 57

I was out walking Willie in the dog run when my cellphone rang.

"You called me?" Sarah asked. "You said it was urgent. What's going on?"

"I need to talk to you. Where are you?"

"I'm at the North Naples Community Hospital."

"Are you all right?"

"Yes, I wasn't in the hospital. I'm just outside it. It's a long story. Krista's called me too. What's going on?"

"Have you spoken to Krista?"

"No, I don't want to talk to her right now."

"Good, I need to talk to you first. Can I come pick you up?"

"I guess so."

"I'll be there in 10 minutes."

Willie never saw me move so fast. Almost dragging him I raced back to the apartment, and before he even lay down I grabbed my reporter's notebook and rushed out.

Sarah was standing out by the road in front of a big sign that said "Emergency Room." She didn't look well.

"Are you sure you're okay?" I asked, as she got into the car.

She took one look at the concerned expression on my face and began to cry.

"What is it?" I said. "How can I help?"

"Can we go somewhere? "she said, between sobs. "Anywhere, but not back to school."

"Sure, ah—" I was trying to think where to take her. "How about the beach?"

"Okay." It was a little girl's voice. Sarah looked like a little girl. Her eye makeup was all smeared like she had been trying on her mother's cosmetics. I gave her a tissue.

I headed for Delnor Wiggins State Park. It was the nearest beach I could think of. Collecting the toll, the park ranger talked to me about what a beautiful day it was. Sarah looked out the passenger window. "You and your daughter have a lovely day," the ranger said.

Daughter? Thanks a lot. Maybe if I had been a teenage mother. I wanted to set the record straight but this was not the time. I simply smiled and drove to the farthest parking lot. There were plenty of spaces. In Southwest Florida, unless it's in the high 80's, full-timers stay away from the beach.

Sarah made no movement to get out of the car. "Want to talk?" I asked.

"You first," Sarah said. "You called me."

"I need to talk to you about what's going on at school. The sorority and all. I think it may be the reason Cara was murdered. But you are so upset about something. Would it help if you talked first?"

"Everything is ruined. This was my last chance. And everything is ruined." She started to cry again. I got another tissue out of the glove compartment and handed it to her.

"I don't understand. What was your last chance?"

"To have friends, to be accepted. I don't know where I'm going to go now."

"Sarah, talk to me. I can help you."

"Nobody can help me." She stopped talking and stared out the window. I waited. Finally, she said "What do you want to know about the sorority?"

"Tell me about the power sex."

"I couldn't do it. Now nobody will speak to me."

"What happened?"

"It was my turn. I had the names. I couldn't do it."

"Could we back up? What names did you have? What are the rules?"

"How much do you know about P.S.?"

"Some things, but it would be so much easier if you would just tell me from the beginning."

"Let's walk." Sarah got out of the car.

We walked down a path through tropical bushes and large trees to the beach. I remembered the story Wit told me about how there had been a plan to rid this park of the tall Australian Pines that offered such great shade to beachgoers. They were "exotics" according to environmental agencies. Only native Florida plants and trees should be allowed in a state park. But beachgoers loved the trees from "down under" because of their shade. They protested the state's policy. While the fight went on, many trees were cut down. Finally the public won, and at the north end of the park near Wiggins Pass, or what we Northerners call the inlet, a few trees remain. Several people were sitting under them. Sarah and I walked out to the water's edge, then headed south toward the condos on Vanderbilt Beach. I again waited for her to speak.

"It was Cara's idea. She started the sorority. She decided on the name. Other girls told me how it was before I got to Triesen's. The girls didn't do much except talk about what they might do. I bet Krista told you it was a fantasy. She always uses that word. Well in the beginning, that's really all everybody thought it was. Until they found out Cara had actually done it.

"When I arrived at school last summer, I was assigned a room near her. I was pretty upset when I got here, and Cara and I would talk and talk. I told her everything about my life. She was good to me. You know Triesen has as many students in the summer as the rest of the year because our parents don't know what to do with us. If girls get their grades up, they can go back home by September. But some of us never go back. It's those girls Cara made friends with. Remember I called us the problem children? Well the P.S. sisters are the worst of the problems at Triesen's.

"When I found out Cara started a sorority, I asked if I could join. Cara didn't want me too. She said it would be too hard for me. I didn't know what she was talking about. Then she told me the rules for initiation."

We were walking past people fishing and sunning themselves. I hardly noticed them. I was trying to remember all this. I knew I couldn't take notes. And I hadn't brought a tape recorder. So I was trying to listen and at the same time remember. What I could use in my articles would be another issue.

"So what are the initiation rules?"

"She named the sorority P.S. To the rest of the world it was Phi Sigma. But what it stands for, I guess you heard, is power sex. To be initiated you have to have sex with a powerful man. He has to be about the age of our fathers, the older the better. You get points for age. You get points for how important he is. I can tell you about the point system later. Cara had the most points. You not only have to have sex but you have to tell about it. I mean really in details you have tell all about it at the initiation ceremony. And you have to bring something back from having sex with the man – some little thing, kind of a souvenir that goes into our awards book."

"And how many girls have done this?"

"Most of the sorority. Right now there are 13 of us. It's been my turn for a couple of days. But I couldn't. I can't." She started to tear up again. I wanted to find out what happened to her, but I also needed to hear more about the sorority.

"And who are the men?"

"Heads of companies, politicians, some sports guys. If they are married you get more points."

"But don't you all understand how dangerous this is? The men can be prosecuted for having sex with underage girls." I had learned that Florida law says any man over 24 who has sex with a girl 17 or younger goes to jail. "Didn't you realize these men wouldn't want people to find out what they did?"

"That's part of the excitement. You don't understand. Our parents have abandoned us. They dump us down here while they go on with their lives. We hate them for that. The thought of doing something that would really upset them, humiliate them – that is like so exciting. I wanted my parents to pay for what they've done to me."

"What I don't understand is Cara's father really loves her. Why did Cara feel that way?"

"Cara said he put everybody else ahead of her, especially that Mara. Then he put her in prison, that's what she called Triesen's. She begged him to let her out. Maybe it was her way of getting him to notice her again."

"Who was the man Cara had sex with?"

"There were several. Cara really enjoyed the thrill of it. You should have seen her telling about it. Her face on the video is like–"

I had to interrupt. "The video? What video?"

"Oh we record all the ceremonies."

"There's a video?"

"More than one. We put all the ceremonies on DVDs so we can have hard copies. And some of the girls even record being with the men. You should see the videos. They're better than a porn channel."

Chapter 58

"It was Cara's idea to record the ceremonies," Sarah continued. "She said 'Think of it, one day, years from now, the guys we have sex with could be even more famous or powerful than they are now. Or our sisters in the sorority could be, and we have the DVDs of what they did. What control we would have.'"

I shook my head. What were these girls thinking?

"Oh not that we would blackmail for money," Sarah quickly added. "Cara just loved the power of it all."

We had walked past several of the gulf front condos on Vanderbilt Beach. Sweat was pouring off my forehead but I wasn't going to stop this tale for anything.

"Where are the DVDs?" I asked.

"I don't know. Cara had them. I guess Krista has the latest one. There's been only one initiation since Cara died. Hayden did it. She was a virgin too. The next was supposed to be mine but..."

"I need to see them, Sarah. Can you help me get them?"

"I don't know. I don't know what I'm going to do now. I was hoping you would help me, not that I was going to help you."

"What can I do to help you?"

We were almost to the LaPlaya Hotel. Blue and white umbrellas lined the shoreline, but few people sat under them. The season hadn't officially begun yet. On the patio, several diners were having a late lunch. "Let's stop here and have a cool drink," I suggested.

"Okay," Sarah said.

We took a table at the far end, away from everyone. I ordered lemonade, Sarah a Coke.

"Tell me what's happened that you're so upset about," I said.

"I can't go back to school. Krista will be so disappointed with me. And when she finds out I told you everything–"

"Krista doesn't need to know you said anything to me. You're a source and I protect my sources. So don't tell her that we were together today. I won't either. But why can't you go back to school?"

"Because I was supposed to do my initiation today and I failed. It's the second time I've failed. I can't do it. Men seem to want to do it. In fact I was with one of them today. But I had to stop him. I can't have sex with a man who's like my father. It brings back bad memories."

What memories? Had Sarah been molested as a child? Should I ask her about it? But Sarah kept talking.

"And if I don't do it, Krista and the other girls won't speak to me. And I won't have any friends. And this is the first time that I've really had good friends. There's no place left for me to go. My parents don't want me back. What am I going to do?" Her voice caught. She was going to cry again.

I wasn't sure how to comfort her. I grabbed in my pocket for the handful of tissues I took from the car. I gave her one, then said, "Okay, let's take this a step at a time. You do not have to tell Krista that you told me anything today or that you even saw me. I'm sure she's going to tell you not to talk to me, just agree with her and say 'okay.'"

Sarah didn't look convinced. I needed to persuade her it was going to be all right. "So you couldn't have sex with an older man who is probably married," I said. "That is not a bad thing. Do not feel terrible about not being able to do that. I think this sorority and what you girls are involved in may have something to do with Cara's murder. It's all going to have to be investigated, so the sorority may not go on much longer anyway. Just make up some excuse about why you haven't done it yet. You said there were three men on their list. Where do these names come from?"

"They're men we researched who are well-known and who would be embarrassed if it got out they had sex with someone young. They're men who we think would have sex with us. We usually choose two and the sorority leader chooses the third. We have to do it with one of them."

"Who were the three on your list?"

Sarah quickly got up from the table. "We should go back." She started to walk away.

"Who are the men?" I had paid the bill, so I got up and started following her.

"Who are the *MEN?*" I asked for the third time.

"I can't tell you."

"Why?"

"I just can't." She started walking faster, back toward the park.

"But you've told me so much else."

"It would make you very upset."

"I don't understand. Why should I be upset who these men are? If they want to have sex with a teenager, I think everybody should know who they are."

"No you don't. You don't want those names out there."

"Why?"

"Because one of them you know."

"Who?"

Sarah stopped walking. "It's – It's—"

"*WHO?*"

"Your congressman."

"Wit? *Wit?*"

"He was on my list."

Chapter 59

I couldn't say anything. And Sarah didn't offer anything more. We walked in silence. Had Wit accepted Sarah's offer to have sex? I knew I should ask. I knew I would eventually ask. But I couldn't right away. My mind kept flashing to our fights and his shouting about going out to screw someone and not caring who it was.

Finally I had to know. "Have you been with Wit?"

"I met him at a fundraiser."

I could feel my stomach in free fall. "What happened?"

Sarah kept walking. Then she said "You're scared, aren't you? You feel like your life is about to change, don't you?"

"Sarah, please tell me."

"The feeling you have right now? That's how I feel. I'm scared and I feel like I'm about to lose the people who are important to me. I wanted you to know how bad it is for me. But don't worry. You're safe with the congressman, at least regarding me. I flirted with him, he flirted a little back, smiling at me, holding the door for me. He walked me to my car, but when I tried to show him I was interested in more, he basically patted me on the head and left. He was not interested."

I felt I could breathe again. We walked in silence until we were almost back to the parking lot. I had one more question to ask about Wit.

"Why did you think he would be a possible target?"

"I didn't. I told you he was a name on the list. He was the third name. Krista is now the president of the sorority. She put his name there. I told her I didn't think he should be there. But she said try him, you never know. I think she wanted to get you."

That she did, I thought, that she did. We were at the car. I felt drained. "Where should I take you?" I asked Sarah.

"I guess back by the hospital. I was dropped off there by the school. I said I had a medical appointment with a doctor in the building next to it."

"Call the school and tell them to come and pick you up. I'll wait with you."

"No, you don't have to wait. I want to be alone. I need to figure out what I'm going to say to Krista and everybody. Just drop me off."

The rest of the drive was silent, each of us lost in our own thoughts. I didn't even realize she was out of the car until I heard the door slam.

Chapter 60

After Sarah left, I drove to another parking lot and started writing down all I could remember from our conversation. The revelation about the sorority and seducing the men put my articles and the murder investigation on a whole new level. I couldn't write fast enough. I kept trying not to think of the part about Wit. The worst thing was when Sarah first said something about him. I believed it was possible. He was mad at me. He was vulnerable. Could he have had sex with a teenager?

But he hadn't, or so Sarah said. I willed myself to not think of him and our relationship. There was too much else to deal with. What to do with this new information? I should probably turn over the facts to the police, but I really didn't have much faith in Folgers, or the sheriff. Especially not the sheriff.

I needed guidance. Who to talk to? Wait a minute. Tess was coming to town the next day. I could run all this by her.

I pulled out of the hospital parking lot and drove to the traffic light to make a right turn onto Immokalee Road toward 41, the main north-south road. I knew I could make a right turn on red in Florida, but it was 4:30, the Naples rush hour. People who were getting off work were heading westbound toward the working class community of Naples Park. A pack of cars came toward me from the east. I would have to wait until they all passed or the light changed in my direction. The first car was a red Focus exactly like my rental car. I wondered if someone actually owned it, or if it was another rental like mine. Next came a black pickup truck that looked like a Texas pimpmobile. It had huge tires and all sorts of chrome. Give me a break. I hate those flashy looking pickup trucks. What are the drivers actually trying to pick up? A truck should look like a truck and be used for work not showing off.

The light turned red as the car and the truck got near me. Both vehicles stopped, the truck nearest to me. I started to turn, and as I did I looked at the truck again. The western sun was shining right at the front window, making the occupants light up as if they were on stage. I couldn't believe what I saw. Driving the truck was Sheriff Bub Walker. Seated next to him was Chasen Wicklow.

Chapter 61

What were they doing together? This day was getting crazier. I tried to stop in mid- turn. Could I follow them? The car behind me honked. I had to make the right turn. Now I was ahead of them. I tried to drive slowly in the right hand lane waiting for their light to change so they would pull alongside. But it wasn't that long a distance to the main intersection at 41, and I was in a right turn only lane.

I pulled off by the entrance to a shopping center and waited until I saw the pickup truck drive by. Chasen was talking excitedly, hands moving like she was making a point. Then she shook her head no and turned in my direction. I ducked down. I didn't know if she saw me.

Now that they were past, I tried to pull back onto the road, but no one would let me in. The sheriff got into the far left lane to turn south on 41. Finally someone motioned to let me back on Immokalee Road. Darn, I was still trapped in that stupid right-hand turn lane. I had to turn right. I watched in my rearview mirror as they turned left and headed south. I had lost them.

What was Chasen doing with the sheriff? My mind flipped back to the Davids fundraiser the first night I met them. The sheriff seemed intent on getting to Chasen. There had to be something there.

Boy did I have things to talk to Chasen about. Not only about the sheriff. How much did she really know about the sorority? Did she know about the recordings of the ceremonies? Did she know where they were?

If all of Cara's things had been taken from Triesen's, where were the DVDs? Could they be in the Wicklow house? Maybe that's where I should go right now. Carson would let me look for them. But what was I going to tell him? That his daughter had sex with his friends? And she made recordings of that? I was already holding back on telling him of Miss Halder's plans to expel Cara. Now there was Cara's involvement with older men.

And who were these older men? I knew about Ross Davids, but Sarah said they were more. How many more? Who were they?

Chapter 62

That night I stayed in my office apartment. I worked late, then tried to sleep on the couch. But I couldn't. I would toss and turn then jump up to write some more. Too much was happening. I kept awake until about 5:00 a.m. when sleep finally came. I had a terrible dream about Wit and Mara using the "sex couch" at his office. A phone ringing jarred me. Who is it? What time is it? I looked at caller I.D. It was Tess. The time said 7:00 a.m.

"Why are you calling so early?" I asked.

"I decided to drive over early. I wondered if you wanted to have breakfast with me. I'm starving."

"Where are you?"

"I'm pulling into the parking lot of Mel's Diner. When I stopped to get gas somebody said it was good for breakfast. It's on the *Tah*-Miami Trail."

I laughed and yawned at the same time. "Tamiami? It's pronounced *Tam-ee-am-ee*," I said. "It's another name for 41. They call it the Tamiami Trail because it runs from Tampa to Miami."

"Oh," was all Tess said.

I yawned again. "Give me about 20 minutes. I'll put on some clothes and meet you there."

"I may order before you get here."

"That's fine. I'll probably just have coffee."

But when I arrived at Mel's and saw the breakfast platter in front of Tess – a special with scrambled eggs, bacon, pancakes and more – I realized I was hungry too. I didn't remember having dinner. Then I realized I hadn't.

"Give me one of those," I said to the waitress, "and coffee, lots of coffee."

We chatted about nothing until my breakfast arrived. I took a few bites then I wasn't hungry anymore. I pushed the plate away.

"That's quite an appetite you have," Tess said. "Stress getting to you?"

We had talked before about the strain with Wit. "Aren't things any better?" Tess asked.

"I don't want to talk about Wit right now, okay?"

"Okay, but you've got to let it out."

"Yes, but not now. I have work stuff I have to deal with and I need to talk to you about it."

Tess signaled to the waitress for more coffee. "Let's hear it."

"I did an interview yesterday and some of the information I got probably should go to a law enforcement official. The problem is I don't know a law enforcement official down here who I can trust."

"Want to run it by me?"

"Yes, not that you would be involved officially, but maybe you could tell me who I should give it to."

"Okay. Are you comfortable talking here? Or do you want to tell me in the car?"

"I think the car would be better. You drive."

"Don't you want to eat anymore?"

"I can't."

We paid our bills and jumped into Tess's rental car. It was a Cadillac, much bigger than my rental.

"This is really nice," I said. "Our tax dollars at work?"

"It was the only thing they had in Miami. I got it for the same price as a compact." She pulled out onto 41. "Where to?"

"Anywhere."

"Okay, I'll head up toward my mother's house. She's not there. She's playing duplicate bridge at the Bonita Bridge Club. She plays *every* day. She loves getting masterpoints."

"My mother plays bridge too. She plays for money. I think she won $6.00 once." We both laughed. But I needed to get serious. "Can you listen and drive at the same time?" I asked.

"I can listen and break a man's arm at the same time."

"Well, you know I'm working on this teenager murder story. One of the girls at the school Cara Wicklow went to told me about a secret sorority they have. There is a special initiation. To become a sister, the pledge has to seduce an older man. It has to be someone prominent who would be humiliated if the story got out. And then the girl has to describe in detail the sex, what happened, all of it. Then she presents to the sorority some kind of token she took during the encounter."

"And how many girls have actually done this?"

"I don't know. I don't think it's been going on so long, so maybe 8 or 9? I don't know. But it turns out Cara, the girl who was murdered, did this initiation several times."

"Couldn't get it right the first time?" Tess started to laugh at her joke, but noticing I wasn't laughing, she quickly added "do you know who the men were?"

"I know one."

"This is definitely something the local police need to know."

"There's more."

Tess looked at me. "What?"

"There are videos of the initiation ceremonies. DVDs were made of Cara telling the girls who she did it with and every detail. If that isn't a motive for murder, I don't know what is."

"Do you have the DVDs?"

"No."

"Do you know where they are?"

"No. But Cara's twin, Chasen, might. I saw her with the sheriff yesterday. What was she doing with the sheriff? She's a strange girl. I think she's definitely hiding something."

Part III

The Lie

Chapter 63

It was all coming undone. Maybe that was for the best. She was so tired of lying, of not being able to mourn for her sister and strangely for herself. A part of her also died that day in the garage when she saw the body of her sister.

She looked in the mirror. It should have been me in that car, she said to the face staring back. I was the one they wanted to kill. They would still want to kill me if they knew I was alive.

She was so sick of it all. Poor Chasen. She wanted to scream, to pound her fists against the wall. But Chasen never screamed. Chasen was always so good. And now, Chasen was gone.

Because of her, because of the mess she made with her life, Chasen was dead and Cara was still alive.

Cara tore off the gray Community School sweatshirt and threw it on the ground. "I am Cara Wicklow!" she screamed into the mirror. "I am alive. Somebody help me!"

Chapter 64

The morning the second article appeared, I wondered what the reaction was at Triesen's. Had Miss Halder read it? Had the girls?

Buiner, the managing editor, placed the story in prime newspaper real estate – on page one above the fold. The shock headline read "Murdered Teenager's Tragic Life." The subtitle was "Private school in Florida hides problem girls."

I had only alluded to the secret sorority and what the members did in it. Those facts would be part of the third installment about the murder investigation. Still, I figured they were probably very upset at Triesen's. And then the phone rang.

"Miss Billings, It's Joyce Janic from Triesen."

Uh oh. Miss Halder probably wanted to give me a lashing. "Good Morning Joyce. Is she finally going to talk to me?"

"What? No, I'm not calling for Miss Halder. I could never get her to call you back. I'm sorry about that. No, I am calling because you did me a favor and now I am going to do one for you."

A crack in the Triesen wall of silence? This was what I was waiting for. "Go on."

"Sarah Van Holben was taken to the hospital an hour ago. She tried to kill herself."

Oh, this was not what I was waiting for. Sarah? Did she see the article? Is that what caused it? "Is she all right?" I asked.

"We have no information yet. She's in the community hospital in North Naples. I thought you might want to find out on your own how she is. Miss Halder and she had a big fight early this morning. It was about your article. I heard them all the way down the hall. Miss Halder called her a snitch and said she wanted her out of the school. Sarah took the pills shortly after that."

I felt sick. "Thank you for telling me. I'll try to find out what I can."

"Miss Billings, I wanted you to know that I think what you wrote had to be said. This didn't come from me, but Miss Halder has too much control over these girls. Some of them are fragile like Sarah. I knew this was going to happen."

"Thank you. But I still feel horrible about this. If I find out anything I'll let you know."

"Please. Thank you. This is a terrible situation." She hung up.

Sarah overdosed? Did I cause it? In the article I tried to downplay Sarah's quotes about the school. Yes, I used her "problem children" line. But I hadn't yet written about the sex initiations. That would be the bombshell. So what caused Sarah to go over the edge?

I called the hospital. They wouldn't reveal any information about a patient unless I was a relative. I decided to wait a few hours then go there.

Several times I've seen patients using a little trickery. I know, I know. That's what makes people not trust the media. Well, this time it was not for a story. This time I simply wanted to find out how Sarah was.

The emergency waiting room was jammed. I went to the sign-in window and asked how I could see a patient who had been brought in. When the nurse asked who, I gave her Sarah's name. "Are you a relative?" the nurse asked.

"An aunt who—" I sniffled. I didn't finish the statement which could have been "An aunt who is coming from New York will be here soon." The nurse assumed I was the aunt. She looked up Sarah on the computer. "She's recovering. She's in room 308."

I went up to the third floor. Would Miss Halder be there? Seeing her would not be good. But no one from Triesen's was in the hallway or the room when I walked in.

It was a private room. Sarah, with tubes in her arm, was bundled up in a bed by the window. She was asleep. I took her hand and held it. I felt so bad that I might have caused this.

She opened her eyes, then slowly smiled at me. "Miss Billings. Thank you. Thank you for everything."

I didn't know what to say. Why was she thanking me? "Sarah, are you okay?"

"I'm going to be – now. I didn't know what to do. I kept lying to Krista about doing it, you know with the older guy. And finally your article came out. But it didn't have everything about the sorority. And Miss Halder was so upset. I thought I just needed some time until you wrote more. So I took some pills. I thought I was taking the right amount to make them leave me alone. I guess I took one or two too many. It was scary for a while. But here I am. And something wonderful has happened."

What was she talking about?

"Miss Halder called my parents. She told them what happened. They're coming. They're coming to see me. It's all because of you and your articles. I spoke to my mother on the phone. She said they would be here in a few hours. Everything is going to fine. My parents are coming."

She looked so happy. "Everything is going to be all right for me now," she said. "Don't you think?"

I continued to hold her hand. "I hope so, Sarah. I hope so."

Chapter 65

Maybe it was time to share with someone the hell her life had become. Cara thought about it for days. She couldn't keep masquerading as Chasen. She couldn't keep avoiding people who might guess. Her father was so lost in his grief that he never realized it was Cara he was talking to. How strange to hear him mourn for herself. And her friends at Triesen? Well, were they really friends? Life went on for them.

Who could she tell? Who would help her? Again and again she thought of Billings. If the reporter revealed all that had happened, maybe that would save her life. Maybe she could start over. She would tell her father how much she loved him, how wrong she had been to distance herself from her sister. She would tell everybody how much her sister meant to her. If she could, she would have died for Chasen, not the other way around.

Should she tell Billings? So much was at stake. Yet she couldn't go on like this. Yes, she would tell Billings. She would tell her everything. And she would do it right now. She reached for her cellphone. Then the front doorbell rang. Marita would get it. She looked up Billings's telephone number on her call log. But now there was knocking on the front door, then a pounding. Why wasn't the housekeeper answering? Oh right. It was

Tuesday, Marita's day off. Days blended together in this life of avoiding the world.

"I'm coming. I'm coming!" she shouted. She rushed to the door and opened it. And there he was.

God, she thought, he has such killer eyes.

Chapter 66

After leaving the hospital, I called Joyce at Triesen's to tell her Sarah would recover. Then I called Tess. I told her I was going to the Wicklow house to see if Carson would let me search for the DVDs. I had to move this story along before something else happened. But Tess said don't do it. Going to the house was not a good idea. First, I would have to confide in Carson a lot of things and was now the time? Second, what if I did find the DVDs? What was I going to do with them? I needed to have an official investigation. If I waited, she would call some associates to find out who to contact on the local police force.

So for the moment I decided to put off searching for the DVDs. Tess asked me to come to Pelican Landing and visit with her and her mother. I said sure.

Pelican Landing is a gated community, which means to enter you have to get past a guard. The keeper of the gate, I thought, as a man in uniform surveyed my dented compact and questioned me. Southwest Florida has all these walled-in neighborhoods with homes, condos, and big clubhouses that look like modern castles. All that's missing is the feudal lord.

Pelican Landing was one of the really nice gated communities. Residents there play golf, tennis and even Bocce. It seems a great place to retire to, which is what Tess's mother and father had done. But her father died from cancer and now her mother was alone, although she said she had so many friends she didn't feel alone. I visited for an hour and then got anxious to get back to work. I told Tess I would meet her for dinner. Wit was busy campaigning.

With the election only a week away, Wit's schedule was so hectic I wasn't even a part of it. If I wasn't so occupied with the Cara Wicklow story, I would probably be miserable. But I realized that was the problem. I should be miserable even with all my work. Instead I felt numb. I definitely had to think about this relationship.

After I returned to the work condo I wrote for about an hour. I had to decide whether to put in Sarah's suicide attempt. I didn't want to affect her life any more than I had. If I found something else, something bigger, I could finish the series without involving her again. If the DVDs were at the Wicklow house, that would be the biggest find of all.

Ignoring Tess's warning, I decided to go there. First I called Carson to see if he was home. Nobody answered the home phone. I called his cell. No answer there either. I left a message for him to call me.

When I got to the house, I rang the bell and knocked on the door. Nobody answered. This was not going to be the day to play Nancy Drew, my mother's favorite detective. Of course my mother was a child when she read the Nancy Drew books. Mysteries were a lot easier to solve back then.

As I walked back to the car, my phone rang. It was Carson.

"Hi, I'm at your house right now," I told him.

"Oh, are you going to see Chasen?"

"Well no one is answering the door."

"That's strange. I think Chasen should be home. Try the door and see if it's unlocked."

I did, and it was. "Should I go in?"

"Sure, maybe Chasen is sleeping. She needs to talk to someone. You're probably the best person. She seems to be honest with you."

I felt bad. I thought how dishonest I was being with him. Honorable nice Carson. I would tell him everything the next time I saw him.

"I hate to be in your house with no one here."

"Why don't you go to Chasen's room and see if she's in there? I'll hold."

I walked down the hall toward the teenager's room. The bed was unmade. A Community sweatshirt lay crumpled on the floor. But no Chasen.

"She's not here."

"Well she must have taken her car somewhere. Do you have an appointment with her?"

I didn't know what to say. Why was I at the house? My initial thought was tell Carson everything now and ask him to let me search. But on the phone? No.

I just said, "I didn't set up a meeting. I was hoping I would catch her. Could I stay here for awhile, in case she comes back?"

"Of course. Make yourself at home. I should be back in about an hour or so. Stay and have dinner with us. We could call Wit to see if he'd join us. "

Calling Wit wasn't such a good idea. "I'm sorry I have dinner plans. I'll wait for a little while and if she doesn't come back soon, I'll call and schedule some time to see her."

"Okay, Maybe I'll see you later."

"That would be nice. Bye."

Well here I was. This was what I wanted, right? I closed the bedroom door, a buffer if I needed it. Might as well start with the dresser. But opening the top drawer made me feel like a burglar. What was I doing? Don't think about it. Just do it.

The drawer overflowed with sheer little bras and panties. It looked like a sale bin at Victoria's Secret. Chasen obviously was not the goody girl everybody talked about. I opened a smaller drawer on the side. It was filled with jewelry. Then another drawer. It was a jumble of two piece bathing suits, little *little* two pieces. I started moving faster. I looked under the bed hoping for a stack of DVDS. Nothing. Then I opened the closet, a big walk-in closet, definitely "closet drink" size. One side was neat with shoes lined up on shelves and short little dresses, pants and blouses all precisely hung. But on the other side the shelves were stuffed with — well it looked like just stuff. I started rummaging through it. Odd. Besides some clothes, there was a combination of Chasen's school work and Cara's. Books from the Community School mixed with papers from Triesen's. Why did Chasen have Cara's stuff here? And why was it all heaped together?

Okay. If the Triesen Academy returned all Cara's belongings, this was probably where everything would be put. And if the DVDs had been at the school, they could be here too. I started searching through the assortment of books, papers and clothing. Would the DVDs be loose? Not if Chasen looked at them. She would have hidden them in something, right? Even if she hadn't looked at them, they would probably be in some kind of container. I needed to find a box or a package.

In the back of the closet, extra blankets and pillows were piled in a mound. For what? A sleepover? I tore at the pile, tossing the pillows out into the room. The blankets got tossed on the closet floor. And then I saw it. Underneath everything lay a big white Fed Ex box. Maybe. Just maybe. My adrenalin pumped as I grabbed for it. I carried it out into the bedroom. Written on the front, in big black letters, was: "Cara Wicklow's Everglades Project. Do Not Touch!" The box was sealed. Should I open it?

I was so fixated on the box I didn't hear the bedroom door open. Suddenly the box was grabbed out of my hands.

Chapter 67

"What are you doing in my room?" Chasen was glaring at me.

"I – I was waiting for you, and I, ah, got curious."

"Waiting? Look at my room. It looks like you were ransacking it."

I didn't know what to say. The only thing I could think to say was the truth.

"Okay, I found out some things today. I think they have to do with Cara's murder. I wanted to talk to you about them. But I thought maybe what we needed to find might be here."

"And what do *we* need to find?"

"The DVDs." I waited to see Chasen's reaction. Did she know about them?

It could go either way. But the way it went was nothing I could have thought of.

She heaved this gigantic sigh and sank onto the bed. Then she began to cry. The crying didn't stop. What had I said? I couldn't figure out what was happening.

"I can't take this anymore," she said between sobs.

"It's okay, Chasen. It's okay. You've been through a lot."

"Chasen is dead."

I didn't understand. I thought she was having a nervous breakdown.

"Chasen, you've got to–"

"I AM NOT CHASEN! I am Cara!"

Chapter 68

Could she really be Cara? I never knew the twins together. So she easily could have fooled me. But what about her father? Her friends?

Stunned, I sat down on the bed next to her. For a minute, neither of us spoke. Chasen, or Cara, kept crying. I got some tissues for her, then sat down again and put my arm around her. I certainly had my share of crying teenage girls. "It's all right," I said. "It's all right. Do you want to tell me what happened?"

She blew her nose. "I've wanted to talk to you for a while. I wanted to tell someone. But I'm so afraid. It was me they wanted to kill, not Chasen. If anybody knows I'm still alive, they will come after me again. But it's so unfair to Chasen's memory for me to pretend to be her."

"Who wanted, or wants, to kill you?"

Cara finally stopped crying. "Maybe I should tell you a few things."

Oh yes, yes. The reporter mode in me went into overdrive.

"I started this group at Triesen's —"

"The sorority?"

"Yes, Power Sex. We called it P.S. or Phi Sigma if we talked about it in public. Our parents were so cruel sending us to Triesen's. We wanted to pay them back. I thought what could be the worst thing to punish my father with? Sex with older guys seemed to fit the bill. So we started the

240

initiations. I went first. It was easy for me. In fact I did it several times. And nothing really bad came from it until I picked the wrong guy."

"Ross Davids?"

"You knew about him?"

I nodded.

"He was pretty upset when he found out I made a video of our night together in the sorority condo. But he wasn't the worst one."

"I don't know about the condo. Where is the condo?"

"Hayden's aunt and uncle own a condo in North Naples. They rarely use it. We had our initiation ceremonies there. Some of the girls also met the men there. We set up a camera, so, if you were really clever, you could get the man there and record the event. I did that with Ross. My mistake was recording other men there."

"Who?"

She studied my face. "Once I tell you, there's no going back for you. You will be in danger just like me."

"Tell me Cara." It seemed strange saying that name.

"Some days I had Big Dick and sometimes it was Little Dick. Bub liked comparing himself to Dick Tracy. He told me Tracy was a detective in old comic books. He wore a special watch. Have you seen Bub's? Anyway he made me call him Dick. He liked the double meaning of that."

"Bub? Bub Walker, the sheriff?"

"Yeah. Once he found out about the video, he went crazy. I gave the DVD to him. But he thought I still had a copy somewhere. And he wanted to know about the other men and if I made DVDs of them. The other day he came here to meet with Chasen 'to warn her,' he said, about things Cara might have hidden. He's so paranoid he thought maybe the house was bugged. So he took 'good ole Chase,' as he called me, for a ride. He asked if I knew of any DVDs Cara made."

"Did you make an extra copy of the DVD with you and the sheriff?"

She looked at me like "Are you kidding?"

"You think I'm dumb?" she said. "Yeah, I kept copies of everybody. But as Chasen I told him I didn't know what he was talking about."

"I think I saw you with him in the truck the other day. I couldn't figure out what you were doing."

"He said he needed to talk to me about the murder. He suggested we get out of the house, that fresh air would do me good. I knew that was just an excuse for his paranoia, but I decided to go with him and see what he really wanted. I asked him if he knew who killed Chasen. Of course I said Cara. He said he was working on it and that the DVDs could give him the answers."

"Do you think he killed her?"

"I don't know who planned it. It could be him, but then it could be a dozen others. I know secrets about lots of people. I haven't been a very good person." She started to tear up again. "I was so angry about everything. I didn't care who I hurt, or what I did. But I don't know what to do about it now. Can you help me?"

"We need to talk to someone."

"No, we can't talk to anyone. You can't tell my father or Wit or anyone. I probably shouldn't have told you. But I was thinking if you could write something and it was published, maybe all this would end. Maybe if people knew I was alive, the killer would be too scared to come after me."

Sarah, Reese and now Cara. They all wanted me to write the story to protect themselves. Were they all threatened?

"We're jumping around here," I said. "But there is so much I need to understand. How do you know that whoever murdered Chasen was really after you?"

"Because I was there. I was there the night they killed Chasen."

Chapter 69

"It was the night of my father's fundraiser. So much had happened in the days before. I had been involved in– I don't want to talk about that. But I had seen something, and I didn't know what to do about it. I needed time to think."

"What did you see?"

She shook her head, then stared at the floor. I waited. Finally she took a deep breath. "You know Chasen was the good twin," she said. "I was the bad girl. I've done things. I probably should have told somebody what I saw. But that would have meant a lot of explaining."

"What did you see?"

"I was with Big Dick. He kept threatening to tell my father and Miss Halder everything about the sorority and what I was doing. I warned him that if he said anything, he'd be the one in trouble. I'm a minor, you know. But he is a bad dude. He got off on this tension between us. He kept wanting to hook up and have more and more sex. And it was exciting for me too. Kind of self-punishment, I guess. The more sex we had, the stranger the things he wanted to do. We were out in a field at night. He liked to keep taking more and more chances. So we were in this field having sex and this guy comes along. He sees us. Big Dick goes ballistic. The guy was on a horse. He takes off and Dick goes racing after him in his truck. I couldn't do anything. I mean I'm naked with a dog collar around my neck."

I must have looked shocked. "I told you he was getting into strange sex," she said. "Anyway, my clothes were in his truck. All I had to cover myself with was the blanket he had thrown on the ground. I mean I couldn't really help the guy and I hadn't really seen him. Just his back as he jumped on this white horse. But Big Dick? I knew he wouldn't let the guy get away, and he probably wouldn't let me either. But where could I go? I was naked. I had no phone. My purse was in his truck too. I sat and shivered and wondered how far a walk it would be to someone's house, and what would I say once I got there? I was so tired of all the lies. So I just waited. I thought this is probably my end. And you know what? I didn't care.

"I had given Miss Halder a reason to expel me by bringing Reese to my room. I needed to get away from Triesen. It was a prison with so many rules. And there was so much hatred between Halder and me. Do you know she locked me in a closet once? But where was I going to go? When my father found out what I had done he would never take me back. And the men, they were never going to leave me alone. You saw that at the fund-raising party. So that night I sat on the ground and waited. About an hour later Dick came back, caked with dirt. He told me to get into the truck. He didn't say anything. And I thought better not to ask him anything. I thought he was going to kill me. But he just threw me my clothes and said 'Where do you want to go?' I asked him to drop me off at the sorority condo. And he did. As I got out of the car, he said 'don't say anything about tonight to anyone.'

"Then came the fundraiser, and my clothes for it were at my house. I didn't want to talk to anyone, so I went to the side entrance by the garage. When I got near, I heard voices inside the garage. I thought they were car repairmen. Chasen had been having problems with her car. I opened the side door. That's when I heard a man say 'Is she dead?' Another man said 'Of course she's dead. The drug only takes 60 seconds.'

"I stood there frozen. They couldn't see me. They kept talking. 'It's sup-posed to look like a suicide,' one said. The other said 'What do you want to do, hang her?' He laughed. The other guy answered 'No, we'll use the car. Turn the engine on. Some people might use a gunshot to the head. But why ruin the face of Cara Wicklow? God, what a waste killing her.'"

Cara was telling this story so calmly, it was as if she was reciting the plot of a movie she saw. I couldn't believe it.

"I remember everything they said," she continued, "including one saying 'maybe we could do her before we leave her.' The other said 'You're sick. She's dead for Christ sake.' I think I was in shock. I was hearing about my own murder. Only it wasn't me who died, which meant they killed my sister. But why would they think Chasen was me? Then I remembered. Chasen asked to borrow my car. Hers was stuck in the garage. She said it had a problem starting and she needed to get it fixed. Since I wasn't using mine, I said sure, take it. They must have thought it was me because she was driving my car.

"I heard them struggling and breathing hard, like maybe putting Chasen into the car. Then I heard them coming toward where I was. I raced to the backyard so they wouldn't see me. They left and I went into the house by the sliding glass doors in the back. I didn't want to look in the garage."

It was hard to comprehend all that she told me. Witnessing your sister's murder and you couldn't help her? And what about the night with Big Dick –the sheriff – and the guy on the horse? That was Cody, of course. That meant Cody was killed by the sheriff. Johnny didn't kill him. Which almost certainly meant the sheriff killed Cassie too. And Johnny's death? Probably didn't happen that way either. I knew I didn't like Bub Walker. But to think of him killing all these people?

"I didn't know what to do," Cara said, bringing me back to her plight. "I was so messed up. Chasen was dead and somebody wanted it to be me. I thought 'I've got to have time to figure this all out.' And then it came to me. I could be Chasen for just a little while until the police found out who murdered her. That night I went to the fundraiser as Chasen and I met you. Later Marita discovered Chasen's body and called the police. I didn't see Chasen dead until I came back from the party with Dad. I really lost it. They medicated me so I could go to the wake and the funeral. I thought I would only have to pretend being her for a few days. But it keeps going on and on. And I try not to see anybody or talk to people. So I do the home-schooling. You know all the rest."

"But there is so much I don't know. Like who wants you dead. Could it be someone on the sorority videos? The videos! Do you still have them?"

"What? The DVDs? They're in that Fed Ex box. You're right. You found them."

"You must have some idea who tried to kill you."

"I don't know. The two guys who killed Chasen, they had voices I never heard before. And I never saw them."

"Then they must have been hired by someone – like Bub."

"I think the only way to find out if Bub killed my sister is to get him to confess and you could record it."

I thought that was crazy. Besides who would we give the recording to? I still didn't know who in the police department we could trust. Sure there were good cops. Wit told me of several he thought were terrific. But they weren't in homicide. If Bub was a killer, who knows who else was? I told her about Tess and that maybe Tess could help us.

All of a sudden I was saying us, because she was right. I now knew things that meant my life was in as much danger as hers.

Then I thought of something else. At the wake she put something in the casket with Chasen. What was it?

"I noticed you right after I did it," she said. "I panicked for a moment. I didn't know if you saw it. And if you had and you told my father, he would know right away."

"What did you put there?"

"Before we were born, my mother bought us each a little baby ring. She kidded my father that if they couldn't tell us apart they could look at the rings. Mine was pale green."

She went to the jewelry drawer and took it out. It was the most delicate little thing.

"Chasen's was royal blue. She loved it so much. It was the only gift we ever got from our mother. Chasen said she would keep it with her always. After she died, I thought she should have it with her."

She gently stroked the tiny ring in her hand. I couldn't think of anything more to say.

A knock at the front door startled us. Then the knocking grew louder. Cara and I stared at each other.

"You stay here," Cara said. "I'll get rid of whoever it is."

Chapter 70

As Cara walked to the front door she looked out the window. The truck was in the driveway. It was the sheriff knocking on the door. What should she do?

"CHASEN open the door. NOW!"

Maybe she could talk him out of his anger. She had done it in the past. Opening the door a crack, she said, "What do you want?"

"I don't think we finished our conversation. You need to know some things about your sister and the men she was with. Then maybe you can be more honest with me."

"I don't want to talk now."

"Whose car is that in the driveway? Is someone here?"

"No," she lied. "One of my father's campaign workers left it here. Leave me alone." She went to close the door. Before she could, he pushed hard against it and barreled his way into the foyer.

"Now that's no way to treat a police officer. We're here to protect you."

Cara erupted. "Protect me? You treated me like garbage and you're the one who probably killed my sister!"

"What's the matter with you?"

"I know how you are!"

"What are you talking about? You don't know anything. You want to be like your sister? Want to be tough, huh? You know what your sister really wanted –" he reached for her.

In the hallway I heard it all and started to panic. Bub was dangerous and Cara was being stupid. I had to get help. I rushed back into Chasen's room and grabbed my cellphone. I dialed Tess. No answer. I left a hurried message. "I'm at the Wicklows. The sheriff is here. I think he's dangerous. We need help." How long would it be before she got the message? I heard more shouting. Oh God, I had to get somebody here fast. What about Detective Folgers? I had to trust someone. I took his card from my wallet and dialed his number. He answered right away.

"This is A.J Billings. I don't have time to explain. I'm at Carson Wicklow's house with his daughter. The sheriff is here. He's threatening us. We need help."

For once he didn't act sarcastic. "The Wicklow house? I'm only a few blocks away. I'll be there in a five minutes." He hung up.

That was unexpected. Good, but unexpected. Did Folgers already know something? Five minutes. He said it would take only five minutes. But five minutes could be an eternity with all the shouting coming from the foyer.

"You're a murderer!" Cara yelled, as she struggled from Bub's grasp.

"I am here to protect you, you stupid little... you were always the dumb sister."

"Chasen wasn't dumb, she was good. And you killed her." Cara started to cry.

"What are you talking about? Have you flipped out? You are Chasen."

"No, I'm not, you idiot. I'm Cara. And I know so much about you."

"I don't believe it. I don't believe you're Cara."

"What about the night you wanted me to seduce the other Dick? You thought it would be funny. Well the joke is on you, because I do it with him all the time now. At least I did before Chasen died. You know what I call him? Big Dick. And you know what we call you? Little Dick, because yours is so small."

He stared at her. Defiantly she stared back. "God, you really are Cara," he said. "Look at you, acting like you're going to fight me. I miss our good times. Little Dick, huh? I'll show you. " He went to grab for her again. But someone rang the front doorbell.

"Don't tell anyone I'm here," he said. He pushed her toward the door. Cara opened it. She couldn't believe it. Now she was really in trouble. Standing there was Big Dick.

Detective Richard "Dick" Folgers, the man with the killer eyes.

Chapter 71

"Get in here in Dick," the sheriff said. "I've got a little problem."

"You've got more than a little one. A.J. Billings the reporter just called and said you were here and threatening her."

"I was what? Are you nuts?"

"I know. It didn't make sense. I was at a house robbery two blocks away, so I came over." He walked into the foyer past the sheriff and Cara's twin. Amazing how much this Chasen looked like her sister. He dropped by earlier in the day just to look at her. He made some excuse about the murder investigation. No question, he was obsessed with these twins. Thinking of Cara and the incredible sex they had always gave him a hard on. He couldn't touch his wife after hooking up with the teenager. After Cara died, he thought about blackmailing another Triesen sorority girl into having sex. Hell, he didn't have to threaten one. They thought they were doing the blackmailing. But when he approached the sheriff with the idea, the sheriff told him to leave the rich girls alone. Bub was acting funny. He wasn't the good ole boy he used to be. What was wrong with him? Did Bub suspect he killed that Cody and Cassie? He might have to deal with the sheriff on that. But right now it was Billings who was trouble. "Where is she?" he asked the twin sister.

Bub closed the front door behind him. "Billings is here?"

"Yeah somewhere in the house, I guess."

"Well let's go find her and straighten this out."

Cara was trying to figure out what to do. "You better not hurt her," she said to Folgers.

"Why would I hurt her?" Folgers asked.

"Don't play your good cop routine on me. You and the sheriff probably killed my sister together."

Folgers laughed. "Your sister was the greatest piece of ass. Did you know that? There wasn't anything she wouldn't do."

"And doing it with you showed how low I would go," the teenager answered back. This time the sheriff laughed. Folgers looked confused.

"Hey Dick," the sheriff said. "Better not say too much about Cara. Cause guess what? This *is* Cara. It was Chasen who was murdered."

"What? No, I'd know Cara." He stared at the blonde teenager. "You're not Cara. Where is Billings?" When Cara didn't answer right away, he grabbed her and pulled her into the living room.

Now it was Bub's turn to worry. Folgers didn't look so normal. When the detective dyed his hair black to try to look younger, the sheriff thought it was funny. Folgers had always been so intense. Maybe he was loosening up. But Folgers hadn't acted right since that cowboy kid Cody disappeared. Then there was Cassie Moran being beaten to death, and the quick confession and suicide of Johnny Moraine. It didn't add up. And Folgers was in charge of those investigations.

The sheriff had gotten suspicious of the detective. He didn't want dirty cops on his payroll. Fooling around with women, or girls, that was one thing. And Cara had approached him, not the other way around. When Folgers started drooling whenever he saw her, Bub thought it would be a good joke to have Cara try to seduce him. He never thought it would work. Obviously it did and Folgers was getting too arrogant. Did he kill that cowboy and the Moran girl? It was time to confront him. But the sheriff's gun was outside in Folgers's truck. He had borrowed the black pickup the day before when his own truck broke down. Folgers seemed anxious to loan it to him, and the sheriff was grateful because he didn't want to drive his official sheriff's car to personal meetings, like visiting the Wicklow teenager. But now he needed to get to that truck and get his gun. He headed for the door.

I was in the hallway hiding behind a large ceramic vase. I couldn't believe what I heard. Big Dick and Little Dick? I thought Cara used both names for the sheriff. But Folgers was Big Dick. So was the sheriff the killer? Or Folgers? They both came into view near the front door.

"Where are you going?" Folgers asked, grabbing Bub's arm.

"Get your hands off me, Dick. Are you crazy? I need to get something in your truck."

"I don't want you to go anywhere." Folgers pulled out his gun and pointed it at the sheriff.

"What's wrong with you Dick? Calm down." As he talked, the sheriff backed toward the door. He was almost there.

"You know, don't you Bub? You know I had to kill those kids. You want to arrest me, don't you? But I'm not going to let you."

The sheriff looked around as if trying to find something to use as a weapon. As he turned, he saw me in the hallway. He mouthed "Run" and lunged for the front door handle. He didn't make it.

I heard a popping sound. The sheriff crumbled to the floor, his uniform turning red with blood. Folgers had shot him. I couldn't help it. I screamed, and Folgers came running.

Chapter 72

"Well Miss New York. Isn't that what the sheriff called you? He said that Billings always turns up when there's excitement. Now we've got a lot of excitement, don't we?"

He turned to Cara. "Get over here by the reporter," he said, motioning with his gun. Cara joined me in the hallway. I was still staring at the sheriff, now dead.

"I'm gotta figure this one out," Folgers said. "Who could have killed the sheriff? Let's get him away from the door. We'll move him into one of the bedrooms. Come on you two, take his feet and drag him."

With the gun pointing at us, there was no choice. I took one leg, Cara the other. The sheriff wasn't light and it took all our efforts to drag him the 30 or so feet across the tile into a guest bedroom. We brought him to the foot of the bed when Folgers said "that's enough."

"Murderer, murderer!" Cara hissed at him. "You kill everybody. You killed my sister, didn't you?"

Folgers made a fist as if to hit her. "I did *not* kill your sister. I'd tell you if I did because now I have to kill you and the reporter here. But I did not kill your sister. I do know, however, who did. And you'd be very surprised who that is."

"And you," he said turning toward me, "You would have quite a story if you knew. But I'll get more out of not telling. Now I have to figure out who did what here. Let me think."

He sat down on the edge of the bed. "What a shame, two pretty girls and I don't have time to do anything with either of you." He stared at Cara. "So it's really you. You didn't care what we did, did you? Your sister was so different. I used to see you two together when you were young. I was your security detail a few times, remember? Boy you had me fooled. You know the night your sister died, the sheriff found this note. Oh wait, our great reporter here, you found the note, didn't you? Well the sheriff showed it me. It said 'We need to talk, important.' I thought you wrote it, Cara, and it was probably better that somebody killed you so no one would find out what you wanted to talk about. But you didn't write it, did you? That means Chasen wrote it. What did she want to talk to you about?"

Cara would never know. Maybe Chasen wanted to mend their relationship. Or maybe she wanted to talk about a new love in her life. The autopsy report said her sister had sex before she died. A guy named Liam kept texting Chasen's phone, begging her to write or call him. Cara never answered. Had Chasen found love?

"Now don't look so sad," Folgers said to Cara. "You don't have to pretend with me. You never really cared about anybody. You only wanted a good time. Wish we had time for that now. But I've got to figure out what to do about the sheriff here. Maybe Bub is who I should frame for Cara's, hey I mean Chasen's, death. Wait until people find out that Cara is still alive." He laughed. "So who killed Chasen? Yeah, the sheriff. Okay. That's good. He was one of the guys you screwed. He didn't want anybody finding out. So he kills Cara, and then he finds out that Cara's not dead and so he comes back here to get the real you, and you shoot him. The gun I shot him with wasn't my County issue. It's for special occasions, like that stupid Cody kid. Yeah Cara, I did kill him. He would have ruined my little games with you. He recognized me, I could tell. A few weeks before that night, I arrested one of the guys he worked with and I questioned Cody a few times. I killed his horse too. You know how hard it was getting rid of both of them? The kid I covered up that night with some dirt. Then later

I dumped him in a swamp. It's got more alligators than mosquitoes. No one will ever find even a part of him. The horse? Well that was tougher. I came back the next day and burned it. They were burning fields nearby. Nobody ever notices anything out there. A few days later I checked again. Just bones. People would have thought it was a cow. I scattered the bones and mixed the ashes with dirt.

"Nobody cared about that Cody anyway, except his girlfriend. What a dumb bitch. Always sticking her nose in things. She tried to get you involved, didn't she, Miss New York reporter? But you were so busy with the "tragic Wicklow murder." That Cassie, she wouldn't stop asking questions. The sheriff warned her. He told her to stop talking to you because something bad could happen to you if Cody had been murdered and his killer was still around. He was trying to protect you! Can you believe it? He had the hots for you, Billings. But then Cassie started in again with this Johnny stuff. Well I had to shut her up. So I did."

"You killed Cassie?" I could barely get the words out.

"I tried to knock some sense into her. I got a little carried away. But no problem. We got that kid Johnny pegged for it. I convinced him he might live if he confessed. I lied. After I got the confession – yeah it was me and not the sheriff like I told people – I got him knocked off in jail. We made it look like a suicide. I've got a deputy who'll do anything for me, like following around that nosey Cassie, and you, Billings. I even had him follow you when you left Cassie's house once. But I decided you weren't important enough to waste my time."

I couldn't speak. Cassie, poor Cassie. Here was her murderer.

Cara was still glaring at him.

"Boy I miss our little games," he said to the teenager. "You are some piece. My teenage slut." He touched her long blond hair. She jerked away.

It didn't faze him. "Okay, now I got the sheriff taken care of," he said. "Now we got you Cara. How do you die? Let's see. So you shoot him, and then I come in and you turn suddenly with the gun in your hand, and you point it at me, and seeing you with a gun I just react and shoot you. It's not great, but they'll accept it. It was self defense. Yeah I can talk my way around that.

"Now what to do with Billings here? That's gonna take more thought. Let's just tie her up for now, shall we Cara? Here use this." He threw her a tennis shoe lying on the floor, then another. "Take the laces out and use them to tie her wrists."

"I'm sorry," Cara said as she bound my hands.

"Now grab that belt and tie her to the chair over there." Cara did as she was told. "Okay Cara time to say bye-bye to your friend. Time to say bye-bye to the world." He pulled her into the hall. I thought it was the end, until once again the front doorbell rang.

"What is this?" Folgers asked. "You got more people coming here than the beach on the Fourth of July. All right Cara, let's go see who this is. I'll be back for you, sweetie." He smiled at me and pushed Cara toward the front door. My chair was at such an angle in the room that I could see the hallway and the door. Please make it be Tess I prayed. And please make her be ready for him.

"Open it and get rid of whoever it is," Folgers whispered to Cara. "If you don't, they're going to die and it's going to be your fault."

Cara opened the door a little. I saw blonde hair. But it wasn't Tess. It was Mara Parkin. Mara—what was she doing here?

"Chasen I need to speak to you."

"It's not a good time. Go away."

"You sound like your sister. In fact you have been acting more and more like your sister and that's not good. I need to talk to you and now." She rushed past her, right into Folgers and the gun he had pointed at her.

"Hi Miss Parkin," he said. "We're having a party here. Want to join us?"

Chapter 73

Tess didn't get Jazz's message right away. She was too busy arguing with her mother over who should be invited to her wedding. She wanted to keep it small. Her mother wanted big.

"You are my only daughter. This will be the only wedding in the family."

They went round and round until Tess asked for a break. "Let me go in the pool and cool off for awhile." In the guest bedroom, she took out her bathing suit. Where to put her engagement ring? She laid it on the dresser next to her cellphone. The phone was vibrating. Someone had called. She looked at the number – Jazz. She had so much fun with Jazz. And now she needed a lighter moment. She called voice mail to retrieve the message. But Jazz was not lighthearted. "I'm at the Wicklows. The sheriff is here. I think he's dangerous. We need help."

Tess was in the hallway in two seconds. "Mom, I got to go. My friend's in trouble." She was out the door before her mother could even ask who.

Chapter 74

"Mara, you never cease to amaze me," Folgers said. "Your timing is perfect."

Cara looked confused. "Oh you don't understand, do you?" Folgers said. "I know Mara Parkin really well. I was just a deputy when you had your fight with her. But we worked out some details so that you would be charged with assault if your father didn't put you in Triesen. We've helped each other out several times since, haven't we, Mara? But now I've got a problem. And it's a very interesting problem. You see Chasen here is not really Chasen."

"What?"

"Well it seems Chasen was murdered instead of Cara. I mean we know it was Cara that was supposed to be murdered, don't we?"

Mara wasn't even looking at him. She was staring at Cara. "You are Cara?'

"Yes, I didn't know what to do. I came home that day and found two men with Chasen. They had just killed her. They were talking as if they thought they killed me. I was scared. I didn't want anyone to know I still was alive. Mara, you have to help us. Dick had Chasen killed. He's going to kill us."

"It's Chasen who's dead?" Mara was having a hard time understanding all this. "But what are you doing here and with that gun?" she asked

Folgers. "I don't understand any of this. I'm getting out of here." She made a move to leave. Folgers waved the gun at her. "Mara did I say you could leave? I said we had things to talk about. And we do."

Cara saw her chance. The detective was talking to Mara. The front door was slightly open. She started to go toward it. No one stopped her. Only a few more feet. She was almost there – then bam, she went down.

"Stupid bitch." Folgers had smashed the gun handle on the back of her head.

Mara walked over to the unconscious Cara as if she was going to help her. Instead she made a race for the door. "Hold it. Don't move!" Folgers shouted at her.

Mara stopped. "I think it's time for let's make a deal, Mara. Now you know some things about me. But I know everything about you. What's really funny is that Cara thinks I killed her sister. Everybody's got some theory about who killed the commissioner's little daughter. But then we know who really masterminded that murder, don't we Mara? So why did you do it? Was it that you couldn't stand the competition for Wicklow? I would have thought you'd have better taste."

"I don't know what you're talking about."

"Oh come on Mara. I know you hired people to kill Cara. I can get anyone to talk. And one of them did. I made a deal with one of the guys who killed – ah – Chasen, and he'll give you up any time I want him too. But I figure we should have a little talk first."

Mara glared at the detective. Then she decided not to pretend any longer. "So you know. What do you want?"

"Now that's a fair question. Money is good. Power is even better. You have both. Boy, you must really hate that girl."

"You have no idea. She ruined the only good relationship I've ever had. Carson was –is - very special to me. With her gone, I think we can be a family again. I thought I could talk to Chasen. She was reasonable growing up. Cara was always the bitch. I hated Cara."

"Well now you're going to help me get rid of her. And then we will have this understanding. And this understanding is gonna last a very long time. You and me, Mara, we're going to have a long term partnership."

Cara regained consciousness. Slowly she began crawling, but this time toward the living room. She was almost out of my line of sight. Get up, I silently willed her. Run. But Folgers put his foot on top of her. "Hey missy, got a headache?" He leaned over to get a better look. His eyes were off Mara. She reached into her purse. Folgers was bent over Cara. "Not so tough now, huh?"

"Hey Dick!" Mara shouted. With a big smile, he turned toward her. He barely saw the gun. He never heard the shot. A bullet tore through his heart and he died instantly. "Poor Detective Folgers," Mara said to the corpse on the floor. "I've been taking target practice. I guess there are some things you don't know about me."

Chapter 75

Cara couldn't believe it. She tried to get up. "Oh thank you Mara, we're saved. Thank you. I was so wrong about you. I hated you for so long."

"You still should." Mara turned the gun toward her. "You're a little bitch, you know that Cara? Your father and I could have been so happy if you hadn't been such a spoiled brat. For years I tried not to think of him and what could have been. But I missed him. And then I saw him in Washington, and without bitchy little you there, we had a great time. I thought maybe we could get back together. He seemed lonely. And we had such a wonderful night together. But in the morning, you know what was the first thing he did? He called his damn housekeeper and asked about you. His darling confused Cara.

"I told him I was coming back to Naples on business and he said we should get together. But all I could think about was how you were going to get in the way again. You always got in the way. I decided it wouldn't happen this time. Some business associates of mine have these men they hire to take care of unpleasant business. And that you are. You see, Cara, I know people who know people who kill. And boy did I want you dead. I hired these two idiots to get rid of you. What did they do? They got rid of your sister instead. Idiots. Now I'm going to have to kill you Cara – again."

Chapter 76

Hiding in the bedroom, what I heard amazed me. Cara had intentionally left all the knots loose, so it took only a few minutes to get untied. My thought was to slip out the front door when Mara and Folgers moved away from it. But I made it only to the bedroom door when Mara killed Folgers. And that was after she announced she was responsible for Chasen's murder. I knew the woman was treacherous, but not like that. Now she was threatening to kill Cara.

"Okay we're going to my car," Mara said to Cara. "I'll let my friends clean up the mess here." I hid behind the bedroom door. Holding Cara up, Mara started toward the front door. I felt my phone vibrate in my pocket. Maybe it was Tess. I tried to find the button to push to answer it silently. I couldn't figure out by feel where that was. Mara and Cara were almost outside. The phone kept vibrating. I couldn't lose the caller. I tapped what I thought was the answer button. But no, I hit the speaker phone. Tess's voice boomed through the hallway. "Jazz, Jazz are you all right?" Mara whirred around and raced for the bedroom. Tess's voice kept bellowing out. "Jazz are you there? Are you okay?"

Chapter 77

Mara pushed the door open, slamming me against the wall. I felt the wind knocked out of me. "Where's the phone?" she snarled as she saw me. Tess's voice kept shouting from my pocket. Mara grabbed at my pants and the phone fell out. She quickly turned it off and put it in her jacket.

"I should have realized you would be around somewhere. You are such a nuisance. I can't figure out what James sees in you. Get up, Get up."

As I slowly rose, I looked at Cara leaning against the wall. How badly was she hurt?

Mara saw the sheriff dead on the floor. "God, you all have been busy here. Who killed Bub? Not that it matters. He was a bother anyway. We better get out of here." With the gun she motioned for us to leave the bedroom.

"Okay," she said, "We're going to my car and if either of you tries to run, you're dead, you understand?" She went to Folgers's body and took the handcuffs off his belt, then searched his pockets for the keys. As soon as she had them, she motioned for us to go out the front door. Mara's beige Cadillac SUV was in the driveway. I helped Cara walk. Her legs were so wobbly she could barely stand.

"Billings, get in the front seat. We'll put Cara in back." She roughly pushed Cara in the backseat, hitting the teenager's head hard against the roof of the car. Cara collapsed, making it easy for Mara to handcuff her wrist to the door.

"Get in the front seat," she ordered me.

I was sure Mara would shoot if anything upset her. "Okay, Okay," I said. "I'm doing everything you ask."

I got in the passenger seat and Mara handcuffed me to the door. Then she ran around to the driver's side and started the car. She gunned it back down the driveway. We were out on 41 in less than a minute.

Chapter 78

Unfortunately it was two minutes before Tess arrived.

She roared into the driveway of the house her GPS announced was the Wicklows. Adrenalin was pumping so hard she felt like she could hardly breathe. She willed herself to calm down and let her police instincts take over. This was no time for emotion. First you observe. There were three cars parked in front of the house. One was Jazz's red Focus. One looked like typical police issue, a late model dark sedan. Was that the sheriff's? The other was a souped up truck with a white stripe on the driver's side. Whose could that be?

Maybe she should call for back up. But who in the local police department should she call? Jazz didn't know who to trust. She didn't either. She decided to approach the house very cautiously.

Taking her Sig Sauer out of her purse, she put it in her jacket pocket. She held her keys in a way that she could easily push the panic button on the remote. If she pressed it, the car would screech a loud alarm. That might give her enough time to overpower any adversary.

At the front door she paused, then knocked. She couldn't hear any movement. She knocked again – nothing. She banged on the door. No one came. Where was Jazz? Where was the sheriff?

She took out the gun and tried the door. It was unlocked. Taking a deep breath she pushed the door open and charged in.

Chapter 79

Silence greeted her. She thought of shouting out Jazz's name, but it was better to search first. With her gun leading the way, she pointed it quickly to the right. Nothing down that hall. Then to the left. Nothing. Slowly she edged into the living room. And then she saw it – on the floor, partially hidden by the sofa – a man's leg jutting out. She rushed into the room. The man lay on his stomach. His dead weight made it hard to turn him over, but she needed to and she did. There was a bullet hole in his chest. Had Jazz done it? She reached into his pocket for a wallet and any identification. She found the badge and his name. It was Folgers, the local detective Jazz mentioned. Where was Jazz? She called out "Jazz, Jazz, are you here?" No answer. Maybe this man's killer was still there. Again with her gun leading, she searched rooms. Nothing in the kitchen, or the great room. She started down the hallway to the left. The tile was sticky. What was that? She looked down. Smeared blood made a trail to a room on the right. Oh my God, Jazz. Please don't let it be hers. She quickly followed the trail into a bedroom. Another body lay on the floor. Thank God. It wasn't Jazz. It was the sheriff. He had been shot too. She needed help with this. She had to have help to find Jazz. She took out her cellphone.

"911. What is your emergency?"

"I've found two people shot in a house on Garder Lane, and one is your sheriff. "

"Our sheriff, are you kidding?" the 911 operator asked.

"I wish I was," Tess answered.

Chapter 80

"Where are we going?" We were headed down 41 on the East Trail, past Fifth Avenue and the heart of Naples. I wasn't sure how long I had before we reached whatever Mara had planned.

"Can't you at least tell me where we're going?" I asked again.

"It's not important to you."

Leaving one hand on the steering wheel, Mara used the other to open her purse and take out her phone. She turned off the car's Bluetooth system. "Some things are best not heard," she said as she speed-dialed a number.

"Hey it's Mary L. I have another job for you. It needs to be done immediately. Are you available? Where are you?"

A long listen.

"Okay that's not that far away. I'm in a car in Naples with a package. I need you to take care of it. Actually I have two packages."

There must have been surprise on the other end, because she quickly said "Yes, two. It's a long story. I can meet you in Everglades City and you can take them from me there."

She smiled as she listened to what was being said, then added, "Yeah, well there are lots of alligators and canals near Everglades City. I think that might work well. Do you know the area? Any ideas where we should meet?"

Another long listen. "Okay that's fine. That's a good spot. I'll wait for you there."

She hung up and let out a deep sigh. "Nothing is easy, is it?"

"You don't have to do this," I said. "Folgers was going to kill us. We could say you saved us."

"Oh right, and what about Chasen's murder?"

I didn't have a quick answer for that. "Right," Mara said. "So much for me trying to save you. You've got about an hour left to live. I wouldn't waste it trying to out think me."

A Walgreen's was coming up on the right. Maybe—"I have to go the bathroom," I said.

"That's the least of your problems."

"No really, I'm going to have diarrhea right here in the car."

Mara glared. "Boy you are something."

I started groaning, grabbing my stomach.

"Okay, Okay. We'll stop here at this Walgreen's. You do anything – I mean anything, you die here, understand?"

I mumbled an agreement.

Mara parked the car away from the building. She turned and looked at Cara, still unconscious in the back seat. "Maybe I won't have to have her killed. Maybe she's going to die anyway. Either way I'll soon be rid of her."

She undid my handcuffs. "Get out and don't do anything dumb," she said. "Or I will kill her right now."

I looked quickly to the right, then left. Nobody was around that I could signal. At least I could talk to someone in the store. I started toward it, but all of sudden Mara was walking next to me.

"I think I will stay with you," she said. "Cara's not going anywhere."

"Where are your bathrooms?" I asked the cashier, who was busy checking a price on a shampoo. The girl didn't even look up. "In the back on the right," she said.

Mara steered me toward the back of the store. We went into the ladies room together.

There were two stalls. "Make it quick," she said, pushing me into the stall on the far end. At that moment a woman came in talking on her cellphone. Mara pretended she was fixing her hair. I looked around the stall. What to do? If I could only write something. But what to write with? And then I saw it. Thank you God. Someone left a lipstick on the little shelf over the toilet paper. A lipstick! I could use it to write on the back of the stall door. I pretended to cough so Mara couldn't hear. Fortunately, the woman on her cellphone was talking so loud as she peed, Mara couldn't hear anything anyway.

Another day, another life, I would have written about what people do in bathrooms. I mean using a phone while you … That had to be so unhygienic. But the woman could sit on the phone for all I cared. I just needed her to keep talking.

"Help," I wrote in bright red. "Kidnapped, call Tess 212-555-4856."

"A.J. I'm waiting!" Mara said, banging on the door. "Time to go!"

I wrote furiously. "Everglades City." The woman on the cellphone left.

"Open this door now!" Mara started pounding on it. I was trying to do a million things. Flush the toilet, pull up my pants, and write on the door. "Killer Ma…."

The door sprung open. Mara reached in and tried to grab me. "Get out of there now." She pulled me out and the door swung closed. Mara pushed me toward the bathroom exit as an elderly woman walked in. Please God, I silently prayed, please let her see my message. As we left, I looked back to see which stall the woman entered. It was the wrong one.

Chapter 81

"This is so silly." Tess sat opposite a detective who had asked her the same question three times. "I told you what I was doing there," she said. "You've verified who I am. We need to find my friend. Whoever killed the sheriff has her."

"We have a double homicide. Two of our police officers were killed, including our sheriff, and you want me to hurry?" The detective shook his head. "Where do you think you are, in Washington, and you're in charge? We'll finish when I feel like it."

He got up and walked out of the interrogation room, slamming the door behind him. Tess had to get out of there. Jazz didn't trust the local police. Now Tess could see why. Why was this detective holding her? Who knew who was involved in these murders? It could be another police officer. She had to get help, but not from here. She still had her phone. Maybe her boss could help. She was about to dial him when the phone began to vibrate. She looked at the number. She didn't recognize it.

"4856," she said, giving the extension of her phone number rather than a hello.

"Is there a Tess there?" A young girl's voice – questioning, unsure.

"This is Tess, who is this?"

A muffled sound, then laughter. "There really is somebody named Tess," the girl said to someone else. Another voice could be heard saying, "No way!"

"Who is this?" Tess asked louder.

"This could all be a joke," the girl said. "But your name was written in a bathroom stall."

Oh here we go, Tess thought. I need this now like I need a hole in the head. What guy would write her name in a bathroom stall anyway? Somebody she arrested?

"I don't have time for this," she told the girl. "I'm going to hang up."

"No wait. I should tell you what it says."

"I don't think I want to hear it."

"It's probably fake. But here's what it says. 'Help, kidnapped –"

Tess felt the blood rush to her head. It had to be Jazz. "Is that all it says?"

"No, it says 'Call Tess, your phone number, then Everglades City.'"

Everglades City? Was Jazz trying to tell her she was in Everglades City? At least it meant she was alive.

"Now listen," she said to the girl. "This is very important what you found. Where are you? Where did you read this?"

"It's in a bathroom stall in Walgreen's on the East Trail."

"Where is the East Trail?"

"The East Trail is another name for 41 south in Naples, Florida. Where are you?"

"I'm in Naples. Do you know the address of the Walgreen's?'

"No, but it's across the street from a CVS. It's near Collier Boulevard. Is there some reward for this?"

Tess lied. "I don't know, but I need you to stay there. I'm a federal agent and I need you to stay there and make sure that no one touches anything before the police arrive. What's you name?"

"Kathy Gladstone. Should I be scared or something?"

"No, you're safe there, Kathy. The police will be there soon. Just stay there, okay?"

"Wow, this something. Okay, we'll stay here. I'm here with my friend Joanne."

"Okay Kathy. I will talk to you later."

She had to get out of this police station, and now.

Chapter 82

Mara was talking now. She seemed to love to talk. All I could think of was the bathroom door and if someone found my message. If they had, would they call Tess? Or would they think it was a joke?

What was Mara saying, something about Wit?

"What?" I asked.

"I said you have no idea what's going on in Naples. This is all so much bigger than you and your little investigation of a teenage murder. What's going to happen in Naples next year, and what it will mean to the nation, well you could have had a *big* story if you were smart enough to figure it out. The election is part of it. But Wit hasn't a clue. And you? You were all caught up in what happened to the little bitch Cara, or Chasen. Not that important, except for me. You had to meddle in my life. And now I'm going to have to go away for awhile. They'll be upset with me for interfering with the big picture. I had everything going so well."

"What's going to happen? Who are they?"

She ignored the question. "Big story, A.J., and I was right in the middle of it. Now I've got to get out of here. You ruined it."

"Me? *You* had Chasen killed."

"But nobody knew about that."

"Folgers did. And you killed him."

"Well, paradise can be deadly. He had to go anyway. He had too big a mouth and too busy a dick."

I couldn't disagree with that. But who were "they?" What was Mara talking about? What was this big story? And how far were we from Everglades City? If somebody had called Tess, she would be at least 15 minutes behind us. Did Cara and I have 15 minutes? Even if Tess was racing toward us, what could I do? I assumed Cara and I would be handed over to the men who killed Chasen. Then what? How long would we be kept alive? Was Cara even alive now? I looked in the back seat. She looked like a sleeping angel, her blond hair spread out, framing her face. Was she breathing? Was her chest moving? I watched for what seemed forever. Finally I saw it rise and fall. She was just unconscious. But she needed a doctor. She needed one soon.

The two lane road kept getting more and more deserted. We passed a marina and homes behind it. Wasn't that the last civilization until the turn-off to Everglades City? I had been there once with Wit. It was old Florida down there, a one street town with the main business being airboat rides. We ate lunch at the historic Rod and Gun Club. We had a wonderful day.

Now I was going back – never to see Wit again, or mend our relationship. I would never find out about the election, or finish my articles. And now, wow, I had the ending to those articles. But it would never get written, because I was going to Everglades City – to die.

Chapter 83

Tess raced toward the Walgreen's. She was going to check Jazz's message and then contact the local police. She didn't want them holding her back any further. Her boss had finally called and talked to the supervising officer. After screaming about interfering with a federal investigation, they let her go. She owed him a big one.

"So what's the investigation?" he asked as she called him from the car.

"I can't explain now. But it involves several murders. I've got to go. I'll call you back later." Up ahead was Walgreen's. Would the girls still be there guarding the bathroom?

As she rushed into the store, she expected pandemonium. She assumed the girls told the manager and clerks and anyone else who was there. But the store seemed calm and empty.

She asked a girl unpacking bottles of Listerine where the ladies room was. "In the back," she said. Tess hurried there. A thin girl, about 13, with dyed black hair and heavy eye makeup, was standing outside. She was dressed in black. Obviously a Goth.

"Are you Kathy?"

"No I'm Joanne. Kathy's inside. Are you Tess? Hey, you're pretty. Where are the police?"

"They're coming." Another lie. "Stay out here and make sure no one comes in."

"I've been doing that," Joanne said. "Is there some kind of reward?"

"I don't know." Tess pushed the door open and entered the small bathroom. There were two stalls. The one by the far wall was closed.

"Hello. Is Kathy here?"

The door to the stall opened. Another girl in black came out. "I'm Kathy. Are you Tess?"

"Yes I am. "

"You don't look like a federal agent. You look like a movie star. I was in there guarding it so no one could see."

"You did a great job. Let me see."

"Let's see a badge first." Kathy and Joanne had talked. If there was a reward they didn't want to have to share it with anyone else. They wanted to make sure this Tess was a real law person.

Tess pulled out her DEA badge. Kathy seemed impressed. She opened the door wider so Tess could read the message. There in lipstick was just what had been recited. It looked like Jazz's handwriting. She had to get to Everglades City and fast. But wait. The message didn't end with Everglades City. There was more. "You didn't read me all of this," Tess said.

"What?" Kathy said. "I thought I did."

"No, you didn't read me the last part after Everglades City."

"Oh about the killer?"

Duh. Yeah the killer part! Were these girls nuts? Jazz had written "Killer – Ma ." What was that?

"Do you know what that means?" Kathy asked.

"I'm not sure," Tess said.

"What about the kidnapping. Who has been kidnapped? And where are the rest of the police? We've been here a long time."

"They'll be here soon. You did great, but I've got to get going."

"To Everglades City to find the killer?"

"I hope so."

And hopefully not to find any more victims.

Chapter 84

Mara finally was silent. I was too. I kept trying to figure out how I could escape. But with my hand cuffed to the car door, there was no way to jump out. And if I could, who would help Cara? She was handcuffed to a door also.

We reached the turn for Everglades City and made the right. I thought we would go down a few miles into the town, but instead Mara made a sharp left only about a half-a-mile from the main road. A sign said Tru-Swamp Airboat Rides. We bumped down a dirt road until we reached a clearing that served as a parking lot. Only two cars were parked there, both near a decaying dock where an old looking airboat was tied up, and a small structure that must be the office. Mara parked away from the cars, at the far end of the parking area.

"Now we wait," she said.

Her phone rang. She looked at the number then answered it.

"Where are you?"

She listened.

"I'm here already. Hurry up. There aren't many people around. I want to keep it that way." She hung up. "They're about 20 minutes away. Then I can get rid of you two."

Cara groaned from the back seat. I said instinctively "She needs help."

Mara laughed. "You've got to be kidding."

Her laugh was interrupted by the slamming of the office door. An old man in denim coveralls came shuffling out. He looked at our car parked over in the corner and started walking toward us.

"This is not good," Mara said. "I'm getting out to talk to him. If you do anything, I will kill him as well as you both."

Clutching the gun in her pocket, Mara quickly got out of the car and started walking toward the old man. I tried pulling on the handcuff to see if it would break free. No luck.

"Hi," Mara said to the man. "I'm waiting for friends and then we may take an airboat ride."

The man looked at the well dressed woman with the designer clothes and flashy jewelry. Surely he must think something is wrong, I thought. But this was near Naples. He probably saw people dressed in every way imaginable. He didn't seem to think anything was wrong. He gave Mara a big smile. How to signal him? I kept shaking my head. No reaction. My eyes raced around the front seat area. And then I saw it. My cellphone was on the floor by the gas pedal. It must have fallen out of Mara's pocket when she jumped out of the car. I grabbed for it. But the handcuff kept me a few inches from reaching it.

"How many of you will there be? I can offer a good deal." The man kept smiling at Mara.

"Six," she said.

I tried leaning, again and again, only an inch now. I kept trying to watch Mara at the same time I grabbed for the phone.

"Well I got a boat coming back in soon. We should be fine. Where did you come from today?"

Mara looked back at the car. I stopped moving.

"Naples," she said. "I'm not really dressed for this, but my friends thought it might be fun."

I tried one more reach. Got it. Now I had to turn it on and dial with my left hand. I pushed the "on" button. Quick, come on. It had to be done fast. It seemed forever before it warmed up. Finally. And now Tess's number. I know it, I know it. What is it? My hand was trembling.

"We're usually busier around this time, the economy you know."

Tess was speed dial number 8. I just hit it. I heard it ring.

"I'm going back to the car. I have a call to make." Mara started walking toward me.

"Extension 4856."

"Tess, we're at an airboat ride place just off of 41. It's like the first left. There's not much time."

"Jazz, Jazz. Oh thank God. Is it Everglades City?"

The man was calling to Mara as she was walking fast toward me.

"Do you and your daughter want to come in and use the bathroom or anything? She doesn't look happy." He was staring at me. I was shaking my head at him, this time to ignore me. That just made him stare more.

"No we're fine, we'll wait here. Goodbye."

Feeling like he was dismissed, the man turned and headed back to the office. Mara was almost to the car.

"Yes, Everglades City, hurry."

Tess asked "Who are you with?" But Mara was too close. I quickly turned the phone off and put it under her seat. Mara got back into the car. "What were you doing, you bitch? Trying to signal that guy?"

"No, nothing," I said.

We sat in silence until we heard the sound of a car coming down the dirt road.

"I can't wait to get rid of you," Mara snarled at me. "And it looks like that will be very soon."

Chapter 85

A black sedan pulled up next to us. Oh please Tess, hurry. Two men got out of the car. They walked over to the driver's side.

"Here they are," Mara said. "The one you were supposed to have killed and this one."

The taller man looked into the back seat. "Jeez look at her, she looks just like the other one."

"They're twins, stupid," Mara said to him.

"What do you want us to do with them?"

"Kill them any way you want, and do it right this time. And by the way, the detective you snitched to, he's dead."

The shorter man looked as if he wanted to question what she was talking about. But the other man quickly opened the back door. Cara lay motionless. "What's wrong with this one?"

"She was hit on the head. That should make it easier for you."

He saw that she was handcuffed. "Where's the key?" he asked.

Mara flipped it to him. "And she's handcuffed too," she said, pointing at me.

The taller man undid the handcuffs on Cara and carried her out of the car, laying her in the back seat of the black sedan. Then he came back and took the handcuff off me.

"Bye Billings," Mara said. "I'll give your best to James."

Oh Wit. I really blew it this time. I had to make a move. I had to try to save myself and Cara. As the shorter man grabbed me and started pulling me to the black sedan. I kicked hard. If I can just get his – yes. He screamed in pain. The old kick-the-balls I learned in self-defense class – my teacher would be proud. I started running toward the office. The taller man started racing after me. He was faster and grabbed my arm. I tried to shake loose.

Then I heard the sound of another car. The man and I both turned to see dirt flying as a large white Cadillac came roaring down the road. It was Tess's rental.

The man holding me let go and took out his gun. The other did the same. Tess kept coming, faster it seemed. Was she going to try to run them down? The tall one shot at the approaching car. Tess swerved sideways and jammed on the brakes. When the car came to a stop, it was sideways, blocking the road. I heard the driver's door slam. Tess was out of the car. The men kept firing.

"Get down Jazz!" Tess shouted to me.

Dumb. I was standing in the middle of the parking lot. I threw myself on the ground as shots rang all around me. I had no protection. I kept my face down in the dirt. I heard the man who grabbed me run to his car. I looked up. He was crouched by the side of the car. He stood up to get a better shot and Tess saw her opportunity. More sound of gunfire. He fell. She had shot him. The other man kept firing. I lay as flat as I could. The cars were starting to look like target practice. Several of the tires on Mara's car were flat. So was one on the men's car. Had Tess done that deliberately?

Off to the side, I saw the driver's door open on Mara's car. Then I saw her stealthily making her way behind the men's car toward me.

I screamed "No! Get her!"

At the sound of my voice, she stood up straight and ran into the open, waving her hands at the same time. Tess could take a shot. Why didn't she? Mara was screaming "Help, Help!" She ran toward the office shack.

"Shoot her!" I yelled, but my voice was lost in the barrage of gun fire between Tess and the remaining man. Why didn't Tess shoot Mara? Didn't she see her?

Chapter 86

Tess not only saw the woman running and waving her arms, she was delighted to see someone escaping. That must be another hostage, she thought. How many were there? She had called the police and sent them to Walgreen's. Now she needed to call them to help her here. For a moment she wondered why the man she was shooting at didn't turn and kill the woman, but he was probably focused too much on her. What was Jazz shouting? It was impossible to hear.

Another reload. She should call for backup. But she couldn't reach the door of her car to get to her phone. She had left it in the car. Stay down, she silently prayed to Jazz. She was so exposed out there. For a second all was quiet. The man stopped shooting. What was he doing? She edged around the car to get a better look at where he was. There was no sign of him.

She wanted to shout to Jazz to ask her what she saw, but she was afraid if she made Jazz speak, the man would remember she was there and shoot her. How to get closer to the car? She had shot out tires on both vehicles, so she knew nobody could get away. But did he know that? The answer came in the sound of an engine as the black car came to life.

He was going to try to get away. He started to back up fast, right to where Jazz was lying.

He was going to hit her. "Jazz, Jazz get out of the way!" Tess yelled. She stood up and fired at the car. It kept backing up.

Jazz had to move. The car was almost on top of her. "Jazz move – now!" But which way? Right or left? Tess closed her eyes as Jazz rolled to the right.

Chapter 87

The commotion of the gun shots was the cover Mara needed to escape. There was no way to leave in the car. She heard the tires blow. How to get out of here? Maybe the old man had a car. He, at least, had the airboat. She would have to get to him. Would that woman cop, or whoever she was, shoot at her? She had to look like a victim. Waving her hands over her head might work. So she ran and waved and nobody shot at her. She got to the shack. The door opened before she even made it to the threshold. The old man pulled her in.

"Thank goodness you're safe," he said. "I called the police. They should be here soon."

"Do you have a car?" Mara asked.

"A car? No, my son drives me here and drops me off. Why are you asking for a car?"

"Because I've got to get out of here."

"But the police are coming, I told you."

Dumb man. "Do you have the keys to the airboat? Do you know how to drive it?"

"Yes, but I don't think we have to go. That woman in the white car already got one of them."

Just then they heard the black car start up and race backwards.

Was a car operational? Could they escape? Mara ran to the window to see what was happening.

Chapter 88

I was alive. I couldn't believe it. I rolled just as the car reached me. I could feel the weight of the tires on the ground inches from me. The car swerved to the left as I rolled to the right. It was now turned toward Tess. She saw her opportunity. As the driver put the transmission in forward, she stood up. She braced herself and took aim at the driver. She only had a second or two before he would start shooting or run her down.

The driver raised his gun and pointed it out the window. Tess took her shot.

Bull's eye. The bullet went through the driver's eye. Blood spattered on the windshield. The car swerved right then came to a stop a few feet from Tess. Slowly she approached it. She pointed the gun into the window, but there was no movement. Cautiously, she opened the driver's door. The man was dead, his head tilted back again the headrest. She let out a deep exhale and turned toward me.

I was slowly getting up. "Are you okay Jazz?" she yelled.

"Yes, I'm okay." We ran to each other. "Oh thank you, thank you, Tess," I said as we hugged. "You got my message."

"Both of them," she said. "Smart girl. But what happened?"

"Cara and I – oh Cara. Oh God, she's in the car."

"Which car?"

I was already running toward the killers' black sedan. I pulled open the back door. Cara was lying on the seat. There was blood. "Cara." I put my fingers on her neck trying to feel for a pulse.

Tess ran up.

"I don't know Tess. I can't find a pulse."

"Let me see," Tess leaned over the teenager. She put her fingers on Cara's wrist, feeling for a pulse. "I've got something. It's weak but she's alive. We've got to get her to a hospital."

"What about Mara? You've got to get Mara. She's the one who brought us here to be killed."

"What?"

"Mara, she's got a gun. She killed Folgers. She took off for the office over there. Why didn't you shoot her?"

"The woman? I thought she was a hostage. She was waving her arms."

Tess pulled out her gun and turned toward the office. Just then we heard the sound of an engine starting. It was an incredibly loud sound.

"What is that?" I asked. I didn't have to wait for an answer. We saw a plume of water as an airboat roared away from the dock.

Chapter 89

Tess and I raced to the dock in time to see Mara and the old man who was driving the airboat, disappear around a bend. For a moment there was only the sound of the engine fading in the distance. Then there was another sound. Police sirens. Two police cars raced down the dirt road toward Tess's car.

"We've got to stop Mara," I said. "She knows about something dangerous going on in Naples."

"I don't know how we could follow her," Tess said. "And we've got to get that girl to a hospital."

The police cars screeched to a halt behind the white Cadillac blocking the road. With guns drawn, two Collier County sheriff deputies raced toward the cars Tess had fired at. They hadn't yet seen us on the dock. And then came another sound. An airboat was approaching. Was Mara coming back? Tess reached for her gun. But it was another airboat, this one driven by a man in his 30's with a young couple on board. As they pulled up to the dock, everybody was laughing at something the driver said. Then they noticed us standing there.

"Do you have tickets for the next ride?" the captain said. He jumped off the boat to tie it up.

"No, no," Tess said. "But I need your boat. We have to catch the other airboat that just pulled out of here. I think the old man driving it was kidnapped. He's in danger."

"The old man driving? The only person that could be is my father. He's in the office. He sells the tickets."

From the far end of the parking lot, the police officers were now running toward us.

The couple hurriedly got off the boat. They didn't want anything to do with this scene. The young man handed a few dollars tip to the captain who absentmindedly pocketed it as he said to Tess, "My father hasn't driven a boat with anyone in years."

"Well he's doing it now and probably with a gun to his back. We've got to follow them."

"Okay, let's go."

Tess jumped in. I didn't know what to do so I started to get in the boat as well.

"Not you. You stay here with the police," Tess said.

"I'm going with you."

Tess saw the officers getting nearer. There wasn't time to argue.

"Okay. Get in, get in."

Tess yelled to the police, "I'm DEA. I've got to catch a terrorist."

I yelled also. "You've got to get an ambulance for the girl in the black sedan. It's Cara Wicklow. She's been knocked unconscious, maybe even shot. Call her father, tell him it's Cara."

The younger officer shouted back, "What did you say? Cara Wicklow? She's dead."

"Tell him –" But the engine started and we took off like a rocket. The police officers disappeared.

Over the roar of the engine, the driver shouted to Tess "My name is John Truman. My father's Jack. He has a heart condition. This is bad for him."

Tess didn't want to say how really bad it could be.

Chapter 90

The airboat pulled out just as the second officer reached the dock.

"Wait, hold it, police!" he shouted. He raised his gun to fire.

"No, no!" The couple yelled together. "They're the good guys," the man said. "I heard the woman say she was a federal agent or something. They're going after the other boat. There's a terrorist on it. The driver's father was kidnapped and made to drive the boat."

"We better call this in," the younger police officer said to his partner. "And we need an ambulance. What did that woman yell to me? Cara Wicklow was in the car? What was she talking about? Cara Wicklow was murdered a few weeks ago. We better get back and check out that car."

Chapter 91

"Do you know where they could be going?" Tess asked John.

"It's just a giant circle with some canals in between," he said. "There's nowhere to go. It's not near a road or anything."

Hopefully Mara hadn't learned that. She was obviously trying to escape.

"Where could he let her off?" Tess asked. She didn't want to tell John that she was sure Mara would kill his father when she felt she didn't need him anymore.

"I don't know. I'd think he'd tell her there's nowhere to go."

That wasn't good for Jack. They didn't have much time.

"How long before they'll come back toward us?" Tess asked.

"Maybe 15 minutes, if my father starts going up and down some of the canals."

"Is there somewhere where we could put the boat so they couldn't see us? Or somewhere where we could stop them?"

"Well they will have to slow down if they get to Homer's swamp."

"What's that?"

"It's a narrow channel that Homer Mulligan made. He thought it would be fun for the tourists to go over almost dry land so he dug this passage from one canal to another. The driver just guns it and the boat goes over about 100 feet of swampy land."

"Would your father go there?"

"He might think that's the only way to jar a gun out of her hand."

"Is there a place for us to hide near there?"

"On the other side of it, but if they make it through, they'll be coming right at us."

"Well I think we've got to try that." Tess looked at me. "I have to take a shot at Mara," she said.

It took us only a few minutes to get to the edge of Homer's swamp. For a second I thought how much fun this airboat ride would be if people's lives didn't depend on it.

We rode over the swampy area that Homer dug out and which felt like we were digging out again. How many people have thought that their boat would never make it over this mound of mucky land and that someone would have to come in and get them? Is this what Jack would try to fool Mara with?

We didn't have long to wait. We could hear the roar of the airboat engine in the distance. John turned his boat around so that Tess could have a clear shot. We wouldn't have much time. Maybe Jack wouldn't even try the Homer's Swamp maneuver. But if he did, the airboat Mara was riding on would make a sharp turn then hit Homer's swamp at nearly full speed. During the turn, our boat wouldn't be visible, but for the few seconds before Mara's boat smashed to a halt she would see us. Could she get a shot off? Tess was taking no chances.

"I want you to hunch down and try to get out of any line of fire," she said to John and me.

The engine roar grew louder. Would John's father think along the same lines as his son? Would he realize this was probably his only chance? Or was he too scared and frazzled to think anything out? Louder, louder. It sounded like a jet plane drawing near. It was rounding the turn. Would it come in or just pass by the opening?

And suddenly there it was, barreling down on us. Jack thought like his son. And it wasn't almost full out. It was entirely full out. They must have been going over 50 mph. Were they going to crash into us? I saw

Mara suddenly realize what was ahead of them – land and then another boat waiting. Her gun had been pointed at Jack. She turned and pointed it at Tess. She aimed. They hit Homer's swamp with a smash, then a giant whoosh as the boat flipped up. Mara went flying out of one side. Jack, somehow stayed in the boat, still holding onto the steering wheel. The boat crashed down and stopped several hundred feet in front of us.

The roaring engine was silenced as it dug backwards into the swamp. The front of the boat tilted up toward the sky. "Forward, go, go! Get to it," Tess yelled at John. He put the boat in drive and raced toward the swamp. As soon as we hit the sloppy earth, Tess jumped off. She sank in about a foot of muck.

"You can't walk on it!" John shouted. "Here grab onto my boat." He pulled the boat next to her, and she grabbed the gunnel as he pulled her in. Her legs were covered in swamp mud.

"Dad, Dad can you hear me?" John yelled to his father. There was no answer from the other boat.

And where was Mara? John inched his boat next to the wrecked boat that now looked like a tilted up statue of an airboat. His father lay crumpled up next to a bench seat.

In the distance we could hear another engine sound. What was that? It sounded like it was getting nearer. I realized it was a helicopter. The police must be on their way. John jumped over the front of his boat onto his father's and rushed to the back. "Dad, I'm here."

"Is he alive?" Tess asked.

"Yes, he's moaning," John said.

The helicopter noise grew louder.

"Where is Mara?" I shouted. I looked in every direction. No sign of her. "I saw her being thrown out of the boat. She has to be badly hurt."

"Dead," Tess said.

"You think she's dead?" I asked.

"She's dead," Tess said. "I know it. Want to bet me a dinner?"

"Any place you want, anytime! How do you know she's dead?"

"Look." She pointed up. I looked up.

In the branches of a pine tree about six feet above, hung a body. Mara's body was like a rag doll, her head at a strange angle as if it wasn't attached properly to her body.

"She must have hit the tree and broke her neck."

"Do we know she's dead?" I asked.

"I don't think anyone could survive that," John said.

The police helicopter now circled overhead. "Drop your guns and put your hands in the air," a voice shouted over a loudspeaker. Tess realized she still had her gun out. She placed it on the boat seat. "I'm a DEA agent," she shouted back. "The kidnapper is up there in the tree."

"We need an ambulance for my father," John shouted too. "Can you get another airboat in here to get him out?"

"We have one being trailered in down the road," the voice came back from the helicopter. "We'll stay by you until it arrives."

And they did. Twenty minutes later we had all been transported on another airboat back to Tru-swamp's dock where an ambulance waited. Jack, the feisty old airboat captain, was quickly placed in the back of it. He had regained consciousness and wanted to be congratulated about his tricky maneuver. Okay, he acknowledged, he did have some pain in his chest and legs. "Don't worry, I'm gonna make it," he said to his son, who jumped into the ambulance with him.

Police gathered around Tess and me. "Could you tell me about the girl who was in the car?" I asked one of the officers. "She's Cara Wicklow, the commissioner's daughter."

"You said that before," the officer said. "Cara Wicklow is dead. You've got it wrong. That must have been Chasen Wicklow in the car. She was unconscious with a head injury and a gun shot wound to the arm, but the EMTs thought she'd be okay."

"Right." I decided now was not the time to explain to the police and the world that Cara was alive. Her father could take care of that when they both were ready.

"I'm going to need you ladies to come with me to police headquarters," the officer said. "We've got a lot of questions."

I bet you do. I turned to Tess. "Mara said there were big things going on in Naples. That something was going to happen next year that would be—I don't know, but very bad for this area and for the country. How are we going to find out what that is now that she's dead?"

"Well I guess you're just going to have to stick around here, huh?" Tess said. "You may become a Floridian."

Me a Floridian? Did I want to be here? My dog Willie certainly did, what with his love for Helga and the beach. Yes, the beach was wonderful. And so was the weather. No snow to drive in, or freeze in, just year-round balmy breezes. It truly was beautiful down here. But then I thought of Wit and our complicated relationship. We needed time and space. I would have to get my own place, and not in a hi-rise.

A.J Billings, a transplanted New Yorker living in paradise. It could be interesting. My adventures in paradise.

Maybe I'd write a book about it.

EPILOGUE

A month after the election Wit and I moved. Not to the same place. I rented a small cottage just off Fifth Avenue in downtown Naples. Wit bought a big house in the community of Pelican Bay, another bird-named neighborhood. After telling off Millstone and the condo commandos, he had no desire to live in a hi-rise full of "Neanderthals" as he called them.

Yes, he came to my defense. And he bought the house so Willie could have a yard to run around in. Willie never had his own yard. He revels in it. I think he's buried something in every corner. But we're not there every day. Wit and I are taking our relationship slower this time. I think we became a couple living together before we became a real couple. So we are dating. I love it. Flowers, and midnight calls and sexy texts. The old joking and passion are back. I know part of our problem was the election and my reporting. Right now we are on hiatus from both.

Of course, you are wondering whether Wit won. No, he did not. In the closest Florida congressional election in decades, he lost by 286 votes. People are still claiming there was voter fraud and Wit should have won. Regardless, Stephen Reynor is the new congressman for Southwest Florida. Wit vows to run against him in two years. In the meantime, he's gone back to being a hometown lawyer. In Naples, that means representing homeowners worth millions. But he is more relaxed, which makes me more relaxed and our personal life is really, really good.

Election night, however, was terrible. Besides the tension over Wit's race, The BBP party won all the local elections. Carson is no longer a county commissioner. But he doesn't seem to mind. He and Cara are learning to value each other again. When Carson found out that his ex-wife killed one of his daughters because of him, he went into a deep depression. In a reversal of roles, Cara is now helping her father find peace of mind. She practically mothers him. It's a tender scene to watch, and one I've watched many times, because Cara and I see each other often. The Naples Lolita and I have become very close.

Many things happened after "Cara's Story" was published. People were shocked that it was Chasen, not Cara, who was killed, so Carson decided to have another funeral. As Yogi Berra said it was déjà vu all over again.

Triesen Academy closed "for the holidays," as the school put it. However my deep throat, Joyce Janic, tells me the school will not reopen, at least not in Florida. All the girls were sent home, but only temporarily. Joyce says that in a few months Miss Halder plans to start another school near Atlanta, Georgia. You would think a sex scandal would put her out of the education business. I guess there will always be a need for some place wealthy parents can dump their disobedient offspring.

Last week I got a call from Sarah, the problem child who coined that phrase. She lives in New York City with her mother. With the help of a psychiatrist, Sarah finally was able to tell her mother what her father did to her. The molestation went on for years. Mrs. Van Holben threw her husband out, but decided not to contact the police. Sarah begged me not to tell anyone either. I won't. She has been through so much. I only hope she finds the peace she deserves.

Then there are the men who molested the Triesen sorority girls. Yes, I called it molesting. Those teenage girls were under extraordinary psychological stress. The men took advantage of that. All should have been prosecuted. But only one was – Ross Davids. The public will never know who the other men were, except for Dick Folgers and Bub Walker. Cara destroyed all the DVDs in her house, then convinced the P.S. girls to get rid of the rest of the evidence. According to Cara, the power sex sorority held one final ceremony where the girls vowed never to reveal who or what was involved in their initiations.

As for Ross Davids, his son Reese was willing to testify against him. So was Cara, because Reese asked her to. But when Davids' big-time lawyer brought up a "blame the victim" defense, Carson felt Cara had been through enough. A plea bargain was reached. Davids got a short sentence with community service. You can see him out on 41 watering the plants with the rest of the Sheriff's work crew.

And Collier County has a new sheriff. It's a provisional appointment. A special election for sheriff will take place next year. Bring Back Prosperity is already fielding candidates. That political party worries me. What are they planning?

I still can't get over Bub Walker wanting to protect me. He wasn't as evil as I thought. I feel bad hating him, yet so many people died under his watch. Why didn't he investigate Folgers sooner? Then maybe Cassie wouldn't have died, or Johnny Moraine. When I found out Johnny's parents couldn't afford his funeral and burial, I paid for his plot in the Vanderbilt Beach cemetery. Johnny might have lived if I hadn't told Folgers about him. I needed to do something for him. Wit supported me on that. He even went with me to the funeral.

As for my work, I've almost finished the book. Somehow writing about my life got easier after talking to Cara about hers. Once the book is published, I may go back to work for The Trib. Buiner, the managing editor, has made me an offer hard to refuse. I would be chief national correspondent. I can write about what I want, when I want, and get paid a lot of money. Buiner says my Naples murder series should win a Pulitzer. He's obsessed with getting another one for the paper.

My biggest prize came here in Naples. Willie is a father. Six little gray and black puppies were born to Helga the weimaraner. They have Willie's big head and Helga's little tail. They are gangly and adorable -- especially this one gnawing on my shoe.

"Do you want to go outside, Maggie May?" Yes, I took a puppy and I gave her two names just like mine, although I think Maggie May is a lot better than Agatha Jasmine.

So my family of three now calls Naples home. Life is quiet here in paradise. But I can't help wondering. What is that big story Mara Parkin said will happen next year?

The End